BRIGHT CITY
DEEP SHADOWS

A Luke Kelly Crime Story

Graham Storrs

This Edition, Copyright © 2020, Graham Storrs

ISBN: 987-0-6484329-2-0

Published by Canta Libre
Cover art and design by Craig Johnson (windowgazing.com)
Interior design by Write Into Print (writeintoprint.com)

Dedication

This book is for my wife, Christine, who is the biggest fan of crime fiction I know and who deserves better from her husband than a constant diet of sci-fi.

Chapter One

The night Chelsea died, I was playing snooker with a bunch of drunken strangers in a pub in Byron Bay. I try not to think about that but it keeps coming back. While my girlfriend was being stabbed over and over in a brutal, frenzied attack, while she was suffering so much pain and fear in that squalid Brisbane alley, as the very life drained out of her body and the certainty of death chilled her soul, I was laughing and joking and drinking, hundreds of kilometres away, spending her money, money she gave me because I'm a useless, worthless waste of space who can't get a regular job and couldn't even be there with her when, for once, she really, really needed me.

Doctor Huber, the therapist I saw for about three visits, told me my guilt was misplaced. She seemed to think I kept remembering that night as a way of punishing myself. I told her she was wrong, that my guilt is well-founded, that guilt is the only rational response to a life like mine and a death like Chelsea's.

It's not like people didn't tell me. They spoke to seventeen-year-old me about careers and job prospects and supporting a family but back then all I thought was important was getting to the heart of things, understanding the world and my place in it. I had nothing but contempt for their mundane concerns. So I went to study philosophy at uni, immersed myself in the complex abstractions that proliferate in the minds of gifted, idle people. I even went on to do a doctorate: "Disambiguating the Notion of 'Posit' in the Epistemology of A. J. Ayer." That was the title of my thesis. Impressed? I was and so were the examiners. Two years later, I was two years into a life of underemployment and mooching off generous others and standing by the grave that Chelsea's mother paid for, listening to some rent-a-cleric droning on about the Life Everlasting. Chelsea didn't believe in any of that crap and neither do I. That whole thing was organised by Stacey, Chelsea's heroic single-parent mum. I was only there, standing in a strange twilight world of misery and isolation, tears rolling down my cheeks, because I didn't have the moral courage to be somewhere else.

Anyway, funerals are for the living, they say. This one was mostly for Stacey, I reckon. Dr. Huber told me it might do me some good, give me closure. I asked her to give me a nice, clear definition of 'closure' so that I could tell if it was happening but she just gave me her sad smile and said, "We've talked about over-intellectualising, haven't we, Lucas."

Yes, we had. *Ad nauseam.*

I was only seeing the stupid woman because my own mum and dad insisted on it. They dropped everything and came over as soon as they heard about the murder. They found Chelsea's mum staying in our unit and me in a motel nearby. Stacey had flown up from Sydney when the police told her and she'd asked them to tell me. I had still been half drunk and was confused to find myself in a hotel room when the Brisbane police woke me with a phone call. I drove back in Chelsea's car – which she'd lent me for the trip – and met

Stacey in the Indooroopilly police station.

The police asked me a few questions about Chelsea, about my relationship with her. *We lived together*, I said. *I don't know what a de facto partner is, I mean, not legally. We lived together. For more than a year. No I don't know what she was doing in Spring Hill. Yes, it's a long way from our unit. No, I was at a conference. In Byron. Yes, I have the hotel receipt. I only checked out a few hours ago.* The conference seemed like an eternity ago, like it had happened on another world. *I was in the bar with… some people. No, I don't know their names. One was called Doug, I think. One was… Steve? I don't know!*

The policeman who interviewed me was called Trevor Reid. He was tall and rangy and looked like he should have been out driving cattle across a dusty plain – except they do that with motorbikes and helicopters these days, don't they, not the horses in my imagination. Funny that they don't have people jumping from motorbikes and helicopters onto terrified cattle at rodeos. Or maybe they do? I've never been to one. I tried to imagine Detective Inspector Reid in a cowboy hat, lassoing cattle from a helicopter. For a moment, I saw myself telling Chelsea about my ludicrous fantasy and making her laugh. She loved stupid stuff like that.

"Do you find this funny, Mr. Kelly?" Reid asked, his face a scowl.

Then the questions turned sharp and insinuating. *No, she didn't have any enemies. We're just ordinary people. Our lives are just… you know… not like that. I don't know much about her work. Yes, I've met some of her employees but they're like mates. You know? Programmers and stuff. They make games. Phone apps. They're all like geeks together. They had a work day out to Comicon last year, for Crissake, all dressed as Star Wars characters. No, there were no money troubles She's doing fine. Doing real good. I – I don't know if there were*

3

loans. You'd have to ask Kazima, she's the accountant, although she likes to be called the Finance Officer.

And, for some reason, just like that, it was all too much. It was the memory of Chelsea laughing with me about Kazima's job title, how silly it all was, and me seeing in her eyes how it wasn't really all that silly but a mark of how her company was growing and succeeding, how well she was doing and how proud she was.

Reid's scowl stayed in place, swimming in my tears. He had big hands, prominent knuckles. He gave me a minute and went on.

No, we hadn't rowed. We were – we were... happy. It wasn't like that. I wasn't at Byron on vacation. It was a work thing. Sort of. I'm – I'm trying different things. Looking for career options.

They let me go, asked me not to leave town without telling them and Chelsea's mum picked me up in the foyer and took control. I told her she could stay at our place and I'd get a motel room. It wasn't generosity. I couldn't face going back home. Not just then. I wanted somewhere small and dark to curl up in until the pain went away.

The interminable graveside service ended with people throwing handfuls of dirt onto the coffin. I didn't join in. I'd seen people do that on American TV shows and I assumed it was another stupid ritual Australians had picked up from that source. I wouldn't have been surprised if two Marines had folded a flag and handed it to Stacey. Maybe if I'd thrown some soil on my dead beloved, I would have got that closure Dr. Huber seemed so keen on. Or maybe I'd have felt more of a fool than I already did, standing there in the bright Brisbane sunshine, waiting for someone to lead me on to the next location in this peripatetic theatre of death.

I saw the big-boned cop in the cemetery as I was leaving.

He was standing at a discrete distance with a woman – another cop I suppose – who looked tiny compared to him. She was dark-haired, about his age – mid thirties – and dressed just as drably as he was. She saw me watching her and for a moment, her large, dark eyes met mine. I looked away quickly.

They held the funeral reception at my mum and dad's house in Kenmore. My dad is so proud of his much-diluted Irish blood I could imagine him saying something like, "Leave all that to us, Stacey. If a Kelly can't throw a good old fashioned wake, I don't know who can. You just get them here and we'll look after them, won't we Em?"

I was still in a daze as I stood there in that house I know so well with people – some of them only slight acquaintances, some of them complete strangers – taking turns to come up to me and tell me how sorry they were for my loss. After a few awkward words, they would leave me to face whoever was next. One or two asked odd questions like, "Have the police said anything?" or, "Are there any leads?" Not really so odd, considering, just a world away from where my thoughts were. But mostly they just said kind things about Chelsea or told me how sorry they were. Sometimes I said the wrong thing back to them like, "I haven't lost her; she's just not here any more," or, "Sympathy really doesn't help." I tried not to be such a jerk. Funerals are for the living, I kept reminding myself. All these other people are also feeling pain. But, if that was true, I couldn't understand why the funeral wasn't for me, too. I'm one of the living, aren't I? Why wasn't all the finger food helping? Why weren't the stilted encounters making me feel better?

I had never been to a funeral with Chelsea. There were a million things we didn't get round to. A million things we would never get to do together. What would she make of it? All the women in their plain dresses, the men in their toned-down smart casual. And me, feeling stupidly overdressed in my black suit and tie. I would never know – not for sure. She surprised me a lot. It was one of the best things about her. But doesn't that mean that I never really knew her? Was she gone before I even got to understand who she was?

The tightness in my chest became overwhelming. I crossed the room to where Mum and Dad were standing together. They must have known far fewer of these people than even I did. Mum put on a sympathetic smile and Dad looked serious, the corners of his mouth turned down. They liked Chelsea. Everyone liked Chelsea. They were sad she's gone but they were more concerned for me, their expressions said. So I pursed my lips and nodded. Yes, I'm miserable, but I'm bearing up, my face said.

"I'm going out for a bit of a walk," I told them. Mum put a hand on my arm to let me know she understood.

"Don't be too long," Dad said. "We have guests."

"Right-o."

The street outside was cluttered with parked cars. I supposed it must have been irritating for people to have to find spaces down the street or round the corner and walk to the house. I tried to resent their irritation, as if they should somehow have put all worldly considerations aside for this day of mourning and reflection, but my heart wasn't in it. It is annoying when you go somewhere and you can't park. It doesn't matter who's died.

I headed away from the shops and the people, wandering off into the quiet suburb, turning at random, only caring to be alone. In my dark suit, people might have mistaken me for a businessman but I was not. I had no business. I wandered along nature strips, gazing at people's gardens. There were yellow flame trees in bloom and pink crepe myrtles. I didn't know the names of trees before I met Chelsea. I knew all about Hegel and Kant but not the names of the trees I'd lived among all my life. While I had focused with blinkered exclusivity on my studies, somehow, she had managed to spread the net of her learning as wide as the wide world. Despite my degrees, I always felt like a dunce when we talked. And the wisdom of Wittgenstein and Russell, for all its logical rigour, seemed oddly sterile compared to the rich and lavish splendour of her own.

She had opened me up. She had shown me a world in brighter colours and bolder strokes. And now, with my education barely begun, it was all over.

I looked around, realising I'd walked a long way and I wasn't even sure where I was any more, possibly in Jindalee, although I didn't remember crossing the river. It was still only late afternoon, not yet evening. I got out my phone and switched it on to call an Uber to take me back to the wake. People would be wondering where I was. But the sight of so many missed calls and messages made me stuff it back in my pocket. I just couldn't face all that. I wanted to be somewhere where people didn't know what had happened, where they didn't keep having to tell me how sorry they were. The Jindalee Hotel – a huge, sprawling pub and restaurant – when I came upon it, seemed perfect. Eschewing the games room and the restaurant, I found a quiet public bar where I could sit alone and drink. I ordered a bottle of Toohey's Old and headed to a table against the wall. My phone rang and I immediately regretted having turned it on. It was Mum. Guiltily, I rejected the call and texted her back with, "I'm OK. Just want to be alone. Love, L." Then I turned the phone off again. I definitely did not want to look at my messages or my social media accounts.

Have the police got any leads yet?

The question popped into my head while I was at the bar ordering my third beer. Why that? Why then? I had no idea but it hit me so hard I said, "Shit!" out loud.

"You all right mate?" an old bloke at the bar asked me.

"What? Yeah, yeah. I'm good."

"If you don't mind me saying, you don't look it." I turned away, not wanting to engage. He was a rough-looking old fella with white stubble on his face and on his shaven head, big build, bit of a bruiser. "Who was it?" he asked. "Your mam or your dad?"

"What?" He was watching me closely with pale blue-grey eyes.

"Well, from your clothes, I reckon you've come here straight from a funeral. From your red eyes, I reckon it was someone close. My guess is you're about twenty-five, so it's not likely to be your wife or a sibling – although that's possible, I suppose."

It was intrusive and annoying, more so because he was pretty near the truth. I'd forgotten about the black suit and tie. I was walking around like a billboard with my grief written in giant black letters.

"None of my business," he said, turning away to cradle his glass of whisky – no, too dark for whisky, must be rum. I realised I'd just been staring at him without responding. The barmaid turned up with my beer at last and I handed her the plastic, ready to go back to my table.

"It was my girlfriend," I said on impulse.

He swirled his rum and nodded, lips pursed. "Chelsea Campbell," he said.

If he'd jumped up and slapped me, I couldn't have been more surprised. "What the fuck? How did you know?"

He turned his pale eyes towards me, his expression grim. "There's not that many brutal murders around here. Your girlfriend's was about a week ago. It was all over the news. Given a slight delay while the police examined the body, that puts the funeral around now."

I was impressed by how quickly he'd put it all together and alarmed that Chelsea's death had become a media circus, broadcast nightly for the entertainment of the masses. "You some kind of detective?" Worse still, maybe he was a reporter.

"Not any more." It seemed to be the end of the conversation, which suited me fine. I was about to leave but he asked, "Who's the SIO?"

"The what?"

"The cop in charge of the investigation."

"Are you a reporter?"

He gave a silent, derisive snort. "Your first guess was nearer the truth. Ex-cop. Ex-PI. Now 'retired'. So who's the SIO?"

I perched myself on the bar stool next to him – not exactly committing to a conversation but not exactly willing to leave yet. Maybe the old fella had some useful insights. "I don't know. There was a big guy called Trevor something. And a little dark-haired woman I just saw at the funeral service."

He nodded to himself. "Looked like the Marlboro Man?"

"I – don't know what that is."

He rolled his eyes. "Kids! Like Clint Eastwood on steroids."

"Something like that, I suppose."

"That'd be Trevor Reid I reckon. The woman was

probably Alexandra Bertolissio. He's a bit ordinary if you ask me. But she's the dog's bollocks. Sharp as a pin, that one."

"Right. And that means what?"

"It doesn't mean anything. I was just curious."

I stared at him flatly for a few seconds, then got up. "Thanks. You've been a great help."

I went back to my table and sucked on the bottle. When I glanced his way again, he was swirling his rum and gazing into its depths. I wanted to google "Marlboro Man" but didn't want to turn on my phone again so I left it. Some ancient cultural reference, I guessed. *The past is a foreign country*, I told myself. Old fossils like the guy at the bar must feel like displaced people, refugees forced to settle in a strange land where they barely speak the language and nobody wants to know them. I tried to guess his age but it was impossible. Somewhere between sixty and three hundred, probably. A strong, tough bastard in his youth, I reckoned, but now finding his joints were aching, the fat was piling on, and his muscles were getting weak and tired. Yet he still seemed sharp. His blue-grey eyes had been keen and steady and he'd pieced together my story pretty quickly. I hoped I would still have all my marbles at his age.

The bottle was empty and I didn't want to go back to the bar and risk getting into another conversation with my friend there, so I left. It was dark outside. The breeze was warm and I felt like walking again. I didn't know Jindalee well, so I was soon lost but that was OK.

Have the police got any leads yet?

I suppose the question was so disturbing because I didn't have the faintest idea. After that one interview, I hadn't had anything at all to do with the police. They must have checked my alibi and realised I was nothing to do with Chelsea's murder. I supposed they'd asked her mum and her workmates questions but I hadn't spoken to any of them, either – except at the wake that afternoon. But now I started to wonder. Was there a suspect? Had they arrested anybody? It was obviously some random crazy – a druggie, or a mugger, or something. Chelsea would have fought them.

It struck me like a punch in the gut. If someone had tried to rob Chelsea, she'd have told them to fuck off. She'd have been furious.

Shit! I should have been there. I should have been with her.

And who was he? Who was the bastard who thought he had the right to take that most precious of all lives? What kind of sick, twisted, evil…?

I was standing rigid and still in the street, fists clenched, trembling with rage. I wanted to know who'd done this. I wanted to find him and look him in the eye and do things to him, cruel, violent things. I wanted to watch him suffer, hear him scream in pain. And then I wanted to watch him die, the way he had watched Chelsea. I didn't just want it, I imagined it, every blow I'd strike, every cut he'd suffer, all the blood and snot and torn flesh, his cries, his pleading, the tears in his eyes, the piss in his pants… I wanted it all. I wanted it like I'd never wanted anything in my whole life. I would have died, smiling, if I could just have that bastard at my mercy before I went. I fell to my knees, screaming in frustration, burning with impotent fury.

I don't know how long I was there. The anger seemed to burn out the core of me until I was hollow and spent, sobbing on the pavement as people walked by and cars passed. I wasn't really myself again until a vehicle pulled up beside me and the street around me began to jitter in red and blue light. I looked up and saw the white police car with its blue-and-white check patterns.

"Been celebrating, have we?" the cop asked, standing over me.

I climbed awkwardly to my feet. He was a young man, about my age, quite a lot shorter but stockily built. His companion, a slightly older man, had also got out of the car but hung back a bit, watching me carefully. I was suddenly hyper-aware that they both carried guns.

"I was at a funeral," I said. He seemed completely unmoved by the admission.

"We've had complaints that you've been howling and screaming."

"My girlfriend was murdered," I said. From the tiny frown that flicked across his brow, I guessed I'd piqued his interest.

"Name," he said, pulling out a notebook.

"Chelsea Campbell."

He stared at me in silence. If he recognised Chelsea's name, he didn't show it. "Your name, not hers."

"Lucas Kelly. Doctor Lucas Kelly." He looked up from his book and pursed his lips.

"Address?" I gave him the address of the motel.

"I need to talk to one of your detectives. Trevor Reid. He's the SIO."

"What about?"

I had the strong impression this young man didn't like me. Maybe he just didn't like anyone he had to deal with for being a public nuisance. "It's... It's about the case. I need to know what's going on."

Again he weighed me up. "Detective Inspector Reid is off duty. How much have you had to drink?"

His whole manner seemed insolent. "I don't know. Four

or five stubbies, maybe."

"Or maybe a dozen, more like."

I felt my anger returning. "And what if I had? What's it to you? From what I hear, it's only black fellas who get arrested for public drunkenness in this state."

I saw a little snarl on his lips. Keeping his eyes on mine, he put away his notebook with slow deliberation. *Well, fuck him,* I thought. *If this little shit wants to get rough, I'm just in the mood.*

"I need you to move along, now, Dr. Kelly," the older policeman said, putting his shoulder between his partner and me. "And I expect you to go straight home. Can I get your word on that?"

The moment of tension ebbed away. I nodded. They watched me as I walked away up the street.

Chapter Two

The next morning I was woken by a knock at the motel-room door. I groped for my phone to see the time but, of course, it was switched off. It was light out but, in a Brisbane summer, that only meant it was after five am. I heard a man's voice outside, deliberately low, saying, "He's got a bloody nerve. We're not his errand boys." The knock came again.

"Doctor Kelly? It's the police."

"Hang on. I'm coming."

I managed to get my jeans on and opened the door. Hot air poured into my air-conditioned room and the bright light made me squint. There were two uniformed police officers standing there – not the two from the previous night, thank heavens.

"Sorry to bother you, sir, only we've been having a bit of trouble reaching you."

I don't know if I've ever been called "sir" in my life. Standing there barefoot, in the T-shirt I'd just slept in, I didn't feel much like a "sir". In fact, the faintly archaic word, used by these two armed men, in a power relationship to me that suggested the exact opposite of deference and respect, had creepy and sinister overtones. It made me think that I wasn't quite human to them, not really someone like them but a "member of the public", a creature that had "rights" that you might need to respect but for whom normal feelings like compassion were not appropriate. It was distancing. It put me in an out-group.

"Doctor Kelly?"

"Yeah. Sorry. Just woke up."

"We haven't been able to reach you by phone, sir. And we didn't have an address for you until this morning."

My brain finally clicked into the here and now. "Is it Chelsea? Have you found something? Do you know who did it?"

"I wouldn't know about that, sir, but if you'd care to visit the station some time today, Detective Inspector Reid is keen to have a word."

"Well… Yes, of course. Did he say what it was about?"

"Sorry." He looked past me at the phone on the bed. "Maybe you could leave that switched on in future. Save us interrupting your sleep." I glanced back at the phone and when I turned back, they were already on their way to their car.

I took my jeans off again and had a shower. By the time I left the room and crossed the hot concrete car park to Chelsea's car, it was eight-thirty and shaping up to be a stinking hot day. The sky was duck-egg blue in every direction and, in the shrubbery around the motel, rainbow lorikeets were shouting and squabbling. The car was already an oven. I turned on the engine and cranked up the air to max. Chelsea had a nice car, a mid-sized SUV – not because she went off-road but because she liked to have plenty of room to carry display equipment to exhibitions and customer demos. She'd wanted an electric vehicle but had to settle for petrol because there just wasn't much option in Australia.

The day she realised she couldn't "do the right thing" but had to go on polluting the world every time she took a drive, she'd not only ranted from dawn till dusk but had called her local MP to complain, called the State and Federal Ministers, and written to every media outlet in the country to express her utter disgust. She wasn't a green activist in any sense but she had absolute zero tolerance for stupidity, corruption, or blind prejudice.

It struck me how much she'd have hated me sitting there in a car park with the engine running, while I reminisced, so I pushed the stick into drive and got underway. The traffic, heading into the CBD in the rush hour was so bad that I pulled over at the first strip mall I found and had breakfast in a little café. I switched on my phone, ignored all the messages, and read the news while I ate. The old guy in the pub had said Chelsea's murder was "all over the news" but it wasn't. Not any more. A week on from her death, the media had completely forgotten, moved on to other murders, found new political scandals, new outrage at the latest Royal Commission findings, new cats up trees and crocs in back yards. A part of me regretted not having looked sooner, to see what people had said about it, but the better part of me knew that would just have been pointless masochism. Going to the funeral had been bad enough. Chelsea's death had been between me and her. It was no-one else's business.

Except, of course, it wasn't. Chelsea's mum had at least as much right as me to mourn her daughter's death. And there were friends and colleagues. Some of the people she worked with probably spent far more time with her than I ever had. Some she'd had with her from the very beginning, people who had been by her side through all the struggles and triumphs of starting and building a new company. I hadn't been with her at the client presentations, at the meetings with venture capitalists and banks. She'd prepared for each with a grim determination, like they were little battles, fought by a small band of heroes, and she'd celebrated her victories and licked her wounds with others, not me.

And then there were the police. Detective Inspector Trevor Reid and his sidekick, the Italian-sounding woman whose name I'd already forgotten. To them and god knew how many others, Chelsea was now a significant person in their lives, the focus of their day-to-day activities, a deep mystery for them to solve. And, finally, there was everyone else – the reporters who'd needed to fill a few column-inches, or fifteen seconds of TV news, the politicians who'd tutted about crime on our streets and used her name to push some agenda about police numbers, or anti-gang laws, or more state surveillance, and the general public, who, for some reason I've never understood, liked to see stories of murder and death in their newsfeeds. Perhaps it gave them a frisson of fear and fed a self-flagellating sense of impotence and vulnerability. Perhaps it reassured them that their god was looking after them and their loved ones and they were all right, Jack. Perhaps it confirmed their moral certainties that people – especially women – out alone at night, were righteously punished for their presumption and, probably, wickedness.

I stood up quickly and left the café. The great flood of traffic had eased back to a more steady flow and I joined it, eager to have the distraction of doing something and going somewhere. The past week had been like living in a dense fog. My thoughts had been overwhelmed by pain and misery. My actions had been undirected. Everything had seemed pointless. Now, my mind was clearing, which I supposed was a good thing, but the heavy blanket of my suffering was being burned off by a growing hot anger. I could feel it writhing in my chest, fizzing in my brain, but it was just as useless, just as unfocused as the pain.

Perhaps when I saw Reid, I would know what to do with the rage building inside. Perhaps if there was a suspect, it would give me a target for my anger. Until then, I just had the stupid arseholes all around me who couldn't drive to save their lives, and the money-grubbing rent-takers who owned the car parks in the city and milked everyone dry, or Detective Inspector Trevor bloody Reid who sent armed goons out to drag me into that scalding heat trap, then had the effrontery to make me sit around waiting to come and collect me at his leisure.

"Thank you for coming, Dr. Kelly," said Reid when he finally turned up. He offered a big, long-fingered hand. "Sorry to keep you waiting."

We went through doors and corridors while Reid made small-talk about how hard it had been to find me, how hot the day was and how the tennis was going. I kept my answers short and told him I had no interest in sports. We reached a small room. This contained a table, with four chairs around it and a couple more nearby. Reid moved a couple of chairs so they faced each other and did not have the table between them. He'd probably learned to do that on a training course. There were two cameras mounted opposite one another near the ceiling and I assumed they would be miked, Someone was recording everything that was said and done in there.

"Where have you been?" he asked, when we eventually got down to it.

"Nowhere."

"You haven't been home. I've spoken several times to Mrs. Campbell. She last saw you on the day she identified Chelsea's body."

"I moved out to a motel so Stacey could stay at the unit until the funeral. It's probably hers, anyway. Chelsea bought it. Her mother is her next of kin. She'll inherit it."

"You haven't seen Chelsea's will?"

"What will? Why would she have a will?" She was only twenty-four – two years younger than me – and I'd never even thought about making a will. Of course, I didn't own a thing. Chelsea had the unit, a car, her business, all kinds of stuff.

Reid watched me carefully. "There is a will. She drew it up about six months ago. Kazima Abbas, the company's Finance Officer, is the executor. You are the major beneficiary."

I was so stunned at the news that it took a while for the implications to sink in. I was probably not going to be homeless after all. I might even have a car. *Thank you, darling*, I thought. God, she was always so thoughtful and so together. I must have seemed like a silly child to her.

Then it hit me.

"You think I've got motive now, don't you? That's why I'm here, isn't it?"

"Where have you been this past week, Dr. Kelly?"

"For God's sake, stop being so bloody polite. It creeps me out. Especially if you're trying to pin a murder on me. Call me Luke." He just looked at me in silence and I remembered he'd asked me a question. "I was in my motel room, mostly, getting wasted and reading Sartre. The local bottle shop and the Chinese take-away up the road will have credit card receipts and all that. The motel cleaners will remember me as the bloody nuisance who never left his room. Anyway, what the hell do you want to know where I've been, for? I assume you checked my alibi for the night she was murdered. Even if I had a motive – and trust me, I don't. An apartment and a car? I'd swap you the whole city and a dozen Mercedes dealerships for one more day with Chelsea. Even if I did have a motive, I was three hundred kilometres away. Shit. Do I need a lawyer or something?"

"We're just having a friendly chat. You can leave any time you like."

"This is insane. How could I possibly have killed Chelsea if I wasn't even there?"

"That sounds like you're challenging me to work it out."

The guy was an idiot. In my growing anger, my thoughts became hard and clear. "So you've been working on this for a week and you have no clue who the killer is. Someone stabbed my girlfriend in an alley in Australia's third largest city, in an age of ubiquitous surveillance and DNA testing, and you haven't got any idea at all who did it. So, in desperation, in the absence of any actual evidence, you want to try and push my buttons in the hope I'll confess? Or what? What's your strategy here?"

"Oh we've got evidence. Plenty of it. We have the murder weapon. We have the clothes the killer wore. We even have his shoes. What size shoe do you wear, Luke?" There was something shifty about him that made me think he was hiding something.

"You have his shoes? Did he change his clothes? Is that it? He changed his clothes and dumped them somewhere – in a bucket of bleach or something to degrade the DNA. Is that what he did? Or did he burn everything, including the knife?" From his uncomfortable look, I could see it was the latter. "Jesus, you really don't have anything, do you? No CCTV, either, or you wouldn't have me in the frame. This guy is going to walk free, isn't he?"

"Your shoe size?"

"Ten, usually. Depends on the shoe. Take a look in the unit. Search the place. Every shoe I own is there, except these." I held up a foot for him to look at.

"We already searched your unit. Mrs. Campbell was most obliging."

"So you already knew my shoe size. Jeez this is so fucked up. Look, maybe I should be talking to the smart one. The woman, Alexandra something Italian."

He seemed quite taken aback by that. I could see his brain churning, trying to find out how I could possibly have known. Maybe I also saw a tiny bit of insecurity there. But he came back swinging.

"You're a smart guy yourself, *Doctor* Kelly. PhD in philosophy, right? Very impressive. I bet you could easily plan the perfect murder. You'd find an accomplice, give yourself the perfect alibi, choose a restaurant away from the CBD with no surveillance cameras, arrange for your guy to meet Chelsea there, some cock-and-bull story about a business proposition or something, get her into the alley behind the restaurant on some pretence, stab her fourteen times so it looks like a crime of passion, then go almost a kilometre through deserted streets to a dumpster, change his clothes for the ones he already left there with the bottle of metho, then douse the clothes and the knife and burn the lot. How am I doing so far?"

I stood up. What he'd just said was loaded with facts I hadn't known. Facts that had set my guts churning. I wanted to get out and get far away from that stupid bloody man.

"Your idea of a friendly chat is about as misguided as your

choice of suspect," I said but my voice sounded a weak and shaky.

He stood up too. I'm quite tall but he had a couple of inches on me and, I suspected, a lot of muscle. I guessed he must play for the police footy team, if there was such a thing.

"I'll get someone to show you out." We went into the corridor and a woman came down the corridor as if he'd signalled her somehow. "Mary, please take Dr. Kelly to reception and sign him out." To me, he said, "Keep your phone on, Luke, and let us know if you change address again. We will definitely want to be in touch soon."

Chapter Three

It was weird going to Chelsea's office knowing she would not be there but I had to see Kazima. My meeting with Reid had raised so many questions. If Chelsea was having a business meeting with someone on the night she died, why wasn't it at her office, or his office? And why not during office hours? Did they have a meal? And did he then take her out to an alley nearby and kill her? Why? I mean a meal suggested someone she knew – an old friend maybe – or a new one. So why would they then murder her? And, even stranger, the change of clothes and the bottle of meths suggested premeditation. Who did Chelsea know well enough to dine out with who would plan to murder her in cold blood? Or a passionate frenzy?

Kazima wouldn't know much, I supposed, but she might know something. Besides – and it made me feel grubby just thinking about it – I was going to need money soon. I hadn't worked for over a week and I was living in a motel. Chelsea had all the money. It wasn't the traditional wife-and-two-veg model of man the hunter and his domestic slave, but it worked for us. She made the money, she paid the bills. I did bits of part-time work, which I dignified by telling people I worked in the "gig economy", and that paid for stuff I needed without me having to ask for pocket money. I had my own bank account with a few hundred bucks in it, and that's what I'd been living on. I'd been avoiding thinking about where I was going to live and how, vaguely hoping that Stacey would let me stay on in the unit until she sold it.

The office was in a white-painted purpose-built concrete-and-glass building in the trendy suburb of West End. I thought the whole area was characterless and sterile, but Chelsea loved it and wanted us to move there. I parked in the little eight-car parking lot under the building in an empty space marked "Visitor". The other spaces were all filled, even the one marked "CEO".

A concrete staircase led up to the main floor which was completely open plan apart from a single office with Chelsea's name still on the door and a small meeting room. Everyone stopped work and looked at me when I walked in. I stopped too and stared back at the staring faces. They'd all seen me here before, picking up Chelsea, or joining her for lunch. They'd all been to parties and dinners where I'd been Chelsea's plus one. They'd all seen me at the funeral.

I couldn't move and I had no idea what to say.

"Luke, hi." It was Kazima, striding across the floor to rescue me. She shook my hand and said, "Let's go into the office." She seemed to understand that I was floundering like a fish on a beach, because she kept eye contact and gently guided me.

"It was hard coming back here, the next day," she said, closing the door.

Her sing-song accent was oddly soothing and I tried to remember her background. The child of Sudanese refugees? Something like that. Chelsea had talked about them all, all the time, yet so little of it had sunk in. "Which one was that?" I'd ask when a name came up I felt I should know, and she'd happily launch into a potted biography, as if I hadn't asked her ten times already. I loved it that she took such an interest in all these people but to me they were just background figures. My only real interest was always Chelsea.

"How are you doing?" she asked. There was a little table with comfy chairs around it and we sat there. I looked at Chelsea's desk. It was smart and new but nothing special. Kazima saw me looking and said, "I haven't had the heart to clear it, yet. The police took her laptop and some other things. I don't know why. I should bite the bullet, I know, only…"

I nodded and we sat in silence for a moment. This was so much harder than I expected.

"Can I get you a coffee or something?" she asked.

"I just dropped by to… I don't know… try and get a few things clear."

"Yes, of course." She sounded pleased, which made me look at her. She wore a serious expression, ready to help.

Veering away from the questions I wanted most to ask, I said. "I hear you're the executor of her will. I – I didn't know she even had one. She was so…" Young. Too young to even think about dying, let alone going and doing it.

"I think it was the insurance," Kazima said. "It got her thinking."

"Insurance?"

She looked puzzled, perhaps beginning to understand just how ignorant I was. "When we had our last round of financing, the VC wanted us to insure some of our key personnel – Chelsea, me and Hong, our lead developer."

"What, like, life insurance?"

"Yes. I thought it was a ridiculous expense but it turned

out…" She trailed off. I suppose she didn't want to say that anything about this was a good thing. "Anyway, she called the lawyer and made a will at the same time. It was very simple. There were a couple of gifts to her mother and other people but, basically, everything goes to you. It's so simple that the probate is trivial."

I nodded. "Does that include her car?"

Again I got the puzzled look. "I've been trying to call you for days, Luke. I didn't want to mention it at the funeral." She took a breath. "It includes the unit, the car, all her personal belongings – apart from the few that were bequeathed elsewhere – everything in her bank account, her investment portfolio, and this company. You own a sixty-nine point five per cent share of everything you can see."

"What? She left me—?" It was the craziest thing I'd heard all day – and that included Reid accusing me of murdering Chelsea. I wanted to get up and get outside fast. I didn't know how to run the company. I only had a slight understanding of what it even did.

"I suppose she wanted to make sure you had money. I mean, you could pay yourself a salary, or even sell your share. Although I really hope you don't do that."

"Sell? I can't sell Chelsea's company. It would be like…" It would be like selling Chelsea's remains. Or Chelsea's baby.

"Good," she said. "Look, we need to appoint a new CEO. I'm keeping things turning over but Chelsea is a hard act to follow. We probably need a full-time Sales Manager to cover her role, unless we can find another superwoman like her. Are you any good in that department?"

"Me?" I stood up and would have stepped back if the chair hadn't prevented it. "I can't do any of this. I'm just a—" I stopped not knowing what I was, quite. But I was definitely not a CEO or a Sales Manager, or anything. "I do some gig work – delivering food, copywriting – I don't run companies."

She looked at me as if I'd suddenly burst into song or grown another head. "Okay," she said, slowly. It made me realise how foolish I must look, panicking at the merest suggestion of taking responsibility for something. I glanced through the office's glass wall and saw a couple of people staring in at me. They looked away quickly.

"Jeez! They know, don't they, that I'm the new owner?" I sat down again. When I left, Kazima would probably have to talk to them, tell them how it went. There were ten people in the company. Each one of them would have been fearful for their jobs and their families ever since they heard about Chelsea's death. What could Kazima tell them? "Well, he freaked out and acted like a ten-year-old sissy with a wasp in his hair, but I'm sure it will all be just fine."

"Sorry," I said. "Maybe I could get that coffee, now?"

She got up and went out to the little kitchen area. They had a big, expensive cappuccino machine – a present from Chelsea to everyone on the day their sales hit some milestone or other. I had teased her that it was a present to herself, really, and she had grinned and said, "Win, win, right?" I watched Kazima's back as she moved about, getting cups and grounds, sugar and spoons, working the machine. She was a tall, angular woman about my age. She was solid and she looked strong and competent. She and Chelsea had met at a trade show and hit it off from the start. The company had been Chelsea and two developers at the time and she had brought Kazima in part-time to look after the finances. Eventually, she also took on the role of office manager and worked full time. Now, she was running the place and, I suddenly realised, feeling out of her depth.

I sat back in my chair and closed my eyes. I had felt so sorry for myself since Chelsea died. I'd been completely overwhelmed by grief to the exclusion of everything else. Now I saw how much of my self-pity was self-indulgence. I hadn't even wondered how the company was getting on, how all those people had been coping with uncertainty. It was just the same as my attitude to the police inquiry. Someone had killed Chelsea – murdered her in cold blood, I now knew – and I hadn't even wondered why or who. All I had cared about was my own unhappiness. What a despicable, selfish piece of work I really was!

"I don't know how you take it," Kazima said, setting down a tray. "So I brought the full kit."

I began spooning sugar from a little bowl into a matching cup. *This is the service they use for visiting customers*, I thought. I was being treated like an outsider, not part of the team.

"I've put together a spreadsheet of Chelsea's estate for probate purposes. If you give me your email address, I'll send you a link. It's all in Google docs." I thanked her and gave her my address. "Her diaries and notes and everything else are in Google docs, too. It's what we use here. I could have just given the police a link and a password and they'd have had it all but they insisted on taking her laptop." I could imagine Reid wanting to carry off something solid and physical, not just a couple of strings of letters and numbers. I took a sip of my coffee. It was the same kind as we had at home. Chelsea's favourite Arabica roast from the shop in Indooroopilly Mall.

"Kazima?" She looked straight at me, her face composed. God knows what she was thinking I might say. "If you had someone to handle sales, could you run this place – you know – well? Make a proper go of it?"

Her brows furrowed and her lips pursed. She nodded slowly. "I believe so. Chelsea and I were pretty much in tune about how things should go and how we should run things. We have a rolling three-year plan that just needs to be executed." She smiled. "That should be good for about six months I reckon. Do you want to see it?"

I shook my head. "You're the new CEO. OK? Get yourself a sales guy. Get yourself whatever you need. I'm going to be no bloody use to you at all, so don't think you have to run everything past me or any crap like that. You were Chelsea's friend. She trusted you. So I'm going to trust you too."

She took a sip of her coffee and watched me over the rim of the cup.

"I guess we're all getting big surprises today," she said. "Thank you for that." She put her cup down. "There's just a couple of conditions before I say yes."

And this is why I'm no kind of businessman, I thought. I had fully expected her to just whoop with joy, pump my hand and crack open a bottle of champagne.

"I want a raise," she said. "Chelsea paid herself peanuts. My salary is OK but, as CEO, I'll expect more."

I shrugged. "Whatever you think is reasonable. You know the company finances. You know what you can afford to pay yourself."

"OK. I want a bigger share of the company."

"Excuse me?"

"I want another ten per cent."

"How does that work, exactly? Do we just sign something to say your share is bigger?"

"No, you sign something to say you're giving me part of your share."

"My share?" I'd only known I had any share at all for about fifteen minutes, so it all seemed a bit academic. "How much did you say you want?"

"Another ten percent. I already have five. It was part of the deal when I joined."

"So you'd own fifteen per cent of the company." She nodded. "And I'd still have…" I'd forgotten how much she'd told me I had.

"Fifty-nine point five."

"Right." I shrugged again. Then it occurred to me that Chelsea might have expected me to be a little less cavalier about giving away big chunks of her company. "What's that worth?"

It was her turn to shrug. "We turned over four million last financial year. This year might end up being double that. We have some pretty cool IP and a great team. The plan is to go for a public offering in three years. It could be worth tens of millions by then, maybe a lot more."

"So your fifteen per cent would be…"

"The kind of incentive that keeps people like me working their socks off night and day to make this company succeed."

Just for form's sake, I said, "Five per cent." I fully intended to cave if she argued.

"Seven point five."

"Agreed."

Her face lit up. Apparently she'd been trying it on. Maybe I should have offered two. She reached out a hand and we shook. Maybe she had taken me for a ride. On the other hand, Chelsea had left me the company knowing exactly how useless I am and she'd left Kazima as the default boss, knowing exactly how hard-headed she was. Maybe she had foreseen exactly the little scene we had just played out.

"I'll draw up all the documents and I'll call you when you can come in and sign them. Just one more thing. I know you want to be hands-off and everything but I want us to meet at least once a month. I'll report the figures and I'll go over the plans, legal issues, HR matters and so on. It's not necessary, I know. I just… I think having to explain myself to someone would be kind of healthy for me. And you'll get to know the business. I'm not asking you to make any decisions or approve anything – except, you know, implicitly – I just don't want to feel, I don't know, untethered." She made a small hand gesture towards the people outside. "This is kind of huge, you know? We can review it after a year."

"No worries," I said, touched by her show of vulnerability. I could sit through a presentation every month if it helped. "Now I need a couple of things. That link and password to Chelsea's diary and notes you mentioned. And is there some way I can get some money for, like food and board? I'm flat broke and it's getting a bit desperate."

A few minutes later, I drove out of the car park with a well-stuffed bank account and a promise of a contract with the company for regular payments as a "business advisor" to the CEO. I drove back into town, parked without resenting the parking fee, and ate a very late lunch at a café by the river.

Chapter Four

I went to the cemetery and found a bench where I could see Chelsea's grave. There was no headstone, yet, but I remembered the way there and the fresh earth made it easy to find. I have no religious feelings at all. Life is just life, death is just death, and there is nothing magical about any of it — except in the poetical sense. But I wanted to say thank you to her for looking after me, even after her death. I had a home, now, and a car, and enough money to go on living a simple, frugal life without ever having to worry about working. One day, if Kazima's IPO ever came off, I'd be quite wealthy. It was weird to think Chelsea's little company was worth so much, even weirder to think she had been thinking about my welfare, planning for my financial security, even while I was drifting through my life hardly thinking at all.

It was impossible not to feel bitter and angry about myself. I was a philosopher, for heaven's sake. My life had been devoted to thinking. Yet I had barely spared a thought for anything that actually mattered. And now, as grateful as I was for Chelsea's thoughtfulness, I could only think about how miserably unworthy I was of the love of such a woman.

"I just thought there was so much time," I told the mound of earth over her body. "No, that's not true. I didn't think about how much time there was at all. I thought I could look around, pick a direction, find something I liked and was good at. We both did. We didn't have to rush to get married, or to have kids. Everything was so relaxed and easy. But now I'm starting to think that was just me, 'cause you were out there hustling. You were building a future, getting things done. And maybe, maybe you were just indulging me, letting me drift along in my little fog of abstractions and self-absorption. I don't know if I really understand anything anymore.

"When I saw your office today, it was like seeing it for the first time. It wasn't just some place you hung out and did boring computer crap, it was like a beachhead in enemy territory that you had fought hard for and won. It was where you were engaged and focused, planning the campaigns that would give you more victories, more territory. I thought you were my partner, my lover, my best friend. And you were. But all the time you were also this warrior woman. And I sort of knew it but I didn't really appreciate it, didn't really understand all that you were."

My face was wet with tears and I brushed them off angrily. More self pity. More pathetic self-indulgence.

"Anyway, I just wanted to say thank you, for taking me on – for adopting me, I guess – for loving me and making me feel secure and loved. You always said love was about caring – caring about and caring for. And you were good at both of those things while I... I don't think I cared for you enough, however much I cared about you. You always said love requires a certain level of competence if you're going to do it properly. And I thought I knew what you meant but maybe I didn't. Maybe I didn't have any real idea how far short I was falling in that department."

What the hell was I doing, sitting in a field full of dead

bodies, talking to a pile of mud? *Mad as a bag of frogs*, I told myself. I thought about going home but I didn't want to sit in that ratty little motel room, or risk going back to the unit and finding Stacey still there. I should call my mum and dad, tell them the news about Chelsea's will. At least that would stop their endless fretting about my long-term prospects. I could call a friend, guilt-trip them into going to a bar with me. But I just didn't want to be around people.

What I wanted, I finally realised, was to start taking control. I wanted to start doing positive, meaningful things. I wanted to get the police off my back. Most of all, I wanted to find out who had killed Chelsea and why.

It came as a surprise. One minute I'm sitting there full of self-hatred and a vague idea that maybe I might do something to distract myself. The next minute, I'm full of purpose and certainty. The police were obviously idiots. Their only suspect was me, so I knew for a fact they were getting it wrong and wasting their time. I could also see it was either laziness on their part or a failure of imagination. Probably the crime statistics said it was usually the partner who did the murder, so that's where they were looking. But I'd be starting from a different place. I knew it wasn't me. That gave me a big advantage and a big head-start.

It also left me with a big problem. I didn't have a clue about how to investigate a murder. I didn't know what questions to ask, who to ask, how to build a case, what evidence I'd need, or… well… anything. But, hell, I'm a bright guy. How hard could it be? I'd just analyse the problem. It's not like I was trying to understand the nature of consciousness, or solve the problem of free will. I just needed to work out a procedure that would help me get to the answers I needed.

I took out my phone, meaning to write down a few notes and it struck me that this was even easier than I thought. All I had to do was google "how to solve a murder".

As soon as I did, I was deluged in information. Most of it was about games and TV shows, there were books on forensic science, interviews with cops, tips on interrogation techniques, articles about surveillance equipment, hints on how to take a good plaster cast of a footprint, discussions of the law around citizen's arrests, what to look for to spot if someone is lying, and on and on. It was hopeless – and, for the most part, extremely off-putting. Even so, I plunged into it. If six years at uni had taught me one thing, it was how to read through piles of crap, sifting it for the nuggets of information I needed. But chasing down ideas in a well-stocked library, filled with erudite and well-indexed books, is nothing at all like ploughing through the ocean of garbage you find on the Web. It was almost dark when I finally stopped. My phone's battery was just about dead and my back was killing me from hunching over a little screen on a cemetery bench.

"All right," I told Chelsea's grave. "It was a dumb idea. I'm not going to learn how to be a good cop by playing murder investigation games online. But I'm going to do this. I'm going to find out who killed you. And I may be a complete bloody loser, and I may have just wasted half a day, and I may be lacking in all the skills and experience I need to do this, but I know a man who isn't."

* * * *

As I reached the car, I got a text message from Stacey.

"I am back in Sydney. The apartment is yours for now.

But I intend to contest the will and my lawyers will be in touch. The police asked me if you could have killed Chelsea. I told them you were too useless to do anything so purposeful. Even so, in the light of her confused and erroneous bequests, I am keeping an open mind. I don't expect we will meet again."

What the…? I fought the urge to send back an appropriate reply like, "I see now why Chelsea moved a thousand kilometres away from you at the first opportunity." But, on reflection, I decided that "Good riddance!" was what I truly felt and that any kind of response was a waste of time. Even so, I was edgy and irritable as I drove out to the motel to collect my stuff and check out.

As I knew it would be, the unit was immaculately clean and tidy and several of Chelsea's pictures and keepsakes were missing. I didn't begrudge Stacey any memento of her daughter but to just take them like that suggested she thought I might try to deprive her of them. It was insulting and petty and so much in keeping with things Chelsea had told me about her. I sat on the edge of the bed, staring at the space where one of Chelsea's favourite childhood photos had hung and let my anger subside.

"If it makes her feel better," I said aloud. It hardly mattered what Stacey did or what she thought about me. Even about contesting the will. I had no idea what the legal status of it was, or what kind of case Stacey would need to make to overturn it. It was only money. I had enough right now, thanks to Kazima, to see me through weeks of investigation and that was all that mattered. It would have been nice to be rich but some part of me thought that maybe Stacey deserved her daughter's money more than I did, anyway. It was probably all for the best.

I threw everything I had worn, including what I had on, into the washing machine and found myself some clean gear to wear. I called an Uber and was out of there in ten minutes flat. Stacey had actually done me a favour. I had been so annoyed by her and her passive-aggressive antics, that I had forgotten to be freaked out at seeing our unit again. I still had to face it properly, bag up Chelsea's things, make decisions about what to do with pictures, face each chair and table we'd bought together, smelling her scent on her clothes… but coming back next time wouldn't be so bad. Maybe.

Arriving at the Jindalee Hotel once again, I went straight through to the bar.

The old guy was there on the same stool, just as I knew he would be, nursing a glass of rum and scowling at the bar top. I took the stool next to him and caught the bar tender's eye. "Toohey's Old," I said, "and another one of those for my friend."

He swivelled his grizzled head to look at me. "What the fuck do you want?"

"I want to pick your brains."

He looked back at his rum and gave it a little swirl.

"I don't have a license any more," he said.

"What?"

He sighed as if I'd irritated him beyond all endurance. "Look, mate, you only know two things about me. One is that I drink in this bar – because you've seen me here. The other is that I used to be a PI – because I stupidly told you. And I only know two things about you. One is that your girlfriend was murdered – because that came up yesterday. The other is that you probably didn't do it – because you're still walking around free, eight days later, and even a useless bell-end like Trevor Reid would have locked you up for it by now if he possibly could have. From those four things, I conclude that you've come swanning in here, shouting me drinks, because I'm the only real-life PI you've ever come across and you want me to help you find the real killer."

"Wow." I was impressed. "You're really good."

"I am so glad you think so. Now piss off."

For a moment I was taken aback, not just because of his openly hostile attitude, but because I'd forgotten what he'd opened with. "Right. Right. The license. No PI license, I get it. But, look, I didn't want to hire you. I just wanted to ask your advice about how I should proceed."

"A hundred bucks an hour, or part thereof, plus expenses."

"What?"

"If you want to hire me as a criminal investigation consultant, that's what it will cost you."

"Who said anything about—?"

He turned his pallid eyes on me in a hard stare. "Don't fuck me about, kid. You think I'm bloody Santa? You think I'm going to give you everything in my sack just 'cause you've been a good little boy? What the hell planet did you come from? Here on planet Earth, we exchange goods and services for money. So agree to my terms, or go pester some other poor fucker."

I realised the bartender had returned with the drinks and had stayed to watch the show, a grin on her face. I took them from her and paid. When she finally sauntered away, I turned back to the old guy. "All right, you're on."

He grinned too and put out a hand. Reluctantly, I shook it. To tell the truth, I expected some kind of macho bullshit like a knuckle grinding power-grip, but it was a perfectly ordinary handshake.

"Right," he said. He checked his watch, downed the rum he'd been nursing and picked up the one I'd just bought him. "Let's go through to the food bit and get some nosh. They do a good feed here. You'll like it."

He made me pay for the meal. "Expenses," he said.

"Alright, let's start," I said, as we sat down.

"We started back in the bar when we shook hands," he said, affably.

Refusing to be wound up, I said, "My name is Lucas Kelly."

"I know."

"What?"

"You don't think I really only know two things about you, do you? Lucas Michael Kelly, born in Brisbane, aged twenty-six, parents Michael and Emily, went to Kenmore High, degree in philosophy at UQ, followed immediately by a PhD, also in philosophy, also at UQ. Met Chelsea Campbell about two years ago. Moved in together a few months later. You're unemployed. She owned a small but fast-growing software company making tools for games developers. That was all easy. Got it from the Web. Why do the police think you killed her?"

He fixed me with his stone-eyed scrutiny as I got over the fact that he could know so much about me so quickly and applied myself to answering the question. "It was the will. I inherited everything."

"What's it worth?"

"I – I don't know. I didn't go into the detail. Millions, probably."

"Nice. What else?"

"What else?"

"What else makes the police suspicious of you?"

"Nothing. I wasn't even there on the night Chelsea died. I was at Byron Bay."

"Convenient."

"What?"

"If I was planning a murder, I'd make sure I was out of town, too."

"What? You mean having an alibi makes me a suspect? What kind of logic is that?"

He ignored the question. "So what else?"

"Nothing. Me and Chelsea were in love. I had absolutely no reason to hurt her. I didn't even know what she was worth and, even if I did, I assumed her mother would get it as next of kin."

"You didn't know about the will?"

"No!"

His eyes never left mine for a second. "Who did know?"

"I don't know. Kazima and the company lawyer, I suppose."

"Kazima?"

"She does the finances for the company. Runs the office. She's the new CEO now."

"How did she get on with Chelsea?"

"They were fr— You can't think Kazima's a suspect."

"Why not? Did they argue? Was she skimming money from the accounts? Were you having it off with her? Was Chelsea having it off with her? Oh don't look so bloody offended. Someone's got to ask the hard questions. What about Chelsea's mother? How were her finances? Jeez, mate, do you spend your whole life sleep-walking? All right, never mind the will. I'll want to see a copy of it. You've got a copy, right? Christ Almighty! OK, well, get one. Tell me about the murder."

I don't think I'd ever been so insulted, belittled, or made to feel so ashamed of myself, by a complete stranger, in my whole life. I wanted to get up and walk out but a part of me was saying, *Suck it up, you dickhead. This is all gold. This is what you need to hear. This is how you'll find the killer.*

"I – I don't know much," I said, hearing myself and realising how it would sound. "She was stabbed in an alley, near a restaurant. She'd met someone there and, afterwards, he killed her."

"Which restaurant? Which alley? Who did she meet? Did she often meet men in restaurants at night? Did he take her into the alley, or did she take him?"

I stood up, outraged at the suggestion he was making. He sat back and watched me. I noticed his plate was half empty even though mine was completely untouched. "I'm not going to put up with this shit." My voice betrayed my righteous anger by wavering.

"Suit yourself," he said. "You owe me a hundred bucks."

"Fuck you!"

I turned and left, feeling every eye in the place watch me go.

Chapter Five

I went over and over the conversation in my head as the cab drove me home, thinking of all the things I should have said, all the things I should have done, and all the many ways it had been a mistake to go and see that crazy old bastard. I stopped at my local Chinese takeaway on the way back and continued to obsess over the encounter as I waited for my meal.

By the time I'd walked the rest of the way home and chewed my way through the lukewarm food, I was exhausted and emotionally drained. I went to bed and slept, not noticing until the small hours of the morning that I was in our bed alone for the first time.

After that, sleep was impossible. I spent the best part of an hour, trawling through the menus on the various streaming channels we subscribed to, looking for something, anything, that might distract and entertain me. It was another complete waste of time.

Whatever my other shortcomings as a human being, I seemed to be excellent at wasting time. It was now almost a full day since I'd been interviewed by Reid and I had achieved absolutely nothing – unless you counted sitting around in a cemetery, talking to myself, and letting some old freak con me into buying him a free meal.

I was still angry about the old guy and his damned insinuations about Chelsea and everyone around her but not so angry any more that I didn't realise there might have been some kind of method in his madness. Maybe he was like the René Descartes of old moochers in bars, applying systematic doubt to everything and everybody in some half-arsed attempt to get down to some universal truth. It was certainly striking how his questions had very quickly revealed my own ignorance about the facts of the case. It was also painfully obvious that he was willing to look at everyone I knew as a potential suspect, to look at people's motives in a cruel and cynical way that I was completely incapable of.

I felt a new energy stirring in me. Maybe Old Moocher had shown me the way after all. He'd asked about people. He was trying to build a list of suspects. And he'd asked about the crime, trying to establish the facts. I stood up, excited. I could do that. I remembered TV shows I'd seen. The police had big whiteboards on which they stuck photos of suspects, drew timelines, wrote down pertinent facts.

I needed a whiteboard and I knew just where to go to get one.

The Officeworks on Milton Road had been one of Chelsea's favourite places. "It's the Magic Kingdom," she'd said. "It's like a lolly shop for grown ups." I'd been with her a couple of times, once to buy stationery and once in search of a cheap printer. Frankly, I had not seen the attraction.

It was ludicrously early when I got there and parked in the empty car park. The clock on the dash said it was 6:03 AM A quick search on my phone told me the shop didn't open until seven. Fortunately, I was in walking distance of the cafés in Park Road, so I went over there and had breakfast among the early-bird office workers while I read the Guardian online.

The news was all politics and sport so I ended up reading opinion pieces about the UK economy going down the gurgler and Aussie farm lobby groups pushing a science denialist agenda. It all felt like despatches from a different universe; one where reality barely impinged on the minds of its narcissistic aliens, all self-obsessed to the point of solipsism.

At last, my alarm pinged and I hurried back to the shop. Bizarrely, there were other cars in the car park by then and I was by no means the first customer. I left with a whiteboard, an easel for it, two packs of coloured felt pens, a pack of post-it notes, a selection of paper notepads and pens, some photo printing paper for my home printer, half-a-dozen file boxes, packs of plastic document sleeves in different colours, and a pack of chocolate biscuits because they were there. I stuffed it all into my car, fought my way through the swelling rush-hour traffic, and managed to get it all into my unit in only two trips from the car park.

I set up the whiteboard, opened a packet of pens, tried one, opened the packet of photo printing paper and put it in the printer, made a cup of coffee and sat down with the chocolate biscuits to stare at the whiteboard, thinking, *What would Old Moocher do?*

Jumping up, I grabbed my laptop and began searching for photos. Chelsea was easy, so was her mother, the delightful Stacey. I found one of Kazima on the company website. I sent them all to the printer. I put Chelsea's picture at the top of the board and wrote "Chelsea" above it. Below it, I put Kazima's picture and Stacey's and wrote their names too. These were my suspects. There weren't many and I knew damned well neither of them had done it but I set that aside. I was being Luke Kelly the hard-bitten, cynical detective, not

Luke Kelly the useless prick.

I drew a line under them and gave it the title, "Timeline". I needed to fill this in, somehow. At the leftmost end, I made a mark and labelled it, "Last time I saw Chelsea alive." That was at 1:30-ish on the Friday-before-last. At the right-hand end, I made another mark, labelled, "Chelsea's body found". I didn't know when that was, exactly, but it was some time on Sunday morning. So I wrote that. I made a mark for "Chelsea stabbed", one for "Chelsea leaves restaurant" and one for "Chelsea arrives at restaurant".

A wave of sadness hit me because I didn't know exactly when she had been found, or who had found her, or how long she had been lying in that alley, or even which alley it was she had died in. I sat down, tears running down my face again. This was all such a waste of time. Such a horrible travesty. I wasn't solving her murder, I was out eating over-priced breakfasts and buying coloured pens. Everything I'd done since she died had been a farce, an insult to her, and now, with my file boxes and whiteboard, a mockery of her life.

I curled up on the sofa and closed my eyes so I couldn't see Chelsea's face smiling at me from the photograph. What had she ever seen in me? Why would a strong, together person like her ever take up with a useless loser like me? It didn't make sense. If I'd died and Chelsea had been left behind, she'd have been on top of the whole situation. She'd be chivvying the police, making sure she was informed of everything they did. She'd have been working closely with them, feeding them useful information, making sure they stayed focused. She'd have used her press contacts to get the public calling in with leads and eye-witness evidence. She might have offered a reward for information leading to the killer's arrest. There was no reason I couldn't be doing all of that, too. And yet I'd spent the week hiding away like a delicate flower and, even when I'd resolved to act, I'd just done stupid stuff and wasted more time. If Chelsea could have seen me curled up on that sofa, she'd have been so ashamed.

Or would she? There was no doubt, she had seen me in a funk many, many times. She'd helped me "defend" my PhD, even though I'd been a nervous wreck at the thought of facing the external examiner. And she'd helped me through the months afterwards as I slowly discovered that everyone had been right all along: I was practically unemployable as a philosopher in the anti-intellectual, austerity-driven world we live in, underqualified for anything that required actual skills and expertise, and overqualified for anything else. By the time I'd been through a dozen interviews for jobs I didn't even want, seeing the same look on a dozen interviewers' faces – the look that said "This guy's a joke. Why am I even wasting my time with him?" – I was a basket case. But Chelsea helped me get up off the ground again. "OK, so those guys don't want what you've got," she told me. "But you've still got it. So take a bit of time, take a good long look around, and work out how you're going to monetise it."

I wished she was there with me so I could ask her precisely what "it" was, because, whatever she thought I had, I was finding it very hard to see what she saw. In fact, I just wished she was there. Full stop.

I suppose I must have cried myself to sleep. I woke up to the sound of knocking at the door and the sticky unpleasantness of drool on my cheek. I called out, "Just a minute," and staggered over to the door, getting all the way there before I realised it should have been the buzzer and my caller should have been out on the street, not standing a few inches away in the hallway. "Who is it?" I called. My door didn't have a spy hole. Why had that never seemed like an issue before? What if it was Chelsea's murderer come to kill me too? It struck me, as it had not until that moment, that there really was a killer on the loose out there, a man who had viciously and brutally murdered the woman I loved. I felt a chill in my stomach and a rush of adrenaline. I ran to the kitchen and grabbed a knife. If this was Chelsea's killer, he was not going to get away with it.

I returned to the door and pulled it wide open in a rush, gripping the knife hard, ready to plunge it into the evil bastard who had come for me. Even as I did it, another thought came to me. *What if it was the police, come to arrest me?* What the hell was I doing? I froze in horror at the insanity of being on the cusp of attacking some random person with a knife.

"Fucking Jesus!" the man in the hallway said, falling back a step and raising his arms as if to fight me off.

"You!" I cried. I almost sobbed with relief. I didn't have to fight a killer. I didn't have to explain myself to the cops. It was only Old Moocher from the bar. He gathered his wits a lot quicker than I did.

"Put that fucking thing down, you fucking boofhead." He looked me up and down, no doubt taking in my dishevelled clothes and wild hair. "Are you pissed, or what?"

"I thought..." I began but was too embarrassed to say what I'd thought. Which made me cross. It was my place and he had no right to take that tone. "What the hell are you doing here? How did you get in the building?"

"Can I come in?"

"No bloody way! How did you even know where I live.

No, wait, you're a detective. What do you want?"

His jaw clenched and he seemed to struggle against an angry retort for several seconds. Eventually, he said, "I came to apologise. I acted like a dick and I shouldn't have." He looked past me into the apartment and his eyes narrowed. "Is that Chelsea?"

"None of your business."

"And those two would be Stacey and Kazima, right?"

"How the hell did you know that?"

I'm not sure how it happened but I kind of stood aside and he walked past me into the room. He went straight to the board and studied the timeline. "I can put some more detail on this if you like."

"What? How? What do you know about it?" I closed the door and followed him into the room.

"Only what I found in the papers and online. But it seems to be a lot more than you know."

I wanted to argue with him and throw him out but instead I put down the knife and picked up a pen. I held it out for him. "All right. Go on then."

He took the pen and started writing things – the name of the restaurant ("Tea For Two"), the time she arrived there (6:50 PM), the time she left (8:40 PM), the name of the alley ("Barnett Lane"), the estimated time of death (8:50 PM), and so on. He didn't refer to any notes and he talked while he worked.

"The name's Ronnie, by the way. Ronnie Walker. And as for last night, like I said, I was a prick, and I'm sorry for that. And I'm probably going to go on being a prick, so I want to apologise for that in advance. Thing is, I've always been a prick. It's what got me chucked out of the navy, and the police, and why I couldn't make a go of it as a PI." His face darkened as he went into what looked like a short reverie. After a moment, he shook his head, scowling. "Fucking clients."

He left the timeline and started to draw a fragment of a map. It had a rectangle labelled "Tea For Two" and, behind it, "Barnett La." Beyond that was a zigzag path through some unnamed streets to another street a few blocks away marked "Torville St." on which was an "X" with the word "dumpster fire" next to it.

"How do you know all this?" I asked again, bewildered.

"News reports. Google Maps. Jeez, mate, it's not rocket science."

"What are you even doing here? I'm not paying you for this."

He put down the pen. "You owe me a hundred bucks for last night. We made a deal. And a deal's a deal." He didn't act belligerent or aggressive but I still felt a curl of anxiety. He was an old bloke, yes, probably over seventy, and at 5' 10" I had at least four inches on him but, while I could imagine people describing him as "stocky" or "compact", "tough" or even "thuggish", those same people would probably describe me as a "beanpole" or "scrawny".

"Today, however, is gratis," he said. "In fact, I've decided I'm going to help you." He put on a big grin. "So, go get the kettle on, and fill a flask, 'cause we're going out."

"I – I haven't got a flask."

"Mate, I'd give you a good slap only I don't want to get idiot on my hand." He pursed his lips as if to stop himself speaking and held up his hands, palms towards me. "Sorry. I just can't help myself. I'm sure we'll get on great once you get used to me. So, why don't you go out and buy a thermos – make it a nice big one – and I'll finish this?" He waved a hand at the board.

It probably seems strange that I let him into my home, put up with all that crap from him, and then left him alone there while I ran his errands. It certainly felt that way to me and yet there was something I needed there. Not just the information he brought, or the expertise he had. What I really needed and was secretly glad to get, was someone who knew what to do and who just took charge. It's kind of pathetic, I know, but that's how I felt.

I got back to the unit half an hour later with my shiny new thermos flask, a bagful of wholesome snack foods and a pair of binoculars. I reckoned he was taking me on some kind of stakeout and I was showing initiative. He was stretched out on the sofa with a coffee beside him and my laptop balanced on his chest. I stomped over and took it off him, cursing myself for forgetting to log off.

"Not a single subscription to any porn sites?" he said, eyebrows raised. "What kind of a bloke are you?"

"One who doesn't want to contribute to the exploitation of women – or children or animals or whatever it is you're into."

"*Touché*! But I see you stand before me unarmed in this battle of wits."

"The old ones are the best, I suppose." I tried to put plenty of scorn into it, guessing that he got most of his wit and wisdom from Internet memes.

"I couldn't agree more but you try explaining that to the young hotties at the pub."

"Did you do anything while I was gone? Apart from poking around in my stuff?" I wasn't actually upset about him finding my porn stash – I didn't have one and, if I did, my tastes were so tame, any such collection would probably rate a

PG classification. It was my fumbling attempts at writing a novel and some poetry that I was particularly sensitive about. I hadn't even let Chelsea look at those.

In response, he tipped his head towards the whiteboard. He'd added a few more details here and there, including lines between pictures labelled with their relationships, but the main addition was an empty rectangle with "Mr X" written next to it.

"Mr. X?" I asked. "That's your contribution?"

He sat up and looked at me seriously. "That's our killer. Today, we're going to find out everything we can about him, hey?"

I shrugged. "Sure."

"Let's go, then." He got to his feet and headed for the door.

"Go where?"

"To the restaurant, first off."

I held up my carrier bag. "But what about the flask?"

He gave me a big, shit-eater grin. "Mate, I just wanted you out of the house for a while so I could rifle through your undies draw."

I stopped dead. "What the fuck?"

"I needed to know if you were Mr. X, yeah? It's not like I could just ask you. Well, now I know. You're a hopeless innocent, who loved your girl, and who writes really bad poetry."

I still didn't move. It was an outrage. It was an invasion of privacy. It was probably a crime. And the crack about the poetry was really unfair. I should have been furious but, again, I was mostly just relieved. Unlike the police, he believed it wasn't me. I was actually grateful for the vote of confidence. Even so, I had to put up some kind of show of disapproval. I opened my mouth to tell him how little I thought of his investigative methods but he cut me off.

"Yeah, yeah, I get it. Moral outrage, blah, blah, blah. Look, it was quick, it was efficient, and it got a lot of bullshit out of the way so we can focus on Mr. X, right? So, are we going, or what?"

I took a long, deep breath. "Right-o." What was the point in arguing? For whatever reasons of personal inadequacy, I'd let this cranky, intrusive old bugger push his way into my life, so now I might as well make the most of it.

We left without another word and made our way downstairs to the hallway. There was a double glass door to the street and as we approached it, like a distorted mirror image, two other men approached from the outside. We all stopped and looked at each other. I had the odd feeling that, if I raised my right hand, one of the men outside would raise his left.

Ronnie broke the spell by stepping forward and throwing open the doors.

"Detective Sergeant Trevor fucking Reid," he said, stepping outside. I followed him and let the doors close.

"That's Detective *Inspector* Trevor fucking Reid to you, Walker." I might not have been there for all the attention the two cops paid me. "What the hell are you doing here? Does he know you lost your licence? It would be too bad if you were passing yourself off as a PI and I had to arrest you for it."

"Always nice to bump into you, Trev. I see you're here without your better half." He gave the other cop a fake smile. "No offence mate but we all know the only way this guy is safe to be let out is with his Girl Friday along to stop him wandering into the road." The other cop worked his jaw, trying not to smile. Pleasantries over, Reid turned to me.

"What's going on? Why is this man here?"

I really did not like this bloke's attitude. "Mr. Walker is a friend of mine. We're a little busy just now. Can I help you?"

"I need to ask you a few questions. Shall we go inside?"

Ronnie stepped forward. "As Mr. Kelly explained, he's busy just now. I'm sure if you were to call and make an appointment, a mutually suitable time could be found for an interview."

"Fuck off, Walker. Mr. Kelly?" He held out a hand towards the door, inviting me to go back inside.

"As I said, I'm busy."

"You don't want to help us find your girlfriend's murderer?"

"If I thought that's what you were doing here, I'd be all over you like a rash. As it is, I think we should start conducting our affairs a little more formally. My lawyer will call you to arrange any further interviews. And he or she will be present at every one."

"On the other hand, why don't I just take you down to the station right now? If you want to be awkward, I can play that game."

"Are you arresting my friend, Detective Inspector?" Ronnie's tone was sweetness itself. "Because, if not, I can't see why he'd agree to that. And, if you are, I reckon my advice would be to keep saying 'No comment,' until his lawyer arrives to get him out and lodge a formal complaint."

Reid's lips tightened into a snarl. He stepped up close to Ronnie, which made my heart beat even faster. "This better be fucking important to you personally, Walker, because I don't like washed-up old has-beens sticking their noses in my business. Do you really want to screw with me?"

"If that's all, Inspector," I said as firmly as I could. "I need to be on my way." I didn't know why I was being so brave. Reid was a big bloke and he could have snapped me like a twig. Also, although this was the second confrontation with the police I'd had in the past twenty-four hours, I assure you, there had not been another in the past twenty-six years. On the other hand, these were not normal times and I was definitely not my normal self.

Slowly, Reid backed down and stepped away from Ronnie. He turned to me and said, "I want to hear from that lawyer today. If I think you're hindering my investigation, I'll have all the reason I need to drag you in in cuffs. Do you understand?"

I wanted to make some defiant, preferably witty, rejoinder but with him glaring at me like that, all I had the nerve to do was nod. As soon as I did, he turned and strode away, his sidekick hurrying behind.

"Jesus!" I said, as soon as he was gone. "That was a bit intense."

Ronnie grinned at me as if it was all good fun. "Don't worry about Reid. His problem is he's actually an honest cop. Makes him a paper tiger. If he was bent, he'd have taken you in on some bullshit charge just for the fun of throwing you in a van so he could rough you up a bit. Then there'd be a resisting arrest charge, too, assaulting a police officer, all the usual crap. No, the one you need to worry about is his buddy Alexandra."

"The little woman you said is clever."

"That's the one. If there's a case to be made and she thinks you did it, she'll have you. She's like a dog with a bone."

My mouth felt dry. Ronnie was painting a picture of a

whole police force out to get me, good ones and bad ones alike. "Well, there's no case. So I'll be all right, won't I?"

"Yeah, sure. No worries." Yet his breezy dismissal somehow failed to reassure me.

Chapter Six

Tea For Two was an intimate little place, vaguely Italian in cuisine and upmarket modern in decor. Even in the middle of a bright Brisbane summer's day, it was cool and dim. The sign on the door said "Sorry, we're closed." but there were still people moving around inside, clearing up after the lunchtime session. My stomach grumbled to remind me I'd been eating erratically for a long time and neglecting its reasonable demands. Ronnie tried the door. It was open, so he went straight in. There was a young waitress, cleaning tables and a young bloke with a broom. They looked at us like startled meerkats for a moment before the waitress hurried over.

"I'm sorry, we're closed."

"Of course," said Ronnie, his voice suddenly modulated and urbane, his face all smiles. "I don't mean to interrupt your work. We're not after food – although it smells delicious. My name is Walker and this is Luke Kelly. Luke is the *de facto* of the young woman who was in here last week, the night she was murdered." The waitress stared at me with widening eyes. The guy with the broom stopped pretending to sweep and walked over to join us.

"Oh my god," the waitress said. "That's so awful. People are still talking about it. We've had police and reporters and all kinds coming here. She was so young and pretty. It's like, you daren't walk in the streets round here no more."

"You saw her then, on the night she died?"

"Yeah, nah. I don't do Saturday nights. Ain't worth it. Jase was on, though, weren't you?"

The young man nodded seriously.

"So you saw her then?" Ronnie asked.

"Hello? Can I help you?" A middle-aged woman in an apron appeared from a door at the back, walking briskly towards us. "Is there a problem?"

"This is that Chelsea's bloke," the waitress said. "They want to ask us some questions."

The woman gave me a careful appraisal, during which Ronnie jumped in with his introductions. "We just learned that Jase, here, saw Chelsea that night. Were you here, too?"

"I'm the owner," she said. "I'm always here. Look, the police have already asked us loads of questions." She seemed to notice her two employees listening in. "Get on with it, you two. I'll handle this." To me, she said, "I'm very sorry for your loss but I don't know what I can tell you that I haven't already told the police at least three times. Maybe you should—"

"We're really sorry to impose on you like this," said Suave Ronnie, in his most regretful tone, "but, to be honest, the family feels the police investigation hasn't been all it could be. The man who was with Chelsea that night, for example, what kind of overcoat did he bring with him?"

"Overcoat? Why would he bring an overcoat? It's the middle of summer."

Ronnie smiled and nodded. "Yes, indeed. Some people

just have cold blood, I suppose." If nobody else heard what he'd said, I certainly did. "Now, try to remember the overcoat."

"There wasn't an overcoat," the woman said, starting to sound a bit tetchy.

"Yes! There was!" It was the guy with the broom. "Sorry, I couldn't help hearing. He did have a coat. I remember it was on the back of his chair, like a big raincoat, black, or navy maybe. I remember thinking that there was no chance of rain, so why was he lugging that bloody great coat around with him. Jeez, I didn't even remember until just now."

I stared at Ronnie in amazement. How could he possibly have known?

"You see?" he said, turning back to the owner, who was also looking at him like a stage magician who'd just pulled out the card she had been thinking of. "That's the kind of detail the police have failed to pick up on. Poor Luke here is going mad with grief and needs all our help finding the monster who destroyed his life. I don't think the police are going to be much use. It's up to us to do the right thing by that poor dead girl. So would you mind if we just asked you and young Jase a few more questions?"

By the time we left Tea For Two, we had a full description of Mr. X and the events of his dinner with Chelsea. He was an Anglo-European male ("No bugger just says 'white' any more," Ronnie had grumbled as we compared notes), average height, average build, mid-to-late twenties, black hair, black suit, pink shirt, red tie, black shoes, and the astonishing black overcoat.

"How did you know about the coat?" I asked as soon as it came up.

"Trade secret," he said, looking away.

58

"Why are you being evasive. What made you think he had a coat?"

"You don't want to know."

"Yes, I do."

"All right, then." He fixed me with his pallid eyes. "If he'd planned to stab her, he was going to get blood all over his clothes. It's why he wore a pink shirt and a red tie – in this bloody heat. To a dinner date. Since he also planned to walk about a kilometre afterwards, a coat would be handy for hiding his blood-soaked clothes." The image it conjured was so vivid I felt puke rising in my throat. I looked away quickly and he said, "Told you."

Mr. X had arrived before Chelsea. The table was reserved in the name of Jones. When Chelsea arrived, she didn't give any name, Mr. X was easy to spot from the entrance and he waved her over before she'd had the chance to ask. They seemed to know each other well. Jase thought they might be "relatives or something" because they were friendly but "not all dopey and smiley like people who come in on dates." I couldn't help feeling a surge of relief. I trusted Chelsea completely but Ronnie's insinuation last night had scared me more than I wanted to admit. It was a mystery to everyone why a woman like Chelsea would take up with a bloke like me. I suppose a part of me had always been waiting for her to wake up to the idea that she could do so much better for herself.

They'd chatted and ordered, laughed even. Jase seemed to have been watching them closely. ("Yeah, watching Chelsea, I reckon," was Ronnie's verdict.)

"How did you know he'd ordered a steak?" I asked Ronnie, remembering him asking the owner.

"Lucky guess," he said. And there was that evasiveness again.

This time, I worked it out. "It saved him bringing a knife with him," I said, weakly.

Ronnie nodded and was silent for a while. "It tells us something about our man," he said. "The guy is the kind of yuppie who has a matched set of good knives in his kitchen – and probably never uses them. If he'd used one of those, the burned remains in the dumpster would have matched the empty slot in his display case. So he needed a different knife. He's a yuppie so he doesn't have camping knives or anything like that lying about, so he'd have to buy one. He daren't go to a shop and do it in case the police can trace it to him. Same with an Internet purchase. Slipping a steak knife up his sleeve was an easy, untraceable solution." He shook his head. "Our Mr. X is one seriously cautious bloke. He's been to that restaurant before, too, to case it, and he's walked these streets, to make sure there are no CCTV cameras and not too many people. A smart guy, a planner, probably with a good dose of obsessive-compulsive disorder. Someone Chelsea knew well. Similar age to her—"

"Older," I said.

"Mate, to seventeen-year-old Jase, you probably look like an old geezer. We need to explore the possibility that she was at school, or uni, with this bloke – as well as all the other possibilities."

After they'd eaten, the conversation had seemed to become more intense. "No, not a blue," Jase had said, "more like they were excited about something. Probably whatever was in the envelope."

"What envelope?" Ronnie and Luke had asked in unison.

"He took it out of his jacket pocket and put it on the table.

The girl – Chelsea – wanted to take it but he kept his hand on it and kept saying no but not in an angry or mean way, just kind of all secret squirrelly. You know what I mean? Like she couldn't look in a busy restaurant but he'd show her later, in private." Later, he'd put it back in his pocket.

Mr. X paid cash. They'd left together. And that was all the Tea For Two staff could tell them.

"Should we tell the police about the coat?" the owner had asked as they were leaving.

"Yeah, you can if you like," Ronnie had said and then he'd become all conspiratorial. "But it would be best if you could avoid mentioning our visit. If they know we're on the killer's trail, they'll try and stop us – even if they're doing a pretty ordinary job of finding him themselves. They just hate relatives sniffing around. They're as territorial as bloody magpies in the mating season."

"So what now?" I asked when we'd been over everything we'd got from the restaurant.

"Now, me bucko, we go to that café over there, and get an overpriced coffee and a pie to set us up for a walking tour of the lovely suburb of Spring Hill."

* * * *

We found the alley easily enough. The crime scene was almost directly behind the restaurant although Mr. X and Chelsea would have had to walk down two quite major city streets before turning off into it. It was obvious, even to me, that Chelsea had gone willingly. You could not have dragged someone all that way on such busy streets without someone noticing. I had expected police tape and maybe a constable on guard but all evidence that a woman had been brutally murdered had been removed from the alley. We went to the place where the stabbing had taken place. Neither of us had spoken since we set off. I stared at the ground, morbidly searching for a bloodstain that I could not see. Ronnie stood nearby, slowly turning as he examined the buildings all around us.

"Nothing," he said in a flat tone.

"What were you looking for?"

"Windows. Places people might have been sitting on balconies. But all we've got are the backs of shops and office buildings. The cops will have gone around and asked for witnesses but they won't have got anything."

"Why here?" I asked. Even in the daytime, it was a forlorn and dismal place. In my imagination, Chelsea lay in a tangle on the pavement, blood all around her. I set off walking. I had to get away from there.

"Oi!"

I ignored Ronnie's shout, didn't really hear it. He shouted again. And again. I stopped.

"You're going the wrong way."

I turned, trying to keep my eyes on him, not on the pavement. "What?" I could see as well as he could that the alley was a dead end. The road stopped not twenty metres behind him. "This is the only way out."

"No it's not," he said. "Think about it. He's just walked in here with a woman. People on the main road might have seen them. Now she's dead and he's covered in blood. He puts on his coat to cover up the worst of it and puts the knife in his pocket. But a curious passer-by might easily spot the mess on his face and hands and they might remember the woman. He can't risk it. If someone calls the police and he's stopped, it's all over. There must be another way out."

I looked past him to where the road ended. Beyond it was a brick wall – the back of another office building.

"Come on," he said and walked towards the wall. I followed, curiosity overcoming my horror for the moment.

There was a door in the wall and several windows. The door looked solid. He tried the handle and it did not open. The windows at street level were barred. Then he spotted something in the corner. There was a gate. It was a metal grille, set in a frame that was about three metres high and topped with razor wire. It was locked with a chain and heavy padlock. Beyond it, a concrete path ran between two buildings, disappearing around a corner.

"This is it," he said. "Got to be."

"I don't see how."

He reached in and grabbed the heavy padlock, pulling it and a length of chain out to show me, The lock looked brand new and so did the chain.

"Our Mr. X came here earlier that day and cut the chain to give himself an escape route. When the police spotted it – I bet it was your friend Alexandra – the owners replaced it with this new, beefed-up version." He got his phone out and pulled up Google Maps. "Yep, this path leads to any number of places he could get out from. Some are practically on a direct route to the dumpsters in Torville Street. Come on."

We went back to the main road and walked in silence along the noisy streets to the front of the buildings Mr. X might have emerged from. The sight of that alley had laid a heavy hand on my mood and my mind was full of oppressive images of it, the litter she must have lain among as her life trickled away, the stark brutality of the buildings all around that were the last things she saw, and her murderer, putting on his coat, probably wiping his face and hands with a cloth he brought for just that purpose, feeling satisfied that his plan was working so well. Did she cry for help? Did she beg for mercy? Was it all so sudden and violent that she had no time to speak?

"Focus on the case," Ronnie said. "You're a hunter now, looking for tracks. You're going to find this man and you're going to lock him up. His life is over. He just doesn't know it yet. That's what you should be thinking about."

Maybe it was, but I couldn't see it that way. It was my life that was over – at least, the life I once had with Chelsea. In a way, I didn't care what happened to Mr. X. He was irrelevant. He'd hit my life like a runaway train. Smashed right through it. Why should I care what happened to the train afterwards?

Ronnie stopped and consulted his phone. "He could have come out here and..." He pointed to a street across the road. It ran between a bunch of small businesses, a plumber, a tile shop, that kind of thing. They would all have been closed for the night when Mr. X came by. Beyond the shops were purpose-built blocks of apartments and a few large houses converted to units. It was all quite up-market and very impersonal. It was the kind of street a man in a black coat could walk along at night and never see another soul.

We followed it and were soon in a suburban maze of rentals with low walls and arrays of post boxes stuffed with junk mail. It was depressing to think that people had come to a place like that and been pleased to find a couple of rooms to live in. Depressing, too, that I had been part of it. Still was, I supposed, when all this was over. Whatever this was. Until then, I hardly felt a part of anything.

"What are we doing, Ronnie?"

He looked at me and kept on walking. "I shouldn't have brought you. Sorry. I didn't expect you to... Anyway, I thought you might see something, have some kind of insight… I dunno."

"Yeah? Even so, what the hell are we doing?"

He looked at me and frowned. "Tracing the killer's route. You know that."

"Yeah, but why? The police will have done this, won't they? They found the cut chain. They know which way he went. They probably had cops knocking on every door in these bloody awful streets, asking if anyone saw him."

"They talked to the people at Tea For Two as well. Does that mean we shouldn't talk to them ourselves?"

"Well… yes, probably."

He shook his head and we walked on in silence. When we turned a corner into Torville Street, he stopped and looked along its length. It was another commercial area, something like the alley we'd left a kilometre behind us, with shops and businesses backing onto it. There were dumpsters here – big metal ones. He started walking again until he found a dumpster-sized gap with black smoke marks running up the wall.

"They took it off to Turbot Street for forensic examination," he said.

"So that's it? A dead end?"

He squinted at me as if trying to puzzle me out. "You need to engage that king size brain of yours, Luke. You're not firing on all four cylinders by a very long way. Did you really think we'd come here to look at a burnt-out metal box and that, somehow, we'd find a clue in it that scene-of-crime and forensics managed to miss?" The exasperation in his voice turned to hardness. "Where are we? Right now, right here. Where are we?"

I shrugged, feeling stupid. "In Torville Street."

"And?"

"Where the murderer burned the evidence. Burned his clothes. Washed his face and hands. Put on other stuff."

"So?"

It felt like one of those awkward scenes from school days where a teacher would keep badgering some unfortunate dummy who hadn't read the book to come up with an answer he didn't have a clue about. The rest of us would all know exactly what the teacher wanted – at least, I always did – but we had to sit there and squirm in sympathy as the dummy was tortured.

"So... he knew the place, knew he wouldn't be seen, knew he could take his time."

"Yeah, yeah. What else?"

It was becoming irritating and I didn't like feeling like the naughty schoolboy. "I don't fucking know. Just tell me." But, even as he opened his mouth to speak, I realised what he was getting at. "It's where he left from to go home. There's a route out of this street and out of this area that takes him to safety."

"At last! But where did he go? Did he walk another kilometre – or more – to get home? Risky. He could have been spotted. Did he have a car parked nearby? Or a long way away? Both risky. Or does he live here? In the next street, maybe, or just round the corner, or even over one of these shops?"

I scanned the buildings around me as if I might see him at an upstairs window looking down at us. "Jesus. Do you suppose the police have thought of that?"

"Of course – and several other possibilities. He could have called a cab. He might have left a bike here. He might have been picked up by a friend. He might have gone to ground in a pub and left the area two hours later. Loads of possibilities. And they will have thought of all of them and they will have had to check up on every single one of them, if it was plausible enough. Don't let Reid fool you. He knows how to run an investigation and he's as thorough and methodical as the next man. If knocking on doors and checking alibis can solve the case, he'll solve it."

"But sometimes that's not enough," I said, making the inference from something in his tone of voice.

"And that's why he needs his little Italian sidekick." He grinned. "And that's why you need me."

Chapter Seven

"Something I don't understand," I said as we sat in a hushed and almost empty Indian restaurant that evening, waiting for our meal to arrive.

"What's that, Grasshopper?"

"This guy, Mr. X, has gone to enormous lengths to hide every scrap of physical evidence of his involvement in the murder, right? It'd be unusual for someone to plan a murder so meticulously, wouldn't it?"

Ronnie nodded. "I reckon. I've got to say, I've never seen it before. Murders are usually spur-of-the-moment things: crimes of passion, if you like."

"Right. So, given all that, why has he been completely relaxed about letting people see his face? I mean, he could have just jumped Chelsea in the street or gone to our unit or something. Why sit around in a restaurant with her for half the night, then walk down busy streets with her before... you know?"

"That's a good question." He sat back in his chair, settling into the role of wise mentor. "Well, I can think of several reasons. The first, and most important, is that his plan went wrong. He knew Chelsea, and he was having a legitimate business or social meeting with her. He took pains not to go anywhere he was known, to pay cash, and all that but, if the cops had gotten onto him, he'd have just acted all innocent and said he left her in the street and walked home. He didn't expect the police to connect the dumpster fire with the murder. If they hadn't, it might have looked like she'd been attacked by some random psycho, or been in a mugging or an attempted rape that had gone wrong.

"You see, all a murderer has to do to get away with it is to raise a reasonable doubt in the jury's mind. There was no CCTV of him and, without it, there's only the evidence of young Jase at the restaurant that it was even him. That kind of thing is easily discredited in court. Besides, it's almost impossible to find a suspect based only on a description of him, especially if he's wearing a disguise."

"A disguise?"

"Sure. He had 'a bit of a beard', Jase said. How long would it take you to grow 'a bit of a beard'? Well, maybe not you, you probably haven't started shaving yet. It would take me less than a week. So Mr. X just had to stay out of sight for a week – go on holiday, go to an overseas meeting, some plausible excuse – and he's got his disguise. Then he shaves it off as soon as he gets home from doing the deed and, bingo, Jase is on the witness stand squinting at the accused and saying, 'Well, I don't know, I'm pretty sure it's him but, without the beard, it's hard to be sure.' I bet you a million bucks Mr. X has been clean-shaven his whole life and can get a dozen intimate friends to swear to it."

"So, knowing what he looks like won't help us." I couldn't keep the despair out of my voice. The description of the man with Chelsea in Tea For Two was the only solid lead we had. Every single thing else was guesswork and supposition.

The meal arrived and we let the waiter put down the

various pots and plates. I was paying, of course, so Ronnie had not stinted himself.

Ronnie began stuffing chunks of meat and naan bread into his mouth. "Thing is," he said as he chewed, "in an investigation, there is almost no fact that doesn't bring us closer to the perpetrator."

I poked at my vegetarian curry listlessly, admiring his enthusiasm – for the meal as well as our hopeless case – but not feeling any of it rubbing off.

"Look at what we know already," he went on, using a fork to emphasise his points. "The killer was a young man who is normally clean shaven. He was planning the murder for at least a week – the time he needed to grow a beard. And he had to stay out of sight for at least the week before the crime. He has visited that restaurant before and walked those streets many times, working out his plan. He visited the alley the day of the crime to cut the chain on the gate he escaped through. We know he knew Chelsea: knew her well. He may have been in her class at uni or at high school even. We suspect he lives very close to Torville Street."

The way he put it really did make it seem like we knew a lot about this man. "So…" I said, groping my way forward. "We get class lists from Chelsea's school and uni. We get the electoral roll for the area around the dumpster fire site? Then we try to find a name that is on both lists?"

"There you go! You're not as thick as you look." He tucked into his food with gusto, as if we'd solved the case and this was the celebration.

"Won't the police have done that already?"

"Maybe. Maybe not."

I remembered standing in the street a couple of hours earlier, looking at the spot where the dumpster had been and thinking we'd gone as far as we could. Had the police done that? Had Trevor Reid felt that same sense of hopelessness I'd felt? Or had his smart little sergeant told him there was still hope? At the very least, they'd have sent cops to knock on everyone's door to ask if they'd seen anything. Perhaps someone had seen Mr. X leaving, dressed differently, with the dumpster burning at his back. But, if that were the case, why did they still want to interview me?

"I need a lawyer," I said, one thought leading to another.

"Yeah, you do. Don't worry, I know a bloke."

"I don't want someone dodgy. I'll ask the company lawyer to recommend someone."

He put down his spoon and waved a piece of folded naan bread at me. "You fucking little turd," he said. "Is that what you think of me? That I'm dodgy? That everyone I know must be dodgy? What the fuck do you know?"

He looked really angry. It was quite menacing. And what did I know? That he'd been kicked out of the Navy, then the police, then couldn't get on with his clients as a PI? For all I knew, he'd beaten his bosses and his customers to a pulp. Even with three careers, he looked old enough to have done substantial jail time in between.

"I – I'm sorry," I said. "I wasn't thinking. I just meant..."

"I know what you meant, fucker." He looked like he wanted to shove that piece of naan bread in my face but, after a moment, he threw it on his plate, fell back in his chair and scowled at me in silence.

I didn't know what to say, or where to look. I didn't want to antagonise him by making eye contact. "The thing is," I began. "I don't really know you. And I don't know why you're helping me. Not that I'm not grateful. I am. Only it's all just a bit..." *Weird*, was what I wanted to say. "I mean, I just met you in a pub two nights ago and here we are…" *Jeez, was it only two nights?*

His scowl became a grimace, then a look of exasperation. "All right. Fair enough. You don't know me. So what have you done to find out about me?"

"What?"

"Have you looked for my Facebook page? Have you searched for newspaper articles about me? Have you even asked me any questions?"

"Well… I…"

"Here." He pulled out his phone and poked at it for a moment. "Here's the folder of notes I've got on you and Chelsea. Your backgrounds." He showed me the screen. A popular notes app was open and the page had my name at the top. There was a list of folders down the side with titles like "Education", "Employment", "Family", "Friends" and so on. He whisked it away before I saw much. "All right. You show me yours?"

"Well, I haven't…"

"No, of course not. So, do a search now. See what you can find." I started to complain. I wanted to make the point that it was an invasion of privacy. But he was getting stroppy, saying, "Go on. Go on."

Reluctantly, I pulled out my phone. I opened Google and typed, "Ronnie Walker" into the search field. There were, of course, tens of thousands of results. The first page was dominated by a singer and an American football player. I glanced at the angry, set face opposite me and tried to refine the search. I added "private investigator" to his name and got ten times more hits rather than ten times fewer as I'd hoped. There were FBI agents, PI companies that happened to employ someone called Ronnie, or someone called Walker, something about UV blockers, all kinds of rubbish.

"Wouldn't it be easier if you just told me?" I said, growing annoyed that he was making me waste my time on this.

"You think so?" He started poking at his phone again. "Maybe you'd like me to take you to the toilet too? Hold your cock so you don't get piss on your feet? Here."

He handed me his phone. This time it was open at a Facebook page. And there was Ronnie's happily-smiling face, flanked by two curly-haired dogs that seemed to be smiling too. There were a couple of short posts visible under the banner. One was a very crude and offensive cartoon about our current Prime Minister. The other was an apology to everyone that he was going to be a bit busy for a few days and the hope that The Dogsbodies could get along without him for a while. I clicked on "About" and found a load of stuff about his volunteer activities with various charities and his great passion for a club called The Dogsbodies. I checked out the "Photos" section and there was Ronnie, mostly with other old blokes and women, grinning and drinking. There were quite a few pictures of dogs, too: dogs on their own, dogs with other dogs, dogs at shows, dogs with Ronnie…

I looked up at him. "What the hell?" It was as if his Facebook page was some kind of secret identity, deliberately hiding the crusty old bastard I knew, behind the façade of a fun-loving, sociable dog-fancier. "So, by day you're mild-mannered Ronald Kent, wit and raconteur at the Jindalee Bowls Club, but by night you become Supersleuth, fighting for Truth, Freedom and the chance of a free curry?"

He grinned at me and held out his hand for the phone. I gave it back to him, reluctantly. I wanted to see more of his incredible double life. "That lawyer I know is…" He scrolled his photos for a second and showed me a white-haired guy whose face looked like it had been ploughed and harrowed. "...this bloke's son. He'd look after you as a personal favour to me, if I asked him. He owes me." That sounded more like the underworld crime figure I thought I was working with. He started poking at his phone again, then lifted to his ear. "Hang on." His voice rose ten decibels. "Terry? Sorry to bother you at home mate. Ronnie Walker." He laughed so loudly everyone in the place turned to look. "Yeah, well, next time you get to pick the strip club." He laughed again, then his voice grew serious and, thankfully, a little quieter. "Mate, I need a favour. Friend of mine's in trouble with the cops. They're trying to pin a murder on him." I sank down in my seat, feeling every eye on me. "Yeah, total load of bollocks but the heat's on. Chelsea Campbell case. Trevor Reid's the SIO. Yeah, that's the one. Can he come see you tomorrow morning?" There was a pause while Terry talked. Ronnie used the time to roll his eyes and make a hand gesture to indicate his friend was talking too much. Eventually he said, "Excellent! Nine o'clock. I'll make sure he's there. Give my love to Olga." There was another laugh and the call was over.

He looked at me meaningfully, then started tapping at his phone as he spoke. "I'll text you the address. I've seen how useless you are at looking anything up. Don't be late. Terry Marchant is the best criminal lawyer in Queensland, so be sure to act grateful that he rescheduled his whole day to fit you in." He turned his attention back to his food and ate with relish. I watched him in silence.

I had a strange feeling of dissociation from my life. Outside forces were pushing me around like a ship in a storm. Chelsea had died and that monstrous catastrophe had cut me loose from everything that had anchored me to solid ground. Now I was drifting farther and farther from shore, helpless to reach any harbour. Not least among the forces acting on me was the police investigation, going on beyond my awareness but ready to stab out at me at any moment, and this crazy old geezer stuffing his face opposite me, organising my days, finding me lawyers, doing me favours...

I pushed my plate away. "I'm off."

He didn't seem surprised. "Nine o'clock tomorrow," he said, sternly. "And then you can start making a list from the electoral rolls. OK?" I hadn't a clue how to do that but I nodded. "I'll go visit the schools and the uni and I'll meet you again at your place at tea time. We'll order in and compare notes, OK?"

"Sure," I said. Why not? I'd just let him organise my life for the whole of the next day but what else was I going to do?

"And don't forget to get the bill on your way out."

It was a warm night and somewhere above the street-light haze was a clear sky. I thought I'd walk home but Brisbane is a city designed for cars, not people. After half an hour of trudging along ugly roads, still full of hissing, growling traffic, I called a cab and gave up. My unit was empty and silent when I stepped through the door. The whiteboard faced me like a challenge, like a rebuke. I put my head down and pushed past it to the bedroom.

Chapter Eight

I rolled over in bed, seeing it was light, and looked to see if Chelsea was still sleeping. Her side of the bed was empty and, for a moment, I wondered if she was up already. I listened for sounds from the kitchen.

And then I remembered.

I got out of bed quickly, struggling for breath as if I'd been hit in the chest. I went to the lounge room and began tidying up. Anything rather than lie still thinking about her. I knew from having done it so many times just how bad that could be. I showered and dressed, put the kettle on, reached into the freezer for some bread. Keeping frozen sliced bread was one of Chelsea's "life hacks" as she called them – little tricks and techniques for coping with her busy, unpredictable lifestyle. I shut the freezer, picked up my phone and keys and left the unit. I needed more and bigger distractions, or this was going to be another Very Bad Day.

In the car park I stopped. What was I doing? Where was I going? It took a while to order my thoughts. My head was full of fluttering, restless birds on the verge of panicked flight. Electoral rolls. That was it. No, no, something else. The lawyer. Yes! I had to meet him. I consulted my phone and found Ronnie's text. Some building I'd never heard of in the

CBD. Nine o'clock. Three exclamation marks, the cheeky sod. But it was already 8:30 and, although I was only ten minutes away on a Sunday afternoon with no traffic, I would be late for sure trying to drive there on a Thursday morning in the rush hour, then finding a parking place and then finding the building. But I just might make it on my bike.

The bikes had been Chelsea's idea too. It was beginning to be obvious to me that I had been something of a passenger in our relationship. Chelsea had definitely been the driver. We were supposed to use the bikes to get more exercise, to make us more grounded, and to help save the planet. In the end, Chelsea had barely ever touched hers, but I found it a convenient way to get around our great, sprawling city. During my PhD, I used to cycle in to the university a lot. A bike's a great mode of transport when you don't have tight schedules and you can ditch it and take a cab when it rains or the wind is high. Weaving through rush hour traffic on one, going as fast as you dare, with every driver likely to jump lanes right across your path at any moment, was too much like a game of Russian roulette: the kind of game where you know, if you play it long enough, you will definitely end up dead.

So I arrived panting, sweating like a pig, and shaken from several near misses, in a George Street low-rise, at five minutes past nine. I left my bike in the entrance, not really caring if someone nicked it, and took the lift up to the offices of Glebe Associates on the fifth floor. The best criminal lawyer in Brisbane seemed to work out of a suite of offices that must have been impressive in their pre-WW2 heyday but which gave me a strong desire to go find Ronnie and punch him in the nose. Dingy didn't quite do it justice. The sour-faced old fossil behind the reception desk was probably one of the original fittings. She looked at my sweaty face with ill-disguised horror and said I should go straight in.

"Mr. Marchant has been waiting," she added and I tried to look suitably contrite.

Terry Marchant's room was brown, lined with brown books and sported a brown polished hardwood desk so heavy it must have taken half an old-growth forest to supply the timber. It made the lawyer, a balding, beaky man in a high-backed leather chair, seem small and out of place. Surely this office belonged to someone large and important. There was a phone on the desk but no computer. Marchant had a massive law book open in front of him and was making notes with a fountain pen on a pad of paper. It was a shockingly archaic scene.

He stood up to shake hands across the desk and asked me to sit.

"I've been talking to our mutual friend, Mr. Walker," he began without introduction. "Sounds simple enough. The cops are trying to fit you up for a murder you did not commit. You have a strong motive but a cast iron alibi. They need to show that you conspired with a third party..." Here he gave a small, wry smile. "...Mr. X, as Mr. Walker calls him, or they have no case at all. By now they will have been through your finances and your phone records, your movements, your associates, and all the CCTV footage they can gather. Yet they have not arrested you. We can assume, therefore, that they have found nothing to tie you to Mr. X. Of course, the case against Mr. X is itself entirely circumstantial. The man in the restaurant may be as innocent as you are."

"I don't think—"

He held up a hand. It was a small, pallid hand. "My job is

to prevent the police from exceeding their authority. I'm happy to do that *pro bono*, as a favour to Mr. Walker. If they manage to make a case against you and it goes to trial, I will need to consult Mr. Walker as to whether he wishes me to proceed. If he does not but you do, I will gladly continue to represent you but, at that point, I will start charging you at my usual rate. Do you understand?"

"Er, yes."

"Good. I'll have my assistant draw up a contract to that effect. I gather that the police wish to interview you. I will be present every time you meet the police from now on. Are you free to see them tomorrow morning, around ten, say?"

"Er, yes. I don't work."

He smiled. "How nice. So, if there's nothing else…"

Again, I had that sense that my life was being controlled by others. "Don't you want to… talk about it?"

"Absolutely no need. Thank you for coming in. I will see you at the Central Police Station at ten AM. Please try to arrive a little early and looking less like you sprinted all the way. We don't want to antagonise them more than we absolutely have to."

I felt that there must be more to say but in the face of his obvious desire for me to leave, I just said, "Right-o. See you there, then," and stood up. He rose too and we shook hands again.

My bike was still there in the lobby when I got down to street level. I picked my helmet up from the floor and attached it to the pannier. I took the bike by the handlebars and wheeled it into the street. I'd barely walked fifty paces when I fell into the first café I came across, leaving the bike on the street. I queued for ages for a coffee and a croissant. The rest of the queue were smartly-dressed and very young;

city workers – mostly public servants in that part of town – who each seemed to be buying for the whole office. I sat down on a hideously uncomfortable chromed steel chair and put my purchases on a matching table. The croissant was in a paper bag and the coffee in a paper cup with a plastic lid. It felt as if the café was doing the absolute minimum it could for my comfort and enjoyment and, although there was nothing unusual in that, it filled me with resentment. Not quite filled, I should say, because there was plenty to spare for Ronnie Walker, who was doing me a big favour I didn't want, and clearly felt no compunction about discussing me and my business with his insufferable lawyer friend.

Who the hell did he think he was? Come to that, who the hell was he? Some guy I'd met in a pub. An entitled, old baby-boomer who felt at liberty to elbow his way into my life. And for what? Free drinks? To amuse himself in his retirement? To cling to the glory days when he was a real investigator? And what was that Facebook page all about? Anybody could tell by looking at Ronnie Walker that he was a thuggish, brutal man. He was built like a bouncer and his eyes would have been more at home watching you from an executioner's hood than in all those smiling pictures with dogs and old biddies.

I sat for fifteen minutes staring at my minimalist breakfast in its minimalist packaging before I calmed down. By then, my coffee was too cool to enjoy and I went up for another.

"Queue's gone," I said to the barista, suddenly noticing the fact.

"Morning rush," he said. "It'll pick up again soon for smoko."

He made a cute leaf pattern in the foam on my coffee and then obliterated it by putting a plastic lid on it. I took it back to my table and took the lid off. I sipped it even though it was too hot. I tore open the paper bag to create a makeshift plate for my croissant and pulled pieces off it to chew on.

OK, I told myself. *The electoral rolls.*

I googled it and had my usual "Why do I bother?" moment of regret. All the links at the top of the page were for ancestry tracing services. I followed the State Library link farther down the page but that only took me to old records. Somewhere on page two of the results, I found the Australian Electoral Commission. I read their pages on the Queensland electoral roll three times before I accepted the fact that what I wanted to do was impossible. Yes, I could go to the local AEC office and look at the rolls but it was a paper copy and I couldn't write anything down, photocopy it, or take any pictures. Yes, there was an electronic version that was searchable but that was only available to candidates for political office and their parties. Why? I could only assume that, among the ranks of unscrupulous advertisers, property developers, and other evil-doers they were trying to keep away from this sensitive information, politicians were deemed less villainous for some reason.

I swigged back my coffee and went outside, my head full of impractical schemes to join a political party for the day – or to start one. My bike was still where I'd left it. Apparently, despite he endless cuts, public servants were still paid enough that they didn't need to steal bicycles. The traffic had eased off a lot and I needed another shower, so I went home again.

My main concern on the way home was Ronnie. He already thought I was a useless dickhead who couldn't run a chook raffle. When I told him I'd given up on the electoral roll thing after five minutes online in a café, it was going to confirm his worst prejudices. Why that bothered me so much, I didn't like to think, but it was probably something to do with my contempt for myself and not wanting to see it reflected in Ronnie's eyes.

I needed some way to get around this but nothing would come. I grappled with it on the ride home, through a long, cool shower, through a cheese sandwich, and a half-hour lying on the sofa staring at the ceiling. Turning up at the AEC offices with a large bribe in a brown-paper bag was the best I could come up with after all that. I even spent five minutes wondering where on earth I could buy a brown paper bag, followed by a brief fantasy about life behind bars. I'd given up and was steeling myself to call Ronnie and confess my failure when another, equally illegal but slightly more promising plan occurred to me.

I texted Kazima at the office to tell her I was coming over and ran down to the car. I was there just before lunch and she greeted me at the door.

"We'll have to save you a parking space if you're going to come over so often," she said. She seemed more cheerful than last time I saw her and the office seemed to be buzzing with activity. It was only reasonable. Making her the CEO had probably ended a week of terrible uncertainty for her and the whole team.

"It's just a one-off," I said. "I'll get out of your hair in a minute. I just need a favour."

"Of course. Would you like a coffee?"

"No, look, I need to borrow one of your developers."

"What?" We reached her office and we sat down. "For how long?"

"Not long. At least, I don't know. Just this afternoon maybe."

She considered me for a moment, her deep, dark eyes

growing a shade more guarded. "Of course, this is your company and you have the right to do what you like with our resources, but you realise we have schedules we're working to, milestones we're trying to hit. We lost a lot of... momentum, I suppose, after Chelsea died. I've been trying to get the team back on track."

"I know. Look, I'm sorry. I wouldn't ask if this wasn't really important. I promise it won't be for long."

She was struggling with the idea and clearly didn't like it. "Who did you want, exactly, and what for?"

"Yeah," I said, grimacing. "I don't know exactly who'd be best. And I don't really want to tell you what for." She didn't say anything but gave me a hard stare, demanding that I say more. "I need someone who's a good..." *Hacker* is what I wanted to say. I needed a hacker to break into a government database and steal information for me. "I need a security specialist."

She nodded. "Why?"

It was best for both of us if she knew nothing about what I was planning. "I'm trying to catch Chelsea's killer," I said. "I think I have a lead but I need someone who can... Someone who's good with computers."

"Don't you think you should leave all that to the police?"

"I'd like to. I really would. But they're getting nowhere."

"And you think you can do a better job?"

"I couldn't do much worse. I don't think that bloke Reid could find his arse with both hands."

A little smile touched her lips. "They came to see me today. Reid and a woman. It's the third time they've spoken to me. Reid asked a lot of questions about you. More than last time."

I shrugged. "What good was that? We've hardly ever met."

"Oh, Chelsea talked about you a lot. I feel like I know you. I had lots to tell them."

"All of it good, I hope." A feeble joke to mask my sudden nervousness.

"Oh yes. Chelsea loved you and she felt loved by you. Inspector Reid was not happy with my answers."

Chelsea felt loved. If there was one thing in the world I wanted to hear right then, that was it. Tears sprang to my eyes and I said, "Thank you," though my throat was trying to close.

"Do you really think you can find who did it?"

I shook my head. "I don't know. I've got a guy helping me. A professional, sort of. He reckons we're making progress. But if I don't get… this security issue solved, we're almost back to square one."

Kazima pursed her lips, then suddenly seemed to reach a decision. She stood up and walked to the door. Leaning out, she shouted, "Karen, can you come here a minute, please?" She came back to me but didn't sit down. "Karen is our sysadmin. I think she's the person you need. She's very, very good and takes an interest in the kind of security matter I think you are talking about."

A small, very smartly dressed Asian woman walked into the office. She was delicate and pretty and looked about fifteen. Kazima introduced me as the new owner of the company and I shook her tiny hand.

"Luke is going to take you to lunch," Kazima told her – which was news to me. "He's going to offer you a bit of work which I'm guessing may not be completely legal." Karen looked at me with wide eyes. "Listen to his proposal and, if you accept the work, you can have as much time off to complete it as you need – on full pay, just as if it was an ordinary work assignment. If you decide you don't want to do it, that's OK. Don't worry that Luke is the boss. Just say no and that will be the end of it. No-one here wants you to do anything you are not completely comfortable with."

Karen nodded and said, "OK." She swallowed hard and her eyes seemed to have set into a look of permanent fright.

Kazima ushered us out. Everyone in the office cast curious glances as we walked past them to the door. "Take him somewhere nice," Kazima told Karen as we left. "He's paying."

We walked about five minutes in the hot sun to a row of busy cafés and restaurants, already buzzing with the lunchtime crowd of local office workers. We walked in silence almost all the way until Karen said, "I'm sorry. About Chelsea."

"Thank you. Did you know her well?"

"I've only been with the company a few months but she was always very kind. Everybody liked her."

She led me to a relatively quiet little place that served over-elaborate salads and twenty kinds of coffee. She caught me staring at the menu boards and asked, "Is this all right?"

I assured her it was. We made awkward small talk until the meal was ordered. She was from Hong Kong. She left after she finished uni to avoid the troubles there. She'd been in Australia three years, she said, as I rapidly reassessed her age. Then she sat in silence, waiting for me to speak. She sat upright, with a straight back, like a young lady from another era. She had square shoulders and a long neck. Under the table, I was sure here knees were pressed together. I had been hoping to be hooked up with some counter-culture type with half a kilo of body piercings, bleached hair and a thrash metal T-shirt, not this prim and elegant escapee from a BBC period drama. It made it almost impossible to broach the subject I wanted to discuss.

"What's a sysadmin?" I asked by way of openers.

"What?"

"Kazima called you a sysadmin."

"Oh, a systems administrator. I look after the network, keep the servers running, you know."

"So, you know all about system security, how to keep hackers out, that kind of thing?"

"Oh yes." It wasn't at all boastful, just matter-of-fact.

"Have you ever done anything like that yourself?"

"Sorry?"

"Have you ever hacked a company or whatever?"

Her face fell. "Am I in trouble?"

"No, no. I – I just want to know if you can do it. I…" Oh what the hell? I leaned into her and said softly, "I need you to hack a government database for me."

If I'd grabbed her knee under the table, she couldn't have reacted any more violently. She leaped to her feet saying, "No, no, no!" and walked straight out of the restaurant. I leaped up too and ran after her.

"Hey!" I caught up to her as she waited to cross the road. "Hey, I'm not asking you to steal money or anything. All I want is the electoral roll for the electorate of Brisbane Central."

She scowled at me. She was really angry. "Go to the library."

"Yeah, well, that was my thought too but it doesn't work like that." She set off across the road and I dogged her heels. "I need to compare two lists of names: one the electoral roll and the other some school records. I'd be happy to do it manually but I just can't get that kind of access."

"Tough," she said, over her shoulder, walking faster.

I ran in front of her and blocked her way. "What the hell is wrong with you? I'm just trying to find out who killed Chelsea. The police are stuffing it up and this might be my only lead. If I could do it myself, I would, but I just don't have the skills."

Her scowl softened. "Why don't you get the police to do it? They could get access to whatever they needed."

"The police think I had something to do with the murder. Look, if you won't help me, I'll probably have to go to them and try to persuade them but, honestly, I don't think they will. They're trying to build a case against me and they'll keep at that until they succeed or they're forced to try some other theory. Meanwhile, Chelsea's killer is out there on the loose. Maybe he'll kill again. Maybe he'll skip the country." Her eyes dropped. She still wore a surly, stubborn expression but at least she was no longer furious. "Wouldn't you like to help me catch a murderer? I know there's some risk involved but, look, if you get caught, I'll tell them I made you do it, threatened to sack you if you didn't do what I said." She kept her eyes averted and her brows pulled down. "Please help me. You're my only hope."

She tilted her head up sideways and eyed me suspiciously. "How do I know you're not a bad man? Maybe you're planning a big office development and you want those names so you can buy people out and threaten them to sell. Maybe you're a stalker and you've got some victim you're trying to find information about? Maybe you're a—"

"Hey! I'm not. I'm not any of those things. I just want to find my girlfriend's killer."

"And kill him?"

"No!"

To be honest, I hadn't really thought about what I wanted to happen to Mr. X. I just wanted to catch him. Killing him hadn't crossed my mind. Well, just once. That night after the funeral but that was, like, a moment of madness. The realisation gave me a rush of shame. Surely, if I'd really loved Chelsea, I'd want to see her killer dead?

Crestfallen, I said, "I just want to hand him over to the police."

Not beat him to death with my fists like some vigilante arsehole in an American movie. What kind of man did that make me? Even though I knew full well that Chelsea would have been repulsed by the idea, I couldn't help feeling that I was unworthy, not man enough, that I'd let her down.

"I knew some bad men in Hong Kong," Karen said. "When I was a kid, they made me do some very bad things. I had to do those things over there. Not here."

I looked into her set, stubborn face. I had no idea what she might mean but it was obvious I'd just kicked over a white ant nest in her life.

"I – I – Look, I don't know about any of that. I just thought maybe you could help me. If you don't want to, that's OK, I suppose. I just don't know where else to turn." My life had become a Jean-Paul Sartre novel. Every life I touched was a chasm filled with angst. Was there some kind of moral or philosophical message I should be looking for in all this, or was Chelsea's death just a big rock of misery dropped into the calm pool of our everyday lives?

"I'm sorry," I said, stepping aside. "I should let you get back to work."

She didn't move. She looked straight ahead down the road. After a while, she said, "I'm sorry too. About Chelsea. I want to help." She kept looking straight ahead. "Tell me what you want to do."

So I laid it all out for her right there in the street. She listened in silence and, when I'd finished, nodded. The sadness in her big brown eyes was hard to look at.

"If you don't want to…" I said.

She looked at me at last, her lips pursed. "No. It's OK. I need to go back to the office and pick up my machine."

"What machine?" I had visions of some high-tech hacking device.

"My laptop. Then I will need somewhere to work."

"We can go to my unit. What else do you need?"

"Just an Internet connection."

"And you can do this? Get the data?"

"Sure." She spread her hand, palm down and made a rocking motion. "Pretty sure."

We started walking again. "Don't you want to go back and get some lunch?"

"Not hungry."

"Right-o." I could make her a sandwich later if she started feeling better about things.

When we got to the office, she went up to get her stuff while I called Ronnie. I felt good about calling him now that I had a plan. But the call went to an answering service. Ronnie's recorded voice said, "If you're selling anything, fuck off. Otherwise, if you really think I'll be interested, leave a message. Don't expect an answer." I thought he would be interested, but I hung up anyway.

Chapter Nine

Karen's laptop was an enormous black slab that looked even bigger against her tiny frame. It had a picture of an alien's head on the lid and, when I said, "Cute," she looked at me sideways as if I might be joking. She settled on the sofa with it and I eventually managed to find her the wi-fi password and fetch her a large mug of coffee.

"Don't you need special equipment, or something?" I asked. "You know, like routers and servers and stuff?"

She grinned at me – the first smile since we were in the café. "For a guy who owns a software company, you don't know much, do you?"

"Yeah, well, I didn't expect to be in this position."

Her smile fell and I regretted my bitter tone.

"All the tools I need are software," she said. "And I have them right here, or I'll get them from the Web."

"How long will it take?"

"Huh?" She was already absorbed in the screen and took a moment to pull herself away. "I don't know. It's quicker if I focus."

"Oh. Sorry."

I wandered around the room a bit, went to stare at the

whiteboard, sat down with my coffee and watched her work, got up, went to the bathroom, came back, stared out the window while I finished my coffee, checked my watch. Just ten minutes had passed. Karen hadn't moved. She seemed frozen in front of that giant screen. If it wasn't for the way her fingers would suddenly flick into action, moving so fast it seemed like a superhuman ability, I would have thought she was in a trance. Her face was blank and she hardly blinked. I don't remember ever seeing such intense concentration.

The urge to ask her how it was going became unbearable, so I went outside and stood in the sun. A bunch of noisy miners were squabbling in the trees nearby. A small flock of cockatoos passed overhead, flapping lazily in the early afternoon heat. On days like this, Chelsea would want us to go out to Mount Coot-tha, get an ice cream and sit by the lake. She loved the water dragons and the ibises, and we'd walk through the cactus house and the succulent beds and the scented garden, where she would touch every leaf and smell her fingers. Sometimes there'd be exhibitions – by the local cactus society, or orchid growers, or some fossicking group – and we'd trail among the trestle tables admiring the weird and wonderful things that people grew or found or made.

I should go there soon, I told myself but I didn't know why. It had always been Chelsea's thing, not mine. I'd always have rather stayed home with a good book. But not going now would seem like some kind of rejection of her. Going would honour her memory. It was weird. She was dead and, to me, that meant gone completely. There was no way that anything I did now could hurt her in the slightest. Yet I was as prey to all these superstitious notions as my poor old Catholic grandma; like it was wired into my DNA and no amount of rationality could quite overwrite it. But I had to admit it was there inside me and I knew I would go back to Mount Coot-tha and walk around miserably and hurt when I saw the water dragons and cry when I smelled the scented geraniums – because that's what Chelsea would want.

I went back inside, wiping the wetness from my eyes. Karen was still frozen in place. She didn't even glance at me.

"I'm off out for a bit. Help yourself to anything you want. I won't be long."

I don't know if she heard me. I had no idea where I'd go or what I'd do but I had to go somewhere and do something. So I walked up the road. I'd come to some shops eventually and maybe I'd get sandwiches and cakes. I pulled out my phone as I walked and tried Ronnie again.

"If you're selling anything, fuck off. Otherwise, if you really think I'll be interested, leave a message. Don't expect an answer."

"You know, you're a total fucking dickhead?" I told his answering service. "Why do you have to be so bloody...?" I took a breath. "Call me when you get this. If you can be bothered."

The shops were miles away. I'd only ever been to them in the car before, I realised, and had grossly underestimated the distance. So I was hot and sweaty and completely knackered by the time I got back.

I found Karen still on the sofa but her laptop was closed beside her and she was watching the telly with my packet of chocolate biscuits on her lap. She'd turned on the air conditioning and was looking cool and relaxed and everything I was not.

"Taking a break?" I asked, trying to sound cheerful.

"Finished."

"What?"

"I've finished. I got in. It was not so hard as I expected." She held up a thumb drive. "It's all here."

I dropped the carrier bag full of food and drink on the counter. "You beauty! You're like a hacking genius or something. My god!" She held out the thumb drive and I took it from her. "It's really here? Will they know you took it? Will they trace you here?"

She smiled. "I was careful."

I stared at the gaudy little stick. "Oh my god!"

She set aside the biscuits and clasped her hands in her lap, leaning forward slightly. "There's more."

"More? I only wanted…"

"I hacked the schools too."

"What?"

"I went to Facebook to see what schools she'd been to. Then I went into their systems. Schools are very easy." It was beginning to dawn on me what she was telling me, why her deep, dark eyes were glistening like that. "So then I had lots of lists: the electoral roll, two high school class lists each for several years and the university enrolment lists for all the classes she took. I wrote a little Python program to search them all, comparing every name in every list to every name on the electoral roll for the Central Brisbane electorate."

"And you found him?" I looked at the little stick in my hand. My heart was racing.

She pursed her lips. "I don't know. Maybe. I found five males who live in that suburb and who either went to school with Chelsea, or shared one of her classes."

"Five?" I was expecting one, at most. Five seemed ridiculously high.

"Brisbane is a small world," Karen said, shrugging. "People here tend to be born here, go to school here and go to uni here. Then they get jobs here. I was surprised at first but when you think about it, it's not so strange." She stood up, obviously preparing to leave. "Anyway, the names are on there, in a file called "Suspects.doc", along with all the data." She picked up her giant laptop. "I hope it helps."

I wanted to print out the file and get to work finding and eliminating each suspect. I wanted to bury that stick and never see it again. Trying to stay calm, I gave Karen a lift back to the office – promising her my undying gratitude all the way and apologising again for raking up whatever it was in her past I had inadvertently unleashed. I drove like a maniac on the way back, though, and ran to my own little laptop, pushing the thumb drive into the slot with shaking hands, turning the damned thing over and over because every way I tried seemed to be upside down. There was one folder, labelled "Research". It contained a couple of dozen ".csv" files, all clearly labelled. They must have contained the data. There was a file called "Namextract.py", which was probably the program Karen mentioned, and, at the bottom of the alphabetical list, there was "Suspects.doc".

I stopped. I daren't click on the file to open it. I wanted to see the names. I wanted to find the killer but the enormity of what was in that file overwhelmed me. One of the names in there was the man who murdered Chelsea, the man who had plotted for weeks, lured her out to that alley and stabbed her over and over, the man who had put on a coat despite the summer heat and walked through the streets of Brisbane, his clothes soaked in Chelsea's blood, the man who had changed into his everyday clothes, gone home, showered and shaved, and had then gone about his life while mine had crumbled into dust.

It was too big, too important. I shouldn't be doing this. I

should take it to the police. I should give it to someone whose job it was to hunt people down and administer cold, hard justice. I had a mind full of subtle abstractions, I pondered the quality of knowledge, the nature of reality, the limits of doubt. The contents of that file were too heavy to be supported in such a fine web of thought. It would crash through, tear and smash everything. Chelsea's killer! It was too real.

I was too scared even to look.

I put my laptop down on the table and pushed it away from me, sat back in the chair and stared at it.

* * * *

I was still staring at it two hours later when Ronnie arrived. I almost didn't let him in.

"The perfect end to the perfect fucking day," he grumbled when I finally buzzed him in and opened the door. He looked pointedly at the laptop. "Not cool, mate, having a bloody wank while I'm left standing in the street like a bloody shag on a rock."

I went to sit down, well away from the computer. He went straight to the kitchen, opened the fridge, the freezer, then started on the cupboards. "Not a beer, not a pie, not even a bloody biscuit? What's the matter with you? Where do you keep your booze?" He scoured a few more cupboards while I watched.

"I hope you had better luck than me," he said. "Bloody schools. You'd think they were protecting the bloody lotto numbers instead of the names of our great state's future burger flippers and dole queue bludgers. You know, one of those stuck up cows threatened to call the police? Practically called me a kiddie fiddler. After I'd spent half the morning laying on the charm with a trowel! And you know how charming I can be." He looked around, as if he'd just realised where he was. "Come on, let's get out of this dump and find some pub grub. We need to drown our sorrows and make a new plan."

He stood up to go. Somehow, his grump and bluster had broken the spell Karen's suspects file held over me.

"I've found him."

He looked at me, possibly seeing me for the first time, too.

"I found Mr. X. He's on that laptop."

He looked at the laptop, then at me, then sat down again. "Go on," he said.

So I told him everything I'd done that day and he listened in complete silence. When I finished, he said. "That was not smart. You committed a crime. You dragged that poor girl into it. You could both end up doing time for this. And now I'm an accessory after the fact."

I said nothing and we sat in silence until he said. "So, who is it?"

I shook my head. "I don't know. I haven't looked yet."

I saw his brow crease, in anger or puzzlement, I couldn't be sure. In a voice that was almost kind, he said, "Go put the kettle on. I'll look."

I tried to ignore him as I busied myself getting cups and grounds and working the coffee machine. In the corner of my eye I could see him pushing buttons and reading from the screen. Then I heard the printer whining and clacking. When I returned with coffee, he handed me a sheet of paper. There were five names on it.

"Do you know any of these people?"

I took a deep breath and looked. "No. No-one." It was a relief.

"Call that woman at the office."

"Karen?"

"The other one. The boss."

"Kazima?"

"That's the one. Read her the names and ask her if she knows them."

"I thought we'd just google them or something."

"This is quicker."

Kazima picked up on the second ring. I told her I had a list of suspects.

"Is that what Karen did for you?"

Remembering Ronnie's admonition, I said, "It's best you don't know what Karen did. Can I read you the names?"

"OK."

I read each one and then waited. She was a long time responding.

"So… do you know any of them?"

"Yes," she said and my heart thumped. She seemed reluctant to say who it was.

"Kazima?"

"What are you going to do?"

"Nothing bad, I promise. I'll just ask the police to look into it. That's all."

There was another long pause before she said, "Simon Anning. He's one of our clients. He runs a games company here in Brisbane. He's big in e-sports, organises the East Coast Gamefest, you might have heard of it?" I hadn't. "Makes *Silent Empire* and a few other titles. All games with in-app commerce, even gambling."

I had no interest at all in computer games and had no idea

what any of it was about. "What's his connection to Chelsea?"

"I'm not sure. Friends from uni or something. We sold him a license for our e-commerce suite and he's building it into the next release of *Silent Empire*. As far as I know, that's our only contact. I never met him in person. Is he the one?"

"I don't know. Maybe. Look, can you dig out the files, see if there's anything in there that might explain why Chelsea was meeting him that night? I'll come by tomorrow and we can chat, yeah?"

"OK. I'll see you tomorrow."

I pocketed my phone. To Ronnie, I said, "Simon Anning."

He nodded, eyes hard. "Now what?"

"I – I thought you'd know."

He studied me carefully for a moment then nodded again. "OK."

With a start I realised what had just happened, what he'd really been asking. "No. I meant what I said to Kazima. We'll just turn him in to the police. I don't want…" Whatever Ronnie was offering.

"The police? Yeah, well, that's not going to happen. Come on. I need a drink."

"I just made you a coffee."

He shook his head as if I'd said something sadly ridiculous.

* * * *

The Brisbane Brewing Company was my local. It described itself as "industrial chic" but that just seemed to mean it had brick walls and exposed beams. We sat in the public bar with a view of the fermentation tanks behind a glass wall and I waited patiently until Ronnie had got most of the sneering out of his system.

"Why can't we go to the police?" I asked.

"They'd want to know how you got Simon Anning's name."

"So?"

"So?"

"I'd – I'd just tell them I remembered something, that she said she was meeting an old friend from uni. And I just put two and two together. What's wrong with that?"

He put down his burger and looked at me, brows creased. "If I was the lead investigator and I'd just started turning the screws on my prime suspect, what would I think if he lawyers up and comes in to see me saying he's suddenly remembered the name of the killer?"

"I suppose you'd think I was trying to throw you off the scent. Or, if Anning really is the killer, that I'm fitting up my accomplice to wriggle out of Reid's grasp. But if Anning really was my accomplice, I'd have to be mad to turn him in. He'd turn on me, do a deal to reduce his time. That kind of thing. But he can't do that because he wasn't my accomplice, so what have I got to lose."

"Oh, I don't know. Let's say I'm Reid and I'm obsessed with locking up some smart-arsed brainbox who thinks he's going to get away with murder. Don't you think I might put it to Anning that, if he stops giving me all this crap about being the only one involved and turns you in, he might get a much lighter sentence? And what would Anning do in that situation, if he has two neurons to rub together?"

The burger felt heavy in my stomach. "Make something up. But that's—"

"Not fair?"

I looked down at the table and the remains of my meal. "You knew we couldn't take this to the cops all along, didn't you?"

"You don't need a PhD in philosophy to work that out."

I ignored the taunt. "So what do we do with it?"

"We do some more investigating." I looked up at him to see if he was joking. He wasn't. "We know who did it. We know how. Now we need to find out why. If we can establish a good, solid motive – one that doesn't involve you – even Reid will have to pull his head out of his arse."

I poked at my burger, picked up a chip and put it down. I was angry. Or maybe I was just frustrated. It should have been over. I should have been able to give the killer's name to the police and get on with my life. And it all felt like it was Ronnie's fault. He was the one who wouldn't let it go. He was the one who kept pushing me to dig deeper into all this crap.

"What's your angle?" I snapped. He was in the middle of pushing the remains of his burger into his mouth. "What's in it for you?"

He chewed for a minute, looking back at me, obviously giving my questions a lot of thought.

"I want to help," he said, at last.

"Why?"

"Because I like you. You remind me of me when I was about six."

I was in no mood for jokes. "Six, eh? And what are you now? Seventy? Seventy-five? Isn't that a bit old still to be playing cops and robbers?"

His brows fell into a thunderous scowl. "Seventy-five, you little shit? I'm sixty-four! And I'm in bloody good shape for my age. I could go ten rounds with any bloke in this bar. Twenty with the likes of you."

I believed him. In fact, I don't suppose I'd have made it through the first round. "Yeah, well, maybe, but you still haven't answered my question."

He sat back, still scowling, and picked up his beer. "You still don't know a single thing about me, do you? I've never met anyone with so little curiosity."

"I'm curious about why you're helping me."

"Really? Yet you haven't tried to find out who I am."

"I know all I need to know. You're just avoiding my question."

"Yeah? Tell me something about me you think you know."

"You were in the navy, then the police."

"Yeah? What did I do in the navy? Whose navy? What was my rank? Which regiment?" I saw him smirk, knowing he'd scored a point. "And what about the police? Which State? What branch? What unit?"

"All right, so I don't know all the details. What's that got to do—"

"You don't care. That's all. Why don't you just admit it? You think I'm some annoying git who's in your life for a few days and then I'll be gone. You don't care who I am or what motivates me because to you I'm just a temporary annoyance you can forget all about soon. The only reason you want to know why I'm helping you is because you'd rather I wasn't. It bugs you that I won't leave you alone to screw things up. It's all over your face. You just want to crawl back into your shell and feel sorry for yourself. You don't give a fuck about finding Chelsea's killer, not really. You're just going through the motions out of some half-arsed sense of obligation."

It was all too accurate for comfort and I felt my defences rising. Either I thumped him or I got up and stormed out.

But he kept me pinned to my seat with his hard, cold stare while he chewed over his next words.

"You want to know why I'm helping you? All right, let me tell you. Murder pisses me off."

I waited for more but it didn't come. "Murder pisses you off? That's it?"

He looked away for a moment, sucked on his teeth and looked back. "I've worked on a couple of dozen murders in my time and they all have one thing in common; for one screwed up reason or another, someone believes that they are so much more important than someone else that they can kill that other person to solve whatever problems they have. Take Simon Anning, for example. Without knowing a thing about him, I can tell you that he thinks a great deal of himself, that he killed Chelsea to fix some problem in his life – probably to do with money, or status, or comfort – and that he probably regrets it but still thinks it was justified. Me? I think life is all we have. Taking it from someone is not just the worst thing you can do, it's an unforgivable sin. People who do it should be caught and punished."

He seemed sincere. He seemed crazy fanatical, in fact. Yet I sensed there was more than he was telling me. "So you're saying—" But he cut me off with a sour expression.

"Look, I've got a problem with it. I know I have. When I was in the police, it became an obsession. It took over my life. That's what ended it for me."

"I thought they sacked you."

"They did because I was too keen to solve cases, so keen I wouldn't put up with their management bullshit, or the lazy, nine-to-five time-servers I had to work with."

"Like Reid."

"He wasn't the worst by a long way." He took a pull at his

beer, brooding. "Anyway, it became a kind of sickness. I knew I was practically certifiable but I just couldn't help myself. I lost my friends, my wife—"

"You had a wife?" It seemed incredible.

"Yes, I had a fucking wife, you ignorant little shit."

"Sorry. That was… Sorry."

He shook his head, irritated but still lost in his memories. "If they hadn't sacked me, I'd have been chewing the padding off my cell walls by now I reckon. Getting out was the best thing for me."

"So why…?"

"Because I could fight the temptation the first night we met. But then you came back again and I could see what a useless bell end you are and what a crap job the cops were doing and if there was ever going to be justice for Chelsea, I was going to have to get back on the fucking horse."

"And now you don't want to get off."

"And now I still can't because, if I don't bring Anning down, no-one will. You'll just get yourself locked up for it while Anning sits back and thanks the gods that protect bastards like him."

His strange confession had taken the wind right out of my sails. Oddly enough, I could actually understand the kind of obsession that might grip someone wanting to get to the very bottom of things. My own experience of it had led to nothing more than late nights in the library and a few missed meals but it gave me a perspective from which I could glimpse the darker, more destructive force that must have driven Ronnie's fall from grace. I thought, vaguely about trying to suggest he stop and leave me to it but it seemed like a dumb idea.

"All right," I said, subdued. "Let's catch him. What's our next move?"

He pursed his lips, thinking. "You're going to see the cops tomorrow, right? Well, don't mention Anning. They'll find him in the end, but they haven't got there yet. That gives us a window of opportunity. We need to start digging into his finances, his business, his associates…" He grimaced in frustration, perhaps regretting the loss of all the resources he once had as a police officer.

"I could maybe ask Karen to take a—"

"No." It was a sharp rebuke. "Nothing illegal. Besides, Anning is some kind of propeller-head himself, remember. He might notice if we set your little bloodhound sniffing around in his business. Do you want her to end up dead as well?"

The suggestion was a surprise, although I don't know why it should have been. For some reason the reality that we were dealing with a killer just wouldn't sink in.

"I don't know how we're going to do any of what you said on our own."

"Let me worry about that. Meanwhile…" He grinned and took a swig of his beer. "Remember that thermos flask I made you buy? Well I hope you didn't throw it away, 'cause you're going on a stakeout."

Chapter Ten

I was at Reid's office at ten AM sharp, looking neat and presentable and ready to face whatever idiotic grilling he had in mind. My hatchet-faced lawyer met me in the lobby looking small and dapper. He shook my hand and gave me an approving look. A young woman collected us with a "Hi, I'm Julie," and led us to a meeting room on one of the upper floors. There was a view across one of the coils of the Brisbane River to the Botanic Gardens. By standing up against the glass, I could see Kangaroo Point and the Story Bridge on the left. Julie disappeared with a, "Trevor will be along in a minute," leaving us to enjoy the ambience.

"Just follow my lead," Marchant said. "Cooperate, tell the truth, and there'll be no problems." I wondered if he said that to all his criminal clients.

Reid came in with an older, balding man in tow. We introduced ourselves all round. The sidekick was called Bronski and was a Senior Detective Constable. I made a note to myself to find out what all the ranks meant. For all I knew, Senior Detective Constable was a higher rank than Detective Inspector, even though Bronski clearly deferred to Reid. When we were seated, Reid made a little speech to the effect that this was a formal interview and that it would be recorded. I looked around and found at least two cameras. In reply, Marchant gave his own little speech to the effect that "his client" was here to cooperate fully and to help the police.

Reid smiled. It was all very polite and friendly.

"We just have a few questions, Mr. Kelly," he said, addressing me directly for the first time. "Tell me about your relationship with Ms Kazima Abbas."

It was annoying and impertinent but I kept my cool. "I don't have a relationship with her. She worked with Chelsea. I met her a couple of times at functions."

"You weren't on more intimate terms with her?"

"My client answered your question," Marchant said as my temper began to rise.

Reid looked at him for a moment with a blank expression before turning back to me. "Can you explain why Kazima Abbas recently transferred a large sum of money from Chelsea's company account to your personal account?"

This one was so ridiculous, I could hardly believe it was serious. "You're really getting desperate, aren't you?" I said. "Is that really the best you've got?"

"You should confine yourself to answering the questions," Marchant said.

I turned on him sharply. "This is a farce. These people have no idea what they're doing."

"Even so," said Marchant, gently.

I drew a deep breath. To Reid I said, "It's my company now and I'll draw as much money from it as I like, up to and including the full sixty-two per cent of my share." I really needed to read up on Australian company law because I had no idea whether that was true. "Kazima is an employee of the company and does what I tell her."

"She's also an equity holder, is she not?"

"So?"

"So, after you took control of the company, you gave her an increased equity holding, out of your own share. You also appointed her the new CEO. A woman you'd just met a couple of times at functions. What was all this extraordinary generosity in return for, Mr. Kelly?"

While I reeled at how such innocent decisions could be so misconstrued, Marchant spoke up. "While my client is more than happy to cooperate, Detective Inspector, this looks to me as if you are on a fishing expedition. Do you have any actual evidence of a relationship between Mr. Kelly and Ms Abbas?"

Reid seemed to ignore him but his next question to me was, "Tell me about the overcoat?"

I immediately knew which overcoat he meant. "What about it?"

"How did you know the killer brought an overcoat to the restaurant the night Chelsea Campbell died?"

"I – Well, I didn't. Ronnie worked it out. I mean Mr. Walker."

"We never told the press about the coat. Funny you knew all about it."

"I told you, Mr. Walker worked it out. Don't tell me that makes Ronnie a suspect too!"

He turned to his sidekick, who had been silent throughout, and nodded. The balding man opened a folder that was in front of him on the table. My heart stopped. If he was going to show me pictures of Chelsea's body… But he didn't. He pulled out a photograph but it was of a dark haired man with a beard. He placed it on the table between me and Reid and turned it one-eighty degrees so it was oriented for my viewing. I studied it carefully. It was a photo of a man in his mid-thirties, the beard was short and neatly trimmed.

"Is this…?" I began but stopped myself blurting out Anning's name.

"Do you know this man?" Reid asked.

"No. Who is it?"

"You tell me."

"I don't know him. Is this the man who…?" *Killed Chelsea.* I couldn't say the words.

"Take a closer look."

It was a ridiculous thing to say. I couldn't have stared more intently at that photo if I'd tried. "Is this him? Is this the murderer?"

Reid gave Bronski another nod and the policeman took the photo back and returned it to his folder. "Don't worry," he told me. "We'll find the connection. You're not as clever as you think you are."

"I think we're done here," Marchant said, firmly.

"I'll say when we're done."

Reid sounded like he meant it but Marchant was completely unimpressed. He stood up and packed his notebook into his briefcase. I stood up too. So did the two cops. Would they try to stop us if we left? To be honest, I had no idea what my rights were. Fortunately, Marchant seemed completely relaxed and confident. He stood his briefcase on the table and rested his hands on top of it. In a pleasant tone, he addressed Reid.

"My client will not subject himself to any further harassment or threats, Detective Inspector. I'm sure you understand. Perhaps, when you've developed your case a little farther, I'll be willing to recommend that he continues to cooperate. Until then, I feel it is in his best interest to decline to comment on any matters you care to put to him."

Reid stood like a boulder between us and the door. "It's in your client's best interest to come clean, right now, and you know it."

"If he were guilty, I would agree. There's no need to show us out, I'm quite familiar with the building."

Reid turned his gaze on me for a moment, looking like he was sizing me up ready to toss me through the big windows. "Wait here. I'll send someone." He flicked his head at Bronski and they left without goodbyes.

"He's not usually this bad," Marchant said, when Reid was gone. "I've encountered him several times before, of course, and he's usually quite pleasant. Maybe it's because he doesn't have his usual amanuensis with him. She seems to be his better angel, so to speak."

"That photograph," I said. I didn't give a damn about Reid's temperament. "Can we get hold of a copy? Can we find out who the man is?"

Marchant chuckled. "I'm afraid not. Why do you want it?"

"Because he matches the description of the killer. Reid must think he's the one who did it."

He put his head on one side and looked at me with a sad expression. "In my experience – and it's quite extensive – trying to exact some kind of vigilante justice is never a good idea. The police can be slow and, indeed, frustrating at times, but they mostly come to the right answer in the end. I had a case a few years ago…"

I wasn't really listening as he rambled on about some loser who'd gone after the wrong guy and ended up doing more time than the actual criminal. I was wishing I'd spent some time online that morning finding out what Simon Anning looked like. Because, if the cops had also realised he was the killer, my vigilante days were over. I'd still have the problem of Reid trying to frame me, but at least I'd be done with all the rest. If the man in the picture wasn't Anning, however, then the cops had focused on some random bloke and were trying to pin the murder on both of us. More time wasted. More need than ever for me to catch Anning.

"Hi. Me again." It was Julie at the door. "If you'd just follow me." We did. "Have a good meeting?" she asked in her sing-song tone, leading us along the corridors. My mind wandered off to Wittgenstein and the purpose of language as Marchant engaged in cheerful small talk.

* * * *

Two hours later, I was in my car with a box of chicken and chips stinking it up. There were half-a-dozen packs of snack foods and two plastic bottles of water on the passenger seat, and a jumbo cup of undrinkable coffee growing cold in the cup holder. I was parked fifty metres down the street from Simon Anning's house, a semi-detached brick house in a suburban street of similar buildings, just two blocks away from Torville street, where Anning had burned the evidence of the murder. I could see Anning's front door. With the binoculars on the dash, I could see the pattern of the wallpaper in his lounge room.

I was on a stakeout.

After leaving the police station, I'd gone straight to the Jindalee Hotel to meet Ronnie. As I knew he would, he had a folder in his phone that contained everything he knew about Simon Anning – including photos.

"It wasn't him," I said, crestfallen. I wanted it to be over.

Ronnie pulled a disgusted face. "Probably got young Jase from the restaurant to look at mugshots and then pulled some poor random crim in from the street to be their new prime suspect – I mean, accomplice of the real prime suspect, the evil mastermind, Luke Kelly."

"Yeah, not funny, mate."

Ronnie was grinning. "Bit funny."

We didn't stay for lunch. I filled him in on the interview as we drove out to Anning's place.

"Jeez, you gotta love that fella," he said in admiration of Terry Marchant. "Pull in there." He was pointing to a fried chicken franchise. When I parked, he asked me for fifty bucks.

"What for?"

"Supplies."

He ducked out and came back with an armload of stuff and no change. At Anning's place, he told me where to park and gave me a few pointers on being inconspicuous. Sitting there in a big white SUV in plain sight of Anning's windows, occasionally peering at the house through binoculars, my car littered with junk food and reeking of fried chicken, I felt anything but inconspicuous.

"You'll do great," he said, getting out. "Remember, you're only here to watch. If he spots you, or anyone else challenges you, just drive away."

The chicken was depressing me. Chelsea had been a vegetarian. She hated animal suffering. I was too, when we were together, but on my own, I ate meat. She knew it and didn't mind, reckoning every little helped and that she'd convert me in the end. The plastic bottles of water were depressing, too. Chelsea had hated the wanton pollution of the world for the sake of a little extra convenience. "They deliver fresh, clean water to every building in the city," she used to say. "It's yours for the effort of turning a tap. Why would anybody want to buy indestructible litter just to get a drink of water?" As with most of her crusades to save the planet, I was happy to go along. And now look at me; bottled water, dead factory-farmed chickens, plastic bags full of snack foods I couldn't eat because every time I looked at them I heard Chelsea saying, "They kill orang utans to grow the palm oil that goes into all that junk food, you know." Even though it had been Ronnie who'd bought it all, I still felt guilty. Even though I was out here trying to catch Chelsea's killer, I knew she'd rather that poor chicken hadn't died in "some mechanised death factory" than I brought her killer to justice. "Justice is just one of your abstractions," she might have said. "Death and suffering are real."

Even with all the windows open, the inside of the car was hot and the smell of the chicken was overpowering. I could see in the rear-view mirror that someone had left their wheelie bin out in the street after the last rubbish collection. They were probably out and they probably wouldn't mind anyway, I told myself. So I gathered up all the plastic and junk food and carried it up the road to the bin. I stared at the house it belonged to for long enough to be sure no irate owner was going to run out and defend the sanctity of his wheelie bin, and quickly dumped the lot.

Feeling better, I turned to go back to the car and stopped dead. Another car was driving past mine, moving slowly; a black, Jeep Cherokee. Its windows were down and a bearded man with long hair was leaning out of the back, staring into my car as they passed. The car pulled up in front of Anning's house and two men got out, leaving the driver behind. One was the bearded guy with long hair. The other had a shaven head. They both wore jeans and T-shirts. They looked all around before heading off up the street. As the shaven-headed guy looked my way, I grabbed the wheelie bin and pulled it after me through the gate of the house. *I'm just a harmless local brining in my bin*, I told the universe. *Nothing to see here.* I kept my head turned away until I was at the garage and sheltered by a large hakea. I let go of the bin and peered round the bush. The two men were through Anning's gate and walking up his short drive. I thought about sneaking back to my car and getting the binoculars but the Jeep was right there and the driver would have seen me for sure.

They knocked at the front door and waited, for all the world like a couple of scruffy, burly Mormons. Did these people know Anning? Did they work with him? Or for him? When I'd asked Ronnie what the point of a stakeout was, he'd said, "We need to know where he goes and who he sees. His social media and workmates will only tell us part of the picture. Something has turned this games developer into a murderer and we'll only find out what that is by putting his life under a microscope."

The front door opened a crack. I couldn't see who was inside but I was very surprised there was anyone at all. Anning should have been at work. He wasn't married, according to Ronnie. The door started closing. With a sudden, violent speed, the bearded guy pushed his way inside, followed quickly by the other one. Whoever had been in the doorway must have been sent flying. In a moment, the door was closed again and the street showed no sign of anything amiss. What the hell was going on?

I kept my eye on the house, pressing myself into the stiff, unyielding bush. Should I phone the police. What I'd just seen was two thugs forcing their way into Anning's house and it did not look like they meant to be gentle with the occupant. Someone was going to get hurt. But, if it was Anning, did I care? Was the enemy of my enemy really my friend? Come to that, were the cops my friend? If someone was beating up Anning and I called the police to lock them up, wouldn't they just say I was complicit, somehow? And wasn't I? Morally? In some convoluted way? It was hard to see myself as outside of it all, hiding in a bush on someone else's property, spying on everyone. With fumbling fingers, I dialled Ronnie, my eyes fixed on the distant doorway.

"If you're selling anything, fuck off. Otherwise, if you really think I'll be interested, leave a message. Don't expect an answer."

I stifled a cry of anger. "Ronnie, you bastard, get over here right now. Someone's just pushed their way into Anning's home – and I think he's in there. I don't know whether to call the cops." I hung up. I was so agitated, I could barely keep still.

Sod it, I thought. *I'm calling the police. They don't have to know it was me.* I typed in triple-zero and stopped with my finger half-way to the send button. Of course they'd know it was me. They'd see my number on the call. There was probably some way I could stop the phone sending my number. I got sales calls all the time from "unknown caller". But did that really hide your number completely? From the police? From the phone company?

As I stood there pondering my options the door to Anning's house opened again. The two men walked out and closed it after them. They walked briskly back to their car, looking all around as they went. The engine was running by the time they reached it and the car was moving before they'd even closed the doors. Again, the street returned to its slumbering, suburban state.

I stepped out of the bush and walked carefully to the gate.

There was no sight of the black Jeep. I went back to my car but didn't get in. What if they'd hurt him? What if he had broken bones or internal bleeding? What if he couldn't get to a phone to call for help? I began walking towards the house, each step debated, tentative. This was Anning, after all; the man who killed Chelsea. Why shouldn't he suffer? Why should I, of all people, help him? I stopped, in the middle of the road. He deserved to suffer. He deserved to be beaten by thugs and left coughing on broken ribs, peering through swollen eyes. I took another step and another, shocked into motion by my own imagination of his battered state. I couldn't just leave him. Chelsea would understand. Of all the people I'd ever known, she was the most tender-hearted. She'd have called the ambulance for Hitler himself. Besides, I reminded myself, I wanted Anning to face trial. I wanted him to be prosecuted and made to face what he'd done. A two-minute beating by a couple of blokes wasn't enough. Not nearly enough.

I went through Anning's gate and up to the door. I tried to open it but it was locked. If Ronnie had been there, he could have picked the lock, I was sure. But he wasn't. Not knowing what else to do, I knocked. There was no answer. I put my ear against the door and could hear no movement within. Somebody had been there to answer the door earlier. Were they hiding now, or injured?

"Anning?" I called, as loudly as I dared. I didn't want nosy neighbours attracted to the sound of shouting. Of course, anybody could have seen me walking up the street, standing like a lemon in the middle of the road. The cops could be on their way right now.

There were bay windows at either side of the door. I moved to one of them and peered in. I couldn't see much but there was no sign of Anning. I went to the other window. Still nothing. I followed a path that led around the side of the house to the back. I suddenly realised that the house was surrounded by neat flower beds full of bright blooms. Anning was a gardener? How could he be a gardener? At the back was a lawn and a little Colorbond tool shed. A patio with garden furniture extended across the whole of the rear of the house. At one side was a free-standing trellis with a dozen pots of orchids hanging from it. The orchids were healthy and lush but not in bloom.

I found a glass double door standing open and stepped through it from the brilliant light outside to the gloom within. And there he was, lying on the kitchen floor, staring at the ceiling, with a bullet hole in his chest.

There was very little blood, which meant, I supposed, that he had died quickly, Shot through the heart. His heart had died and stopped pumping blood. But how could his heart die when it was already dead? Only someone with a dead heart could have sat for ninety minutes chatting and laughing with Chelsea and then stabbed her in an alley. My eyes moved to his face. Clean shaven, of course. A young man. Not bad looking. Perhaps he had a twisted, ugly picture of himself in the attic. I wanted to kick his face, stomp on it and make it look the way it should.

My phone ringing snapped me out of my bloody reverie. It was Ronnie. I stepped away from the body and took the call.

"Luke? What's going on?"

I told him.

"Jeez, mate, get out of there now. Right now. Get in your car and drive home. If anyone asks, you've been home all day, hey? No, no! I mean, since you left the police station. Wait a minute! Did you touch anything? Have you touched the body? The doors? Windows?"

"Yes," I said. "The front door."

"Wipe it. Christ, you're a pillock! What the hell made you go over there?"

"I thought he might be injured."

"You—?" He was actually speechless. "Fuck me! Just get out of there. Are you moving?"

"Maybe…" The thought came to me out of nowhere. "Maybe I should search the place, look for evidence."

"Are you out of your tiny fucking mind? You want to leave your bloody prints and DNA all over the dead man's house? The dead man you have the best motive in the world to have killed? The dead man you didn't tell the police was a suspect this morning? The dead man whose house you were parked outside of with a pair of binoculars? Does that sound like a good idea to you?"

"I won't get another chance?"

"Leave it. Get out. The police will search his house. Just wipe the door and go."

"OK," I said and hung up.

But I didn't go. I looked around the kitchen. I picked up a tea towel and used it to cover my fingers so I could open a drawer. It contained cutlery. I opened another. It contained more domestic stuff. What was I looking for? A folder full of incriminating notes? A diary? A laptop? A phone? None of these would be in kitchen drawers. I looked again at the body. It was dressed in cargo shorts and a T-shirt. No socks. No shoes. The phone was in the left-hand side pocket of the shorts. I hesitated to get so close to the dead man on the floor.

My phone rang again. I answered it. "Where are you?" Ronnie asked. "You're not driving."

"I'm still here. At the house."

He swore, long and hard. "Have you touched anything else?"

"A tea towel." There was a long silence, so I said, "His phone's in his pocket."

Another long silence. "Listen to me, you fucking drongo, if you nick his phone, the cops will trace it. If you disable it so they can't trace it, it's as useful as tits on a bull. So just leave the fucker alone, hey? Listen, mate, you remember all the preparation this bloke made for the murder. You don't think he's going to have left evidence around in his own home do you? Just give it away, mate. There's nothing you can do there that won't just make things worse. Do you hear what I'm saying?" I nodded. "Luke?"

"Yeah. Yeah, yeah. I'm going."

"Good. Take the tea towel with you. Wipe the door with it. Keep it. Don't stand in any blood."

I looked at the floor. There was no blood except on the body. "Right-o." I hung up again.

Just a quick look around. I went through to a hallway that connected all the rooms. I knew already what was at the front. Next to the kitchen, with a view onto the garden, I found Anning's home office. No little laptop there! A big metal rack contained six or eight large slabs of computing equipment. Lights flickered on their front panels and wires criss-crossed and tumbled in thick bundles. On a plain desk stood three huge screens with two keyboards, half-a-dozen game controllers and other weird input devices. I sat in the high-backed, winged office chair and sank into its deep upholstery. There were filing cabinets and other tables and cupboards, every surface was littered with electronic gadgets – including at least three tablets, two pairs of VR goggles and some high-tech gauntlets. *Games*, I thought. *A man who plays games.*

Scanning the desk, I finally found a sculpted, multi-coloured puck that I correctly guessed was a super-fancy mouse and gave it a nudge. The three screens sprang into life. Anning must have been here when his own murderers came knocking. And he'd left himself logged on.

A first person shooter game was running on one screen. The ray-gun toting space commando ran through a post-apocalyptic terrain while alien creatures with terrible aim leapt out from behind half-demolished buildings and fired at him. I watched until he was hit and fell down. Other space soldiers gathered round him.

"What the fuck, man?" one of them asked, clearly put out.

"Yeah, not cool," said another. "You're supposed to body swap if you're having a crap or whatever. Now we're a man down for the raid."

On a whim, I reached out to a microphone on the table and pushed the button to speak. "Help me, I'm dead," I said in a croaky voice.

One of them swore and walked away.

"You need to take this more seriously," said another, "or you're off the squad, man. There's a lot of people got money on this."

I left them to their grumbling and looked at the other screens. There were windows full of code, windows full of stats, windows full of stuff I couldn't make any sense of, but nothing that looked like a diary or a contacts list. I clicked on a few things but I was hopelessly out of my depth.

The game screen changed and drew my attention. It was now some kind of scoreboard, with a list of teams, their rankings, various stats, and the current betting odds. At the bottom of the screen was an archer logo and the slogan, "Powered by Archerfield. Gamble securely. Win big."

Well, I hope they didn't pay their corporate branding company much for that, I thought and got up again. There was nothing to find here. Nothing a useless, technically illiterate, unemployed bum like me could find, anyway. I reached the hallway before I remembered I'd left my tea towel behind. I went back in and retrieved it, wiped the microphone and the chair arms, giggling as I remembered the Hitchhiker's Guide. All I needed to be Arthur Dent was three pints of beer, a packet of crisps and an electronic thumb. I already had the towel.

In the hallway, near the front door, I caught a reflection of myself in the mirror hanging there. It was amazing how pale my face looked, as if all my blood had drained out, like I should be lying dead on the kitchen floor alongside Anning. Shrugging, I left. I wiped the door, like Ronnie had said, and walked back to my car. I got in, started the engine and sat there with the engine running.

My hands were gripping the wheel so tightly my arms were trembling. My breathing was fast and shallow. *Shock*, a voice said in my head. *It's only shock.* But that was silly. Just because Anning was dead and I'd seen the body lying there with its eyes open and a hole in its chest and looking like it was asleep but all the life had gone and it was really dead. A dead thing. Just meat. Meat on the floor. A pile of meat that looked like a person. Like Chelsea had been. Like Chelsea had been. Like—

The police siren cut through my fugue like a jolt of electricity to the brain. The white saloon, decked out in blue checks and black writing rushed to a halt outside Anning's house, headlights on, red and blue lights flashing. Two cops in peaked caps got out in a hurry and ran to Anning's door.

They knocked and waited. Then one ran around the back. Seconds ticked slowly past, then the other got a call on his radio and also ran to the back. I put the car in gear and drove up the road, passing the police car and its epileptic light show and carried on up the road, round a corner, then another, then another until I was far, far away.

Chapter Eleven

I went home. I sat on my sofa and stared at my shaking hands until the tremors passed. Ronnie called about ten times but I didn't answer and he gave up. I lay down on the sofa. Later, I curled up and fell asleep.

I was woken by Ronnie placing a large rum on the coffee table beside me. I looked around, confused, and sat up.

"Get that in you, mate," he said, taking a chair opposite me. He also had a drink.

It was still light. Early evening. How did Ronnie get into my home?

"I remember my first time," Ronnie said. "I wasn't even your age. Northern Ireland, during the Troubles. We were… But that's all classified. I ended up in a ditch in the dark with a dead bloody Mick on top of me. I still see that face in my dreams, even though I've seen a lot more since, some of them mates." He looked down at his drink. "Best thing for it, the only thing that does any bloody good, is to get completely fucking hammered."

The smell of the drink was making me feel queasy. "I didn't think it would be so…"

"Yeah, well. You live and learn."

"Do other people… you know…?"

"Flip out like you did? Some. Everyone's different. What happened after you stopped taking my calls?"

I told him. It was like recalling a dream. I wasn't always sure that it had all really happened and in what order.

"Bloody hell," was his only comment but I caught the undertones. I had been lucky. Incredibly lucky.

"I wiped everything down, like you said."

"We'll see."

"What does that mean?"

He picked up his glass and looked into the brown liquid. "Well, the cops are going to work out that Anning was the man in the restaurant – the one they think is your accomplice."

"How? How could they possibly link him?"

He frowned, like I was being stupid. "Same way we did. Even if they don't use the class lists and electoral rolls, the coincidence of a body turning up just a block away from where the evidence was burned is going to make a cop like Bertolissio take his picture to our friend Jase to get an ID. Once they connect Anning to Chelsea, they'll be round here like a shot to get your prints and DNA, your clothes and your alibi. They'll scour Anning's place for anything and everything that might connect you to him."

My clothes? Even if I'd shed fibres like a dog in moult, my shorts and shirt were common brands. It would only be a weak link. But what about skin flakes and hairs? Was my DNA all over the dead man's house?

"Shit."

"Shit, indeed," he said. "You don't have an alibi and I bet half a dozen traffic cameras – if not nosy neighbours – put you at the scene at the right time. Worse still, the cop car will have had a camera and the two cops might have had their body cameras running. If they think to check the footage, which they will, they'll see your car right there in the street where the murder took place. Worse than all that, you didn't report the crime when you discovered it. You ponced around in his house, played with his toys, and snuck away past the cops."

Now I really felt sick. "Oh God. What should I do?"

"Mate, there's not much you can do. You've probably got a day at the most before they put it all together and come for you. Give Terry a call."

"Terry?"

"Your lawyer. He'll probably recommend surrendering."

I did not want to do that. Sitting in a police cell while Reid stacked up evidence against me seemed like the worst thing I could do. I couldn't deny I was there with the body and I had such a great motive for killing him.

"What about the gun?" I said. "I don't own a gun. I wouldn't even know how to get one. How could I have shot him without a gun?"

"Yeah, the gun. What do you suppose Reid's going to say about that? Why don't you tell us where you dumped it, Kelly? Is that why you were so keen to sneak past the cops at the crime scene, so you could dump the murder weapon?"

"Jesus."

He picked up my glass and his and took them to the kitchenette where he started pouring the booze back into the bottle. "Looks like this wasn't such a good idea after all." He stopped and looked straight at me. "Seriously, you should call Terry, try to get out ahead of all this. The kinds of things I can do for you right now would only make things worse."

"Like what?" Surely, anything was better than being arrested?

"Oh, like showing you how to go underground, getting you a new identity, that kind of thing." Maybe that was worse, maybe it wasn't. "Go on, call him."

So I did. Marchant's first reaction was, "You need to turn yourself in, right away. I'll meet you at the station in one hour. Is Ronnie with you?"

"Yes."

"Well, tell him to keep out of it and to make sure his alibi for the murder is rock solid."

"OK."

"I thought this one was going to be easy but now… Ah well, I shall look at it as an opportunity to enhance my reputation. Will you put Ronnie on?"

"OK."

I handed over the phone and Ronnie said things like, "I know," and "Tell me about it!" They obviously made an agreement to meet up. Ronnie said goodbye and gave me an appraising look.

"Right-o, mate," he said. "Take your clothes off. Everything. Stick the lot in the washing machine. Shoes too."

"No, it's all right," I said. "I've already thought about that. All my clothes are common brands. It won't prove anything if they find fibres."

He sighed. "And what about any fibres or hairs or whatever they find on you that you picked up at the house?"

"Ah. Right."

"Change into something that looks the same. Tell the cops you've had the same clothes on all day. It shouldn't matter but, if this ever goes to court, the more doubt and uncertainty you can muster, the better."

I grabbed some clothes, went to the utility room and changed. The washing machine still had a load of damp washing in it that was beginning to smell musty. I dumped it on the floor, put my clothes and shoes in, and set the machine working. I went out to find Ronnie doing something with my phone.

"I'm deleting your call logs," he said. "And mine too. It won't stop them finding out how often I called you while you were at the house but it will slow them down a bit. I'm going to need a bit of time. I want to find out who those guys were that killed Anning. It's the only thing that will get you off now."

I sat down, feeling tired. "I thought it was all over when I saw Anning dead. I thought all this was finished."

"Yeah, well, it's not. Not for me, anyhow. You get to spend a short vacation at the ratepayer's expense but I've now got two killers to track down." He sounded almost happy about it.

I checked the time. "I'd better get going."

"I've already called you a cab."

"Thanks. Is there, like, anything I should take with me?"

He shook his head. "Nah, mate. They'll supply all your needs."

He came with me in the taxi and I couldn't help wondering if he thought I might chicken out. When I looked back from the police station doors, he was still there in the cab, watching me. Marchant was already in the foyer and greeted me with a handshake.

We were met by our old friend Julie. "Hi, I'm Julie," she said. Neither of us bothered to remind her that we'd already met. "If you'd like to come this way."

She took us to the same room we had been in before. I went to look out of the window while Marchant unloaded his briefcase and made himself comfortable. I wondered how many times a week he went through that same ritual. A woman came in and said, "Hello, I'm—"

"Detective Sergeant Alexandra Bertolissio," I said.

She smiled. "Fame at last." It was a lovely smile and quite threw me. "I'm afraid Detective Inspector Reid is out of the office at the moment but if I can help in any way…"

"He's probably attending a crime scene not far from Torville Street," Marchant said.

She looked at Marchant with a keen eye. I could almost hear the pieces falling into place. Then she turned that intelligent gaze on me. "Won't you sit down, Doctor Kelly?" I did and so did she. To Marchant, she said, "I gather you're here with some important information."

I began to speak but Marchant put a hand on my arm to silence me. He then proceeded to explain how, "in the course of my client's investigation into the murder of his girlfriend, Chelsea Campbell," I had stumbled upon the body of Simon Anning and, "naturally, being shocked and disoriented," had left the scene without reporting it. "However, as soon as my client came to his proper senses, he called me and, well, here we are."

The pretty little detective looked at me throughout Marchant's spiel, not just looked at but studied with a deep, penetrating stare. After he'd finished, she asked me, "Is there anything you'd like to add?" I shook my head. "Mr. Marchant, you realise that I will have to detain your client. I note that he came in voluntarily and is co-operating."

"Thank you," said Marchant. "Can I hear your grounds?"

She sighed. "Well, the DI may want to arrest him on suspicion of murder but that's up to him. For now, let's just say it's for leaving the scene of a crime."

Although she was about to lock me away and begin a

process that might end up with me spending decades in jail, I found I liked this woman. Just from her tone of voice and her facial expressions, I felt reassured. However dumb and pig-headed Reid was, this one was reasonable and fair. I could trust her. On the other hand, maybe I was already suffering from Stockholm Syndrome and my plight was so dire, I'd trust any of my captors who wasn't actively hostile.

"Will you be questioning my client any further this evening?"

Bertolissio said no. "I'll just take him down for processing and put him away for the night. The DI will no doubt want to see him in the morning."

"Oh good, I have a dinner engagement. But, just so we're clear, my client asserts his right not to be questioned without me present."

"Is that what you want?" she asked me but, before I could answer, Marchant jumped in, fixing me with a meaningful look.

"Yes, it is. And, in my absence, the only answer my client will give to any question will be 'No comment. I want my lawyer present.' Isn't that right, Mr. Kelly?"

"Yes," I said, glumly.

"Then we're done," said Bertolissio brightly. We all stood up. Marchant seemed satisfied with the proceedings and so did the detective. She left us in the meeting room and, to my surprise, came back with a uniformed policeman. Then we all left together. It had seemed formal but quite amicable until the policeman took me by the upper arm in a firm grip.

* * * *

Ronnie had been right that they would take my clothes.

Everyone spoke from a script as they explained what was happening at each stage. They scanned my fingerprints and took a cheek swab for DNA. They photographed me and asked me my name, address and date of birth. They checked my understanding of everything they told me. They made me sign for my "personal belongings". Some of the people dealing with me were police officers, some were "technicians". I didn't bother to ask what it meant. Bertolissio left early in the proceedings and a uniformed sergeant took charge of me. "You are being held for questioning," the sergeant told me when I asked if I was under arrest. "You're not under arrest, yet." When I asked what the difference was, he said, "Not a lot." After all the rigmarole, I was taken by a policeman to a cell. It was clean and had a bed and a toilet and a basin. There were no windows. I had nothing to read – probably for the first time in my life since the day I learned. There was no TV, no radio, no Internet. It was cruel and unusual punishment for someone like me. I tried to amuse myself, remembering Plato's description of Socrates' inspirational courage in prison. But that had ended very badly for the great man and I regretted my choice of exemplar. Chelsea had sometimes tried to persuade me to try meditation but the idea of clearing one's mind of thought appalled me. I used to tease her terribly about it. Alone in my cell, I regretted not listening to her. What a blessing it would have been not to think about anything at all.

Chapter Twelve

The next morning I lay awake on the thin mattress, unable to tell what time it was, or if the sun was up. But I knew it was morning because at some point in the night the shouting and clangour of drunks and doors had given way to relative peace and then the noise had slowly started up again. It felt like many, many hours since that had happened and I began to wonder if maybe it was almost lunchtime.

I had, literally, nothing to do. It occurred to me that being there was not at all like being a monk, something I'd often thought might be a good thing. Yes, I had all the time in the world to consider the deep problems of existence but a monk would have had religious observances, he would have had the monastery bells to toll the hours, his days would be structured and purposeful, and, if he got lonely, he could always talk to God. All I had was endless monotony and a gnawing worry that this might become the rest of my life.

With a crash that made me jump, the bolt on my door was thrown back and a uniformed cop took me back to the sergeant's desk. It was a different sergeant, different shift, but the strange, scripted interaction continued. He handed me a folded pile of clothes – not the clothes I came in with but mine, all the same – with a bag of my "personal items" on top and made me sign for them. The cop took me to a cubicle and told me to get changed. I asked him what was going on and he said, "Don't ask me, mate. I only work here."

Dressed in clothes that were far too warm for the day, I was taken up to a floor I hadn't visited yet. The officer took me into a small room that was clearly an interrogation room and told me to sit. He took up a spot by the door and stood there. It was intimidating. My stomach began to grumble with hunger and anxiety.

"Is Reid coming?" I asked.

The policeman looked bored. "Someone will be along in a minute, sir," he said. I assumed his more formal tone meant that we were now under observation.

I heard voices in the corridor outside. The door opened and Reid walked in followed by my lawyer and Bertolissio. They each took their places around the table as if they'd rehearsed it beforehand, Marchant next to me, Reid opposite me, and Bertolissio next to him. The uniformed cop stayed by the door. Perhaps they expected me to become violent and had the crazy notion that Reid alone wouldn't have been enough to subdue me.

Bertolissio went through some spiel for the record and then looked at Reid. This was his show. I expected him to come on hard and aggressive but he seemed strangely subdued. I looked at Marchant and saw a hint of puzzlement in his face.

"I'd like you to tell us again, in your own words, exactly what happened yesterday at Simon Anning's house," he said to me. I took a breath and began with the point that I believed Anning was Chelsea's murderer and I'd decided to put him under surveillance. I didn't mention Ronnie. I ran through the sequence of events, throwing the food in some stranger's bin, seeing the black Jeep arrive, the two thugs, going over to Anning's house thinking he might be hurt, finding the body...

I stopped there. My behaviour from that point on was weird. It was embarrassing to think about, let alone say out loud. And it sounded so crazy. I walked around his house looking for evidence. I sat in his office, watching a game unfold. Played a prank on the other players. Wiped all my prints. Went to my car. Went home. Fell asleep. Jeez, I must have been completely out of it.

I took another breath and told them everything.

I tensed up, waiting for the real interrogation to begin, the shouting, the drama, the angry faces. But it didn't happen. I saw Bertolissio turn to Reid and raise one eyebrow. Reid's lips tightened angrily but then he gave a tiny nod. To me, he said, "We have a lot of things we can charge you with, Kelly – failing to report a crime, for starters – but we're letting you go for now."

"What?"

Reid scowled. "You heard." To Marchant, he said, "Your client is free to go. Make sure he doesn't leave the city without my knowledge." The two detectives stood up and Bertolissio began her "interview terminated" speech.

"What?" I said again. I was free to go? Just like that? I had questions. I had a right to an explanation. I took a breath preparatory to demanding to know what was going on but Marchant did his hand-on-arm trick and silenced me.

"Thank you," he said to Reid, nodded to Bertolissio, and led me out. The cop took us to the main entrance and I was free again.

"What the hell happened?" I asked, the minute we were

clear of the doors.

"You need to ask the mysterious Mr. Walker," he said with a grin. He called me last night and said, if I recall, 'No need to pull any shyster stunts tomorrow, mate, they're going to let Luke go. It's all sorted.'" He raised his eyebrows. "Ronnie has a strange view of what my job is. Anyway, if he tells you, I'd like to know. I've never seen anything quite like that. Anyway, call me if you need me."

He marched off towards the CBD and I stood there watching him, dazed, confused and woozy with tiredness, carrying a brown paper bag with my belongings in and starting to sweat in the morning heat. I caught a cab home, showered and changed. I called Ronnie and got his "get lost" phone message. I told him I was home, probably asleep and he should come round and explain the miracle he had just worked. But I didn't go to sleep. I put on the telly and watched the ABC news – mostly dismal stories of people doing horrible things to one another, the dismal state of the economy, and the miserable cruelties being perpetrated on poor people by our overfed, sleek and privileged government. I'd just decided that watching a cookery show where insanely excitable people shout and cry over sponge cakes would be less awful, when the doorbell rang. I dragged myself over to the intercom by the door and said, "Yes?"

"Mr. Kelly? It's Detective Sergeant Bertolissio. May I come in?"

I was so surprised, I almost forgot to push the button to unlock the door. "Sorry. Yes, of course."

I looked around. The place was a mess. Had I done any housework at all since Stacey left? Well, it was too late now. I unlocked and opened the unit door and waited.

The detective, when she appeared, smiled and held out her

hand to shake mine. She was small and neat, black hair, olive skin, and intelligent eyes. She dressed the way I imagined an executive PA would; comfortably and tastefully. She was probably ten years older than me but had such a confident air, she made me feel like a kid.

"I'm sure you've seen enough of the police to last you a lifetime," she said as she went inside. Her eyes flicked about the room, lingering on the bottle of rum, still by the sink, the laptop on the floor, the packaging for a vacuum flask in the bin, and coming to settle on the whiteboard with its pictures and map. She made an effort not to stare at it. "But I hope you won't mind if I ask you a few questions. There are a couple of things I'd love to clear up, just for my own sake."

"I'm not supposed to talk to you without my lawyer here," I said and felt like a complete fool.

"If you'd rather I left…"

"Nah. Sorry. I suppose I trust you not to beat a confession out of me." She smiled but said nothing and I felt even worse. I offered her a coffee. The biscuits I'd bought the other day were on the chair where Karen had left them. I picked up the packet to offer her one only to find it was empty. She watched me fumbling around, trying to be polite, with a silent indulgence.

"Maybe we could just sit down," she said.

"Oh God. Sorry. Please…" I indicated a chair and went quickly to sit on the sofa.

"Mr. Kelly—" she began.

"Luke," I said. She nodded.

"What led you to Simon Anning?"

"Why did you let me go?" I'd blurted out the question before I realised she'd just asked me one.

"You don't know? Mr. Walker hasn't told you?" I reckon

my expression was all the answer she needed. "Your friend turned up a witness – a neighbour of Simon Anning's. She came in last night and made a statement. She saw the two men you described in the victim's kitchen with the victim. She saw the muzzle flash from the shot that killed him. About five minutes later, she saw you enter the kitchen, stand for a while, and then disappear into the house. Ten minutes after that, she saw the police arrive."

"Holy crap."

"Her story and yours match in every detail. At the very least it gives you reasonable doubt. Even my boss could see the public prosecutor wasn't going to pursue a murder charge, given the new evidence. As for failure to report a crime and the rest, it's still a possibility but, given the circumstances of your bereavement and the strong possibility that Anning is our killer, I personally can't see that a prosecution would be worth our while – or the right thing to do."

I was so stunned to learn that I was actually off the hook – at least for Anning's murder – that I forgot the detective had asked me a tricky question.

"So," she said, repeating it. "How did you get onto Anning?"

"It – it wasn't me. Ronnie worked it out. Do you know Ronnie?"

"Only by reputation. Quite a detective by all accounts. Admired and hated in equal parts, I'd say."

"That's pretty much what he says about you. Er, except for the hated part."

"So, how did he work it out?"

And I saw in her face that this interview wasn't about me or the case at all. It was about a professional so wrapped up in her craft that she had to find out how a fellow magician had performed his trick. So I told her the whole story of our investigation. When I got to the part where Ronnie stood in Torville Street and said the killer must live nearby, she said, "Of course!" When I recounted our conversation in the Indian restaurant, she nodded in approval.

"But how did you get the information?" she asked, zooming in immediately on the part I wanted to leave out. "The class lists, the electoral roll? And how did you compare them? You don't have the resources." She stopped. Her face cleared. "Of course, you do, don't you?" I tried to keep my expression neutral. She smiled. "It's all right. I won't be pursuing it. I just wanted to know."

"Someone did me a huge favour," I said. "I don't want them to get into trouble."

She nodded. "I won't even be writing a report of this conversation. It's off the record. OK?"

"Thank you."

"How do you know Ronnie?"

"I don't really. He's just some bloke I met in the pub. When he told me he'd been a detective once, I asked him to help. After that, he sort of latched onto me."

She stood up. "Lucky for you, he did. I must meet him sometime, pick his brains about some cases I'm working."

"Just hang around here for long enough," I said. "He seems to think he has the right to come and go as he pleases. I think he's made himself a key." Bertolissio frowned, not sure if I was joking. "It's OK," I reassured her. "After what he just did for me, I'm thinking of marrying him and having his babies."

She laughed and made for the door. As I let her out, she said, "One last thing. Do you or Ronnie have any idea what

Anning's motive was?" I shook my head. "What about the two men who shot him? Do you know ho they were?"

"No idea. I bet your DI thinks they were mates of mine."

She laughed again but she didn't deny it. "So this is the end of your investigation."

It was more of a statement than a question, perhaps even an order. "I suppose. It's not like I care why Anning was shot."

"And Ronnie?"

I pulled a face. "He's a bit like one of those dogs whose jaws lock shut when they bite onto something and can't let go."

"That's a myth – about dogs. It may be true about Ronnie. Do him a favour and try to distract him or something."

After she'd gone I rushed around the apartment, tidying and then cleaning. Bertolissio's visit had felt like closure. She was right. It was over. I'd found Chelsea's killer and, as an added bonus, he was dead. There would be no trial, no appeals, no release date to look forward to. I'd been spared years of anguish. In the utility room, I took out the clean washing and the ruined shoes, picked up the smelly old washing from the floor and stuffed it back in the machine. I started to feel good for the first time in almost two weeks. I threw in some powder and chose a wash cycle at random. I was going to have to learn how to use this thing properly. I was going to have to get a grip on my life. I was living alone now. I'd need to take care of myself, like a responsible adult should, like Chelsea would have wanted me to. I'd need to find work – proper work, not all this gig rubbish – and I'd need to decide what to do about the company, and Stacey, and the unit.

I was making the bed when I heard Ronnie's voice in the other room, shouting, "Honey? I'm ho-ome!"

Chapter Thirteen

"I never thought I'd be a free man tonight," I said, raising my beer to salute Ronnie.

"Fuck's sake, give it a rest, mate. If I'd known you were going to slobber on about it all night, I'd have left you in there."

We were in a hotel restaurant on the South Bank. Ronnie's choice. It was a place posh enough to serve your beer in glasses but not posh enough to care what you wore while you drank it. The food was OK and the waiters were attentive.

"Well, I won't forget it." I'd had too many beers already and I knew I was being a bit effusive but I didn't care. "You showed me the way, you tracked down the man who killed my one true love, and you saved me from a life of misery and incarceration. I think that calls for one or two thank yous, don't you?"

"Have you finished?"

"No, I have much more praise to bestow, my modest friend."

"I meant, have you finished eating."

I looked at my plate. The remains of a sticky fig pudding looked back. *Like the abyss,* I thought. "If thou gaze long into the sticky fig pudding, the sticky fig pudding will also gaze into thee." I looked up to find Ronnie's grey-blue eyes staring into mine. "That's about how fighting monsters will turn you into one yourself," I told him. A slight tightening of his brows was enough to make me realise what I was saying. "Oh God, no. I don't mean you. You're my hero. You're not…"

"Come on," he said, standing up. "If you're going to get pissed and philosophical, we need to find a better place than this. Settle the bill."

I did and we walked out into a beautiful sub-tropical Brisbane evening. He led us towards the river, broad and calm and bright with the reflected light of the city centre. South Bank has a covered walk – covered by bougainvillea in bloom that night – that winds through parkland along the river. The uplit foliage trembled in the breeze and huge flying foxes could be seen hanging in the palm trees along the way. Cicadas chirruped and people talked and laughed in the warm air.

"I love this city," I told Ronnie. He looked at me sideways. "Don't you?"

"You've seen one city, you've seen them all," he said.

"Nah, this one's special."

"How would you know? How many cities have you ever lived in? Or even visited?"

I stooped and rounded on him. "Why the hell are you being such a bloody sook? You did a great job. You solved it. Can't you just be happy for one single night?"

He looked shifty, guilty even. "It's not over."

"What?"

"It's not over. All we've got is half the story. Not even half. We still don't know why Anning did it. We still don't know why Anning was taken out, or by who."

"Whom."

"Right, my grammar is so fucking important right now."

"Sorry. It's like a reflex. But who gives a stuff why he did it, or what he's mixed up in that got him killed? I don't. Why should I?"

"You should care because it mattered to Chelsea."

"What? I mean, what would you know about what Chelsea cared about? I mean – Jesus! – to you she's just a picture on a whiteboard. I'm the one who knew her. I'm the one who lived with her, shared her life. You're just some bloody stranger who doesn't have a fucking clue who she even was."

He was staring at me, his face set hard. I realised I had been shouting and, sure enough, when I looked around, people were staring at me.

"You know I'm right," he said. "That's why you're being such a prima donna. You act like a complete wanker but you're not as stupid as all that. Not by a long way. Why did she meet Anning? What was in the envelope he used to lure her into that alley? Why does a respectable businessman, a young Turk, going places, suddenly risk everything to kill some woman he hasn't even seen in years? What did she know about? What was she going to find out that scared him so much? And who were his accomplices? And why did they have him killed?"

"Accomplices?" I had to admit, I'd asked myself all the same questions he was asking me – maybe not in such a clear and pointed way, but they had been rumbling around in my head for the past few days. But accomplices? "Why should Anning's murder have anything to do with Chelsea?"

"Oh, come on! Don't be so bloody obtuse. You think it's a coincidence? And that car you described, that big, shiny black Jeep? Do you know what those things cost?" I began to make a guess but he talked over me. "A lot more than a couple of scruffy thugs can afford." He stepped closer and lowered his voice. "This is gang-related, Luke. Organised crime. Chelsea was onto something big and someone with a lot of clout wanted her out of the way. That's why it isn't over, Luke, because Anning was just a link in the chain."

"That's — that's just wild speculation. You've built this whole edifice out of one car? What if one of them works in a garage and they borrowed it for the day? What if it was a hire car? What if one of them got it as a great second-hand bargain after a crash and restored it? It could be anything. We just—" A sob caught in my throat and I had to stop. Ronnie looked as surprised as I felt. I forced myself to go on. "We found Chelsea's killer. Why can't we just leave it at that?"

"You're really asking me that?"

A wave of exhaustion washed through me. "I thought I could just stop all this, start..."

His face hardened. "What? Start rebuilding your life? Start moving on? You're going to stand there spouting women's magazine crap at me? You saw Anning's body. This shit is real. There are two killers on the loose. They work for somebody who lends them nice cars for doing his little errands. He's probably the one who decided Chelsea had to die. Don't you care that he's out there, thinking he got away with it?"

Dammit but he knew how to press my buttons. "If you want vengeance so much, you go and hunt down Mr. Big. This is your obsession, not mine. Oh, no, wait. If I drop out you've got no excuse to go tracking down killers, have you? If I let it go, you're just a sad old geezer with a vigilante complex."

He took a step towards me, fists balled, head down. I was sure he was going to hit me and, if he did, I was sure I'd need an ambulance. He was built like a brick dunny and, despite his age, looked like he could bounce me like a ball if he felt like it. For a second he glowered at me from under his brows and I held my breath. Then he turned quickly and walked away. My heart was hammering and my breathing was short. I felt sick. But he'd gone. Gone for good, I hoped.

* * * *

I woke up the next morning on the sofa, the half-empty bottle of rum on the floor beside me. I had vague memories of throwing up in the bathroom – thank goodness for small mercies – and watching idiotic American cop movies on Netflix, cheering through the endless fight scenes. I'm not a big drinker, never have been, so the hangover that assailed me that morning was cruel and pitiless. The carolling magpies outside seemed intent on driving their long beaks through my skull and the smell of cleaning products from yesterday's housework made my fragile stomach heave.

I made it to the bathroom with the help of furniture and walls to lean on and was hit by the stench of vomit and booze. I dry-heaved for a long, miserable time, then managed to find some pain killers and fill a glass of water from the tap. I was sure my skin smelled of rum, oozing out through the pores.

I made it back to the sofa, clutching a second glass of water and lay down, waiting to die.

The doorbell hit my ears like a thunderclap.

"Go away!"

The doorbell rang again. And again. And again. And—

"What?" I gasped into the intercom, having staggered all the way to the door.

"DI Reid, Mr. Kelly. Can I come in?"

"You can, but you may not. I'm not feeling very well. You'll have to come back."

"I need to talk to you about the Anning murder. I promise I won't keep you long."

I buzzed him in, pretty sure that the pest wouldn't go away and it would be better to get it over with. I left the door open and went to sit in an armchair, feeling the need of something to prop me up.

Reid came in with a detective I'd never met, who closed the door behind them. He looked disgustingly fit and healthy, clear-eyed and energetic. He took in my dishevelled state and the rum bottle on the floor at a glance.

"Been celebrating your release," he said. Perhaps seeing there was only one glass, he added, "Drinking with the flies were you?"

"Look, it's none of your business but, yes, I had a bit of a bender and got shit-faced. Now I feel like death warmed up. So, can we get through the questions real quick before I start chucking up again?"

He sat on the sofa and the anonymous sidekick got out his notebook.

"First off," Reid said, "I'd like you to come in as soon as you can and spend a bit of time looking at some mug shots. See of you can identify either of the men you saw at Anning's house."

"Yeah, sure."

"And, if that doesn't go well, maybe you could sit down with our artist and try to put together pictures of the two men."

"All right." I was sure I'd feel up to it in a couple of days. "Didn't you get their rego from traffic cams or something?"

"We did, but they'd used false plates." He gave a winsome smile. "Millions of dollars worth of surveillance cameras and computers, hundreds of man-hours spent scouring the video, and they can beat it in one minute with a screwdriver and a bit of painted tin."

I closed my eyes, just to get a rest from the light that was searing my retinas, and wondered how long it would be until the painkillers kicked in. "Is that all?"

"Just a couple more things. When you were in Anning's office, you said you looked at his computer. Can you tell us what you saw on the screen?"

"What? You've got the computer. You can dig around in it at your leisure, surely?"

"You'd think so, right? Only it seems our tech guys are having trouble getting in. Super-strong encryption on the hard disk, they tell me. So, you're the only one whose seen whatever he's got in there."

I shook my head in disbelief and immediately regretted it. "I don't know. There was a game – some kind of multi-player shooting thing."

"*Silent Empire?*" the other cop asked, checking his notes.

"What?"

"Was the game *Silent Empire?*"

"I don't know. I have no idea. I don't play computer games."

"So, what else was there?" Reid asked.

"I dunno, loads of windows that looked like they were full of code or something. I'm not much of a computer user. I poked around a bit but it was all really strange, not like the computers I'm used to."

"A different operating system?" the guy with the notebook asked.

I shrugged.

"Anything at all you can remember?" asked Reid.

"No, nothing. It was all gibberish to me. And I was, you know, in shock or something. I wasn't really taking much in."

Reid pursed his lips and nodded. I wondered if he thought it made him look deep and thoughtful. "Right-o then, we'll get out of your hair." He stood up, as did his companion. I got up too. Almost over. Soon I could lie down again. "If you want to know a great hangover cure, I recommend—"

"No thank you. If you so much as mention raw eggs or oysters, I might puke on you in self-defence."

"Fair enough." In the doorway, he stopped. "Just one more thing. Can you come by at three this afternoon to take part in a line up?"

"In a what?"

"An identity parade?"

"You want me to pick out the shooters? You've got some suspects?" If he did, what was all that stuff earlier about mug-shots and artists?

"No, no. We need you to be in the line-up so our witness can confirm it was really you they saw at Annings house."

I stared at him, stunned, as the implications of what he had said sank in. "You still think it was me?"

He smiled. "We just want to be sure. That's all. See you at three. Bring your lawyer if you like."

* * * *

I lay in a stupor, feeling awful and fretting anxiously for a couple of hours. For lunch I had some toast and a boiled egg. The eggs were past their 'best before' date but the one I had seemed OK. I really needed to get myself together. I needed to do some shopping, take out the rubbish, put the clothes I'd washed twice now into the dryer and, after last night's excesses, clean the loo. I got as far as shuttling the washing from the front loader to the dryer above it before my anxiety got the better of me and I had to call Terry Marchant.

"It's voluntary, you understand?" he said. "Unless they change their minds and decide to arrest you."

"So... should I do it?"

"I'd recommend that you don't. There's always a chance this woman is a complete flake and fails to recognise you. That wouldn't be good."

"No, it wouldn't. I suppose I'll have to call them."

"Don't worry, I'll do that. It's always better coming from your lawyer."

I hesitated. "I should tell you, I'm not investigating Chelsea's death any more. As far as I'm concerned, I got what I wanted."

"A wise decision. These things are best left to the proper authorities."

"Unless they're trying to frame you for the crime."

"Quite."

"So... that means I'm not working with Ronnie any more."

"Hmmm. So you think that means I should drop your case?"

"Well, I suppose."

"Well, don't worry about it. I agreed to be your lawyer in this matter – which, it appears, is still very much active – and I'll see it through to the bitter end. Is that all?"

I thanked him profusely and immediately returned to fretting again. Had I made the right decision, cancelling the line up? If the witness said I wasn't the man she saw, I'd be in deep trouble. But if she identified me correctly, even Reid would need to get off my back. The way things were, I was in limbo again. And didn't it look suspicious, not doing it? And what if the witness would have identified me today, but then they arrested me and made me do it a week or a month from now and she couldn't remember?

I needed to get out and do something or I'd drive myself mad second guessing myself. I'd packed up the whiteboard and had all the folders and file cards and all the rest of that now-useless junk in a big plastic bin bag. I grabbed it all up and struggled out to the car with it. It was all going to the op shop. Maybe some school kid could make good use of it all.

I headed out towards Ipswich, thinking I'd get out of the city and spend some time in a quiet, regional town but, part-way there, I remembered how dismal and run-down most regional towns were and turned off the road. I passed through Kenmore, telling myself I'd go and see my mum and dad but I kept on going, winding along country roads until I ended up in a suburb called Karana Downs. This had a little park – Kookaburra Park, according to the sign – and I parked there and got out. It was actually really pretty. The Brisbane River there was broad and slow and opened into a wide pond where a flock of black swans and a couple of pelicans were floating about. The park was deserted and I was very grateful for the peace and solitude. I walked along the water's edge, at one point disturbing a big brown snake that wriggled away into the rough grass. I found a tree to give me some shade and sat under it, watching the swans, trying to absorb some of their perfect serenity.

But it wasn't working. Reid was still on my case, still convinced I was some kind of crazy arrogant killer, thumbing my nose at the ignorant cops, trying to show them how smart

I was, still trying to discover how I was doing it. Somehow I'd colluded with Anning to kill Chelsea. Somehow I'd tricked a witness into giving me an alibi for killing Anning. Or, and I supposed this possibility must have been driving Reid crazy, the witness was real but I'd paid those two thugs to shoot Anning and then turned up at the crime scene just to get my supervillain kicks at the cops' expense.

The problem with the elaborate conspiracy theory Reid was spinning was the same problem all conspiracy theories had; once you go off down that rabbit hole, any and all evidence can be twisted to fit the theory. I could tell that Bertolissio wasn't buying it but maybe Ronnie was exaggerating her influence over her blinkered boss.

So where did that leave me?

Sitting in a park watching the swans, still waiting for the axe to fall.

And then there was the other thing, the thing I'd got myself stupid drunk to avoid thinking about. My last conversation with Ronnie. I hated to admit it, but Ronnie might just have been right. Until I knew why Chelsea had been murdered, nothing was really over. All my life I would be waiting for the second shoe to drop and it never would. I remembered a story about some great composer or other who, after he'd gone off to bed, heard a friend noodling around on the piano downstairs. The friend played chord progressions but having moved to a point where the final closing cadence should have brought the sequence to a satisfying end, he suddenly stopped and went to bed. The great composer tossed and turned in his bed, every fibre of his musical soul yearning for that final, closing chord. In the end, he had to get out of bed, go down to the piano and play the damned thing.

Well, Ronnie was right. I'd never have any peace until I went down and played that chord.

I got up. I took a pace or two back towards the car. Stopped. It was still unfinished, still to be done. I had to get on with it. But what was I going to do? The last few days of being a detective had been an emotional roller-coaster I just didn't want to get on again. It had been a period of fear and horror, punctuated by the thrills of success and the shame of my own incompetence. I'd pushed a woman into breaking the law for me. I'd looked into the glazed eyes of a dead man. I'd spent a night in a police cell, not knowing if I'd ever be free again. Was finding the truth worth the risk of plunging myself back into all that?

And where would I even start?

Ronnie would know.

No. I'd burned that bridge. If I was doing anything at all, I was doing it alone.

My phone rang.

"It's Kazima. I've got those documents ready for you to sign if you'd like to come by the office."

"Great," I said and meant it. I needed something to do that didn't involve standing in the sun, dithering. "I'll be right over."

"No rush."

"Give me twenty minutes."

Chapter Fourteen

It was more like half an hour before I turned off Coronation Drive, crossed the river, and threaded the streets to the office. The visitor's parking space was full so I had to block some people in by parking behind them. *No-one is going to complain*, I told myself, feeling guilty. *I'm the boss now. The whole car park is mine — well, sixty-two per cent of it, anyway.*

Kazima waved me over from her office when I arrived. Karen spotted me as I walked across the room and I thought she looked worried to see me there. I gave her a smile but walked on. There was a man in the office with Kazima, a tall, cadaverous creature in a grey suit. She introduced him as Tony Longman, the company lawyer and I tried not to grin. At least his name would be easy to remember. Longman was as dry and humourless as he looked. We got straight down to business. He showed me several multi-page documents with little plastic "sign here" tags helpfully stuck to the pages.

"Can we really do this before Stacey's appeal is heard?" I asked. I then had to explain that Stacey had threatened to challenge the will.

"She hasn't lodged any challenge," Kazima said. "As executor, I would know. I see no point in waiting, just in case."

"She really has no grounds that I can see," Longman said. "Being upset is not something the courts consider sufficient." I think that was his idea of a joke. He handed me the documents firmly with a "stop messing about and get on with it" air.

I started turning pages. He urged me to read them carefully and I made a show of at least skimming them as I flicked through, scribbling my name with the lacquered, Parker ballpoint he handed me for the job. It took about five minutes. After that, Kazima signed some things. Then he took his pen back and witnessed the documents. It seemed too easy. In just a few minutes, with just a few strokes of the pen, I'd taken ownership of Chelsea's company, given a chunk of it to Kazima, and become the owner of Chelsea's unit, her car and the contents of her bank account. You'd think I might have been elated but I wasn't. After Longman left, I tried to explain to Kazima my feeling of having got the prize by cheating.

"Impostor syndrome," she said. "Believe me, I feel like a complete fraud sitting in this office every day."

But it wasn't that. It was like buying raffle tickets to help a charity, then winning the prize you didn't want or need, knowing so many people who entered would have been so grateful to have won.

I would have left then, but Kazima kept me there, asking about Anning and how he had died. She even wanted detailed descriptions of the two men who killed him. It seemed overly morbid but I assumed she too wanted to understand everything about what had led to Chelsea's death. After a while, something made me ask, "Are you OK?" Maybe she wasn't coping with all this as well as I'd thought.

"Of course." She actually pulled back, as if I'd offended her.

"The police are hunting those guys down," I said. "They had some connection to Anning. Some reason to shoot him. It's not like they're randomly killing IT company CEOs."

"Or owners," she said, darkly.

"Right." Her response left me confused. "Look," I said, tentatively. "If you know something about the people who killed Anning, you should go to the police. At the very least you should tell me."

She put on a big smile and stood up. "Of course. Look, I really need to get to a meeting. Thank you for all that." She nodded at the pile of signed copies on the table in front of me. "I promise you I will take good care of Chelsea's baby."

It didn't occur to me that she might have meant me until I was in the car and on my way home.

I lugged the whiteboard, the easel and the bin bag full of stationery back up to my unit and set it all up again. I pulled the photos out of the waste bin, cleaned the board with a handful of tissues and started again. At the far left, I put up Chelsea's photo. To the right of that I put a photo of Anning which I took from an online magazine article. Between them I drew a line and wrote "murdered by" above it. To the right of that, I put two boxes, one above the other. In each, I drew an egg-shape. On one of the eggs I drew a beard and long hair. The other I left as it was. I labelled them "Hairy" and "Baldy". Then I added the line between them and Anning and wrote "murdered by" on that one too. To the right of them, I drew another box and another egg shape. On this I drew a big, curly moustache, like a Victorian stage villain, and labelled it "Mr. Big". The line between Mr. Big and the two thugs, I labelled "works for". Finally, I put Kazima's photo above the two thugs and wrote a big question mark next to it.

This was good. I was on the trail again. And, this time, I was going to do it better. I wrote "dead" under Chelsea's picture and Anning's. I didn't even consider putting Stacey's picture back up. I was hunting Mr. Big, and that was definitely not some bitter, middle-aged lady with a toy poodle and a liking for celebrity chef TV shows. The idea that Stacey could have hired two professional assassins over the phone from Sydney was ludicrous. Not because she wouldn't have it in her, but because she wouldn't have had a clue who to kill and even less idea than me about how to arrange it.

I put Stacey's photo back in the rubbish bin.

What would Ronnie do? Well, last time, he'd focused in hard on the unknown quantity – Mr. X. *Just like a mathematician*, I realised. Except now there were two unknowns – the thugs and Mr. Big. Solving an equation for two unknowns was much harder than for one. I tried to remember my high school algebra and ended up wasting about ten minutes considering substitution, elimination and graphing methods before I angrily made myself stop. As intriguing as the metaphor might be, it was getting me nowhere.

So I started again thinking about what Ronnie had done. He'd gone back to the crime scene to gather evidence and seek insights. He'd interrogated witnesses for the same reasons. He'd developed lists of suspects by considering motivations. But what could I do? I'd seen the crime scene. I was the main witness. I'd seen the killers. The police had asked me whether I had a dash cam but I didn't. That would have helped. I could maybe go to the police station to look at mugshots and provide artist's impressions. I checked the time. It was already half-past four. I was pretty sure Reid would be working late into the night, but the police artist was probably a nine-to-five guy and he'd be gone before I got there. So, tomorrow then. In the meantime, what evidence did I have that wasn't already in my head?

I sat there wracking my brain for ages but came up with nothing. All right, I needed a different approach. I looked at the whiteboard for the thousandth time and realised there was a set of lines missing that would connect all the people there. There were relationships between each of them and at least one other. I jumped up and began drawing them in. The first was the easiest. I drew a line from Chelsea to Kazima and wrote "worked together, friends". The line between Chelsea and Anning I labelled "university friends, doing business". Anning to the thugs got a dotted line and a question mark. The thugs to Mr. Big lines were already in place. Finally, there were dotted lines between Anning and Mr. Big, Chelsea and Mr. Big, and Kazima and Mr. Big, each with a question mark. Were there any relationships between any of those people? I didn't know but it raised all kinds of questions and possibilities.

It also triggered my memory. I had Chelsea's diary and access to all her work-related documents. Excited, I rushed to my laptop, retrieved the links and passwords from my phone and began searching. There was a lot of material. Chelsea's diary alone was a nightmare. I'd never kept a diary. If I ever had an appointment per week, it was unusual. But Chelsea's was full to bursting. Every single day had every half hour blocked out for something or other. The weekends and evenings stood out as periods of relative calm in the maelstrom of her frantic life. It made me stop and marvel all over again at this busy, complicated life she had led. I only ever saw the calm, uncomplicated parts of it. How hard did she have to work to make that possible? Was her time with me dead space, or was it blessed relief from the whirligig of client meetings and marketing presentations, code reviews and process audits? I wished... I wished I'd appreciated how hard her life had been, and how easy mine was by comparison.

Sifting through all the names and dates and places in the diary was slow and tedious. I drew up charts on lots of pieces of paper, connecting people to products, to companies, to addresses. I started three months before her death. It was a bit excessive, I realised by the time I had worked through a few weeks. The sheaf of notes it generated was probably just noise, more likely to mask the information I was after than to reveal it. But I pressed on to the end.

It was dark by then. I got up and put the light on, made a coffee and went back to work. The other documents amounted to hundreds, possibly thousands of separate files. Fortunately for me, Chelsea had a neat and clear filing system. So I was able to ignore swathes of material relating to internal company matters – project reports, staff appraisals, product design, and so on – and focus on the externally oriented ones, like sales and marketing. I found the files relating to Anning quite quickly. She'd had only had three physical meetings with him; an initial presentation of the company's electronic payment products, and two meetings that progressively narrowed the "scope of supply" as she called it, and the price. There were also several phone calls. Chelsea and Kazima were both in the habit of making notes in preparation for all these meetings and for the pre-arranged calls, along with notes of everything that was said. It was a fascinating insight into how these things worked but, otherwise, not very helpful. Nothing that was discussed – at least nothing that ended up on the record – hinted at anything other than a perfectly normal business relationship.

I'd almost given up. It was late and I hadn't eaten. I was now so desperate, I was flicking through slide decks from the presentations and idly thinking about ordering a pizza, ready to call it a day, when something tugged at a memory. It wasn't the slide I was looking at, it was something earlier. One by one, I went back through them. And there it was. On a slide with the title "Fully Integrated" a set of coloured blocks were shown fitting together like pieces in a game of Tetris. Each block had a line to a product name and company logo. Chelsea's finance engine was in there and, snuggling up against it was another block linked to a logo I'd seen very recently, a silhouette of an archer, along with the slogan, "Powered by Archerfield. Gamble securely. Win big."

I stared at it and blinked. It was the slogan I'd seen at the bottom of Anning's game when I was in his house. For a moment it seemed massively significant but then I began to realise that, if Chelsea's slide was simply showing how her software would fit well with the rest of the products Anning's company was using, it was hardly a surprise that it was there. Archerfield was not a major new lead, it was just a name I'd seen before.

Even so, I did a complete text search of every document in Chelsea's whole file system, looking for the word "Archerfield". There were about twenty files flagged as containing it, which surprised me, but most of them were saved emails and internal memos about an internal investigation checking on "compatibility with exposed interfaces", whatever that was. It was incredibly technical stuff that I could not believe had anything to do with murder. One document, however, was a note Chelsea had made. From the date, it was just after the last of her phone calls with

Anning. It wasn't part of an official meeting note, but was added as a separate, personal note. All it said was, "Talk to Simon re Archerfield db tables. Poss source of errors."

It was nearly ten o'clock but I phoned Kazima anyway.

"Luke? What's up?"

"Tell me about the errors in the Archerfield database."

"Archerfield?" Did she sound nervous?

"Yes. They're something to do with the gambling in Anning's games."

"Yes, I know who they are."

"So?"

"So what?"

"So what about the errors in their database?"

"I don't know anything about that. I don't have anything to do with the software. Didn't, anyway."

"Chelsea found errors. She was going to talk to Anning about them."

"Why?"

"Why? I was hoping you could tell me."

"Archerfield is nothing to do with Anning. It's a completely separate company. We don't have any business with them at all."

"Who is…" I scrolled through the emails and memos. "Sanjay Patel? His name comes up a lot in discussions about Archerfield."

She hesitated. "He's our systems integration specialist. It's his job to make sure our products work with all the third-party software they have to coexist with."

"I need his number."

"What? Do you know what time it is? Why don't you come in tomorrow and see him?"

"Would he know if there were any concerns about the Archerfield software?"

"Yes, if anybody would but—"

"Then I need his number. Please."

With a heavy sigh, she told me to wait. I heard the phone being set down and, a minute later, being picked up again. "He's a bit…" She seemed to have a lot of trouble finding the word. "Touchy," was her eventual choice.

"I'll try not to upset him too much."

"Please do. Running an office full of sensitive geniuses is a bit like running a kindergarten sometimes." She gave me his number and with a curt "goodnight" hung up.

Her reaction surprised me. Was it so bad that I'd called her so late? Or that I was going to call Sanjay? Chelsea used to mock me sometimes because I didn't always keep the same hours as other people, working when the enthusiasm or the inspiration took me, sometimes working through the night and getting out of bed not long before she got home from work, completely out of sync with the world. But this wasn't so extreme, was it? So maybe it was something else. Maybe Kazima liked to keep home and work strictly separated. Maybe I'd broken one of her rules. But this wasn't work. This was about Chelsea. It just happened to involve that part of her life that overlapped with Kazima's.

It was not good. I couldn't account for her moodiness. I dialled the number she'd given me.

"Yeah?" said the voice on the other end.

"Sanjay Patel?"

"Who's this?"

"It's Luke Kelly. I – I was Chelsea's *de facto*. I'm sorry to call so late but I wonder if I could ask you a few questions."

"Questions?"

"Yes, about your investigation of the Archerfield software."

There was a long silence. "Does Kazima know you're calling me?"

Talk about cagey! "She gave me your number."

"Right, you're the new owner."

"Is there some reason you don't want to talk about Archerfield?"

"No. Why should there be?"

"I don't know. You just seem to be... Look, I came across some internal memos and emails where you seem to suggest there are problems with the Archerfield software. Something about errors in the database?"

"Yeah. So?"

It was becoming difficult not to shout at the bloke. I took a deep breath. "So I wonder if you could explain to me what that was about."

"What do you know about relational databases?"

"Nothing."

"Then I can't possibly explain it."

You arrogant little shit! "Perhaps you could dumb it down for me?"

"Do you know about remote procedure calls?"

Wearily, I said, "No."

"What about stored procedures?"

"Never heard of 'em."

"Then I don't know how I can help you."

For a moment, I fumed in silence. "All right, what if I asked you a few simple, non-technical questions?"

"Like what?"

"Like, could the errors in the Archerfield data be caused deliberately?"

"Why would they be?"

"I don't know. Could they?"

"Yes, of course, if someone had modified the code to make that happen."

"Did you inspect the code?"

"No, of course not. That's proprietary. We get the APIs and the test data."

"So you don't know what the software is doing but it doesn't seem to be doing what you'd expect." He didn't respond. "Have you ever played *Silent Empire*?"

"What? Yeah. Sure."

Of course you have. "Have you gambled with it?"

"Nah. Gambling's for plebs. I always join one of the combat teams. I've got a six-point-three rating, which isn't bad. Most people are spectators. They're the ones that gamble."

You need to take this more seriously, or you're off the squad, man. There's a lot of people got money on this.

"People take it seriously, don't they?" I said, remembering. "There's a lot of money involved."

"Oh yeah. A winning squad can pick up big prizes."

"Anning didn't seem rich," I said, thinking aloud. "His house was nice but nothing special. So where did all the money go?"

"Back into the business, of course," said Sanjay, as if I was an idiot. "The IPO is the prize these tech entrepreneurs are working towards – or maybe a buyout from Apple or Google – and Anning was still years away. Like Chelsea. I bet your house is nothing special, either, right?"

I nodded. "Right." We were worth millions and we lived in a one bedroom unit in Indooroopilly.

"Is that it?"

"Sorry?"

I was caught up in thinking about Chelsea again. Had she ever tried to talk to me about her plans? She'd mentioned IPOs and growth targets and raising capital and so on but had I ever listened? Had she found my responses so uninformed or lacklustre that she'd left me out of all that? Was this another way I'd let her down?

"Any more questions?"

"Yeah, nah. Look, maybe I'll talk to you again tomorrow."

"Yeah, whatever," he said and hung up.

I sat for a while, staring at the interior of the room reflected in the black glass of the window. Sanjay was a dick and he hadn't told me anything useful, but he'd nevertheless helped me see things more clearly. It was all about gambling. That's where the money was. That's why Anning was dead. That's why Chelsea had died. I hadn't got a clue about any of the details yet but this was all about money. Stinking, filthy greed. Anning was mixed up in something. Chelsea was asking too many questions. Mr. Big had told Anning to eliminate her, then he'd killed Anning to tie up loose ends. And Mr. Big was connected to Archerfield and probably to organised crime.

Ronnie had been absolutely right. And I had been a jerk. I'd been selfish, wanting it all to go away. I'd been a moral coward, not wanting to face the reality of what Chelsea had got herself mixed up in. I'd stuck my head in the sand but the world had just used that as a good opportunity to kick me in the arse.

At least now I knew what I needed to do. I had to dig into Archerfield. Dig deep. Turn over every rock and stamp on everything that slithered out from under them.

Chapter Fifteen

I had breakfast in a café in Rocklea, just across the Ipswich Motorway from the industrial wasteland of Archerfield. It had come as a surprise, although it shouldn't have, that the gambling software company was named after the suburb that housed it and not the owner. It was hard to find much information about Archerfield online. Their website was minimal and they were rarely in the news. Fortunately, I remembered I could get information about a company from the Australian Securities and Investment Commission. From the ASIC site, I discovered that the owner and CEO was a bloke called Noah Lee.

I'd previously only known the area as a long row of retail outlets and engineering works on the main road and the small airfield tucked away behind them. Archerfield Enterprises Ltd., was a two-storey, white-painted building, with a dozen or so cars in the car park in front of it and a massive plastic archer logo that was way too big for the building. I drove past, slowly, telling myself I was doing reconnaissance, but, in reality, just stalling. There was a very nice Jaguar saloon parked near the entrance, as well as a couple of other expensive-looking European cars. Anning and Chelsea may have stinted themselves to build their businesses, but I had the strong impression that was not the case with Mr. Lee.

Telling myself to stop pratting about, I parked near the Jaguar and went into the building. Instead of the relaxed, open-plan office I was used to, I found myself in a small reception area with a desk, a gorgeous young receptionist, another outsize archer logo and, to my left, a solid, windowless door.

"I'd like to see Noah Lee," I said, pleasantly.

"Do you have an appointment?" the receptionist asked, just as pleasantly.

"I'm afraid not. Could you ask him if he'll see me anyway?"

"I'm sorry, Mr. Lee doesn't see anybody without an appointment."

"I've come a long way," I lied. "Could you at least ask him?"

"I'm sorry, Mr. Lee is out at the moment."

"Really? When will he be back?"

"If you would just make an appointment..."

"It's all right, I'll wait." I looked around but there were no chairs in the little room.

The solid door clicked and opened. A young Asian man came through and closed the door behind him. He was dressed in a black suit and red tie but he did not look at all like a businessman. His brows were heavy, as was his build, and his nose seemed not just to have been broken but mashed repeatedly. If he'd had the word "Bouncer" tattooed on his low brows, he could not have been more obvious. He didn't look at me but at the receptionist.

"This gentleman would like to see Mr. Lee," she said, pertly. "I told him Mr. Lee was not available without an appointment."

The bouncer turned to me, looked me up and down and said, "What's your name, mate?"

"Alfred Whitehead."

"You a cop?"

"No."

"You press?"

"No, I just wanted to talk to—"

He stepped forward. "OK, you should go now."

I thought about arguing but not for very long. "Fine," I said and left. The bouncer stood in the doorway and watched me drive away. I went back to the café and mulled over what had just happened while I ate a soggy muffin and drank a surprisingly good cappuccino. Perhaps Noah Lee was chronically shy, or chronically busy. More likely, the business he was in involved setting bouncers on uninvited guests. Maybe Lee was Mr. Big.

It occurred to me that it was exactly this kind of blind, intuitive leap that I'd been berating Ronnie about the last time we met. All I actually had on Lee was that his company did business with Anning and he was in the gambling business – an industry I had always associated with corruption and crime. It really wasn't much. The bouncer's behaviour had been weird but maybe they had some legitimate reason to keep Lee away from random callers with no appointments. It was also true that Archerfield didn't actually do the bookmaking – as far as I knew – they just processed the bets with their software. There was probably some big, legitimate bookie behind them, setting the odds, handling the money, covering the risk. I should probably look into that and find out if that was true because, if the next step in the chain was Ladbrokes, or Golden Casket, or some other corporate giant, my whole house of cards came crashing down – unless Lee had some way of skimming the bets that the corporate auditors hadn't noticed.

I decided to make some notes. The café didn't have wi-fi but I had a good strong phone signal. I downloaded the app I'd seen Ronnie using – it was as good a recommendation as I could get, I reckoned – and fiddled about, learning how to set up folders and make simple notes. By the time I was ready to write down my thoughts, I'd forgotten half of what I'd wanted to record. In the end, my only note was, "Gambling license?"

I bought one of the soggy muffins and another cappuccino to take away and went back to my car. There was a plumbing place, just opposite Archerfield Enterprises, the kind of place that is mostly for tradies but which has a bit of a showroom for the public too. I parked in their car park, facing the road. I was a little far away but I had an unobstructed view of the entrance and what I guessed was Lee's Jag. I put my phone on the dash in front of me, ready to take pictures and settled down for a wait. My muffin was long gone, as was the coffee, and I was seriously in need of a pee before anything at all interesting happened. But, when it did, it was a whopper.

A white Holden RS Cosworth pulled off the road into the Archerfield car park, its big engine growling like a caged leopard. It prowled across the tarmac to the main door and stopped, disdaining the marked spaces. The engine grumbled into silence and the driver and passenger doors swung open. Two men got out. They wore jeans and T-shirts. One had long hair and a beard, The other had a shaven head. They strode into the Archerfield office as if they owned the place. I could just make them out through the glass. Once inside they turned left, towards the inner door, and disappeared from view.

Well, I guess they had an appointment, I thought.

Too late, I realised I hadn't taken their picture. I grabbed my phone, fumbling in my excitement. I launched my news reader by accident, had to wait infuriating seconds while it loaded before I could shut it down again, and finally got the camera going. Hairy and Baldy were already coming out of the door. They were carrying a holdall they had not gone in with. I snapped as many pictures as I could as they got back in the car, revved the engine, made a turn and drove back to the road. I ducked down as they approached, holding the phone up above the dash and kept clicking like a paparazzo until they were gone.

I scanned through the pictures as soon as they were clear. Most of the ones of them getting into their car were no good. The two thugs were tiny and, when blown up, too blurry. There were a couple, taken with me cowering below the dash, that were just smears or nice shots of clear blue sky. But there, right at the end, was the money shot. Hairy and Baldy, in their car, about to turn into the road, both facing forward and with the registration number perfectly legible. I hadn't even thought about getting the rego, but there it was, and it was a thing of beauty. I sat in the plumber's shop car park, grinning at it, my heart still pounding, feeling on top of the world.

I had to tell someone. I had to tell the police. They'd know what to do with this. They'd look up the rego, find who owned the car, bring in the two thugs for questioning, unravel the whole case. I'd give them the Archerfield connection. They'd give Noah Lee the third degree. They'd get Mr. Big. This time... this time it really was over. And I'd done it. I'd cracked the case.

In your face, Ronnie Walker! And yours, stupid Reid!

I looked at the photo and felt a twinge of anxiety. I sent a copy to my cloud storage. This was an incredibly important piece of evidence. I knew I should take it straight round to the cops but, I have to admit, a small part of me wanted to take it to Ronnie, get him back on the case so we could work it all out together and take it to Reid all wrapped up in ribbons. But it was a pretty small part. The rest of me was starting to think my phone had become a hot potato and the sooner I could drop it, the better.

The rap on the window made me jump like a cartoon cat with its tail in a mousetrap. A man was staring in through my side window. It took me a moment to realise it was Hairy himself. My heart stopped, my breathing stopped, but my body went into overdrive. I lunged towards the other door, only to find Baldy peering in at me. I pressed the starter. I had to get out of there. I yanked the stick into reverse and an alarm went off. I looked at the rear camera and the view was filled with the front end of a white Holden saloon. I was blocked in. How had I let them sneak up on me like that?

The driver's and passenger's doors opened at the same time and I realised that I should have locked them before I started trying to escape. I had the presence of mind to drop my phone onto the floor as a meaty hand grabbed me by the front of my shirt and dragged me out of the car.

"Who the fuck are you?" Hairy asked, pushing me back against the car.

"I – I –"

"I've got the phone," Baldy called from inside the car.

"Well?" Hairy insisted, giving me another shove.

"I'm a reporter," I said. "I'm doing a story on the

gambling industry. Do you work for Noah Lee?" I was so proud of myself for a moment to have invented a cover story and got in character so smoothly. Then Baldy strolled around the car, holding the phone and I realised my invention wasn't going to last five minutes.

"Says he's the press," Hairy said.

In reply, Baldy held up my phone to show his friend the photo of the two of them in their car.

"What the fuck is that then?" Hairy said, slamming me against the car yet again.

"I was just taking a few pictures. For the piece I'm writing."

A fist hit me in the stomach like an explosion. My breath left me in a rush. My legs turned to spaghetti and I fell to my knees.

"Hey! What the hell's going on?"

I turned to look at where the voice had come from but my eyes were watering so much I couldn't make anything out.

"Fuck," Hairy said. "Some fucking do-gooder."

"There's a couple of blokes come out of the shop, too," said Baldy. "What do you reckon?"

"Time we were gone."

Without another word to me they both walked away, back to their car. I climbed to my feet and wiped my eyes. There were, indeed, two men in the doorway of the plumbing shop. One was making a phone call, presumably to the police. I looked for the other man and had to do a double-take. Ronnie Walker was striding towards my two attackers.

He reached Baldy, as he was opening the door of the white Holden and, without a second's hesitation, thumped him hard in the kidneys. Baldy, who had a good few inches on Ronnie and was forty years younger, to boot, turned to face his assailant looking more surprised than injured.

"Deck the bastard," Hairy shouted, impatient that his exit was being delayed by what was obviously such a minor inconvenience. Baldy, who was clearly a bit of a body-builder from the way his muscles bulged under his tee, pulled back a fist like a sledge hammer to do just that. I started moving. Ronnie was going to be pulped and some insanely suicidal part of me decided I needed to be there when it happened. Even as I broke into a run, feet skidding on the car-park gravel, I watched in fascination as Baldy's fist began its strike. Ronnie seemed as mesmerised as I was, he kept his eyes fixed on Baldy's, as if he was oblivious of the doom that was about to descend on him.

I blinked and everything changed.

Ronnie somehow had a hand up, blocking Baldy's blow. His other hand flashed out and back and Baldy froze, eyes wide, mouth open. Ronnie stepped back a pace and Baldy clutched his throat and sank to his knees, gasping for air. There was a roar from Hairy. The big bruiser leapt over the bonnet of his car and reached Ronnie at about the same time I did. With a forearm that felt like a log, he brushed me aside, sending me sprawling to the ground. I landed close to Baldy who was choking, his eyes bulging. Hairy charged at Ronnie like a bull, a long knife blade glinting in his right hand. Ronnie watched him with that same unnatural calm with which he'd faced Baldy. As the knife came up towards his chest, he swung an open hand, almost casually, and moved Hairy's arm aside, stepping away to let the bigger man go stumbling past. Ronnie was some kind of martial arts expert!

The realisation seemed to shake me out of the terror that had gripped me. I glanced at Baldy. He was on his knees, red-faced and coughing. My phone was on the ground beside him. I scrambled to get my feet under me and ran towards him, snatching up the phone as Hairy came back at Ronnie with a wild swing of the knife. The old man didn't flinch. As soon as the blade passed him, Ronnie stepped in close and hit the big guy in the ribs with a short, fast punch. I wasn't sure but I thought I heard a rib crack. Hairy staggered back two paces, pain on his face. Ronnie took a fighting stance, feet apart, one slightly back from the other, fists drawn up to his chest, both clenched and ready. He looked like he was made of granite. Hairy, took a long, desperate look at him and made up his mind.

"Get in the car you useless fucking dick," he shouted at Baldy, who was just getting to his feet and still not breathing well. Hairy ran round to the driver's side, clutching his ribs and hung on the door while Baldy climbed in. "Youse bastards are dead men," he yelled. He got in and they drove away with a lot of engine revving and flying gravel.

In the sudden quiet, I looked at the two men in the shop doorway. They had been joined by three women. All of them had their phones up and were filming us. All of them were staring at Ronnie. The old copper was still standing as if he was waiting for the two thugs to come back but, with a big sigh, he unfroze, dropped his fists and relaxed. Turning to me, he said, "You OK?"

My stomach felt like it had been pushed out through my spine, my hands and knees were grazed and bloody where I'd fallen, and there was an electric current echoing around inside my body, but I didn't even think of complaining.

"Fucking hell, man," was all I said.

Ronnie walked quickly to the car, tipping his head towards the crowd in the shop doorway. "We should probably go. Are you OK to drive?"

"Yeah, no probs." I actually felt light-headed and was beginning to tremble all over.

"Let's go then."

We climbed in and I started the engine. I reversed out of the parking spot but, as I stopped, there was a banging at the window on my side. I almost jumped out of my seat. I turned to find one of the shop guys. I didn't open the window. He waved a phone.

"It's the police. They're on their way. They say not to let you leave."

Ronnie leaned across me. "Wind down the window." I did. To the man outside, he said, "Tell them thank you for their concern but we won't be pressing charges." He smiled a grim smile. "And we won't be hanging around for those two thugs to come back with a bunch of mates with sawn-off shotguns." The shop guy went pale and stepped back. I drove way. In my mirror I saw him running back to the shop.

Chapter Sixteen

By the time Ronnie and I had reached a café, far from Archerfield, and the waiter had brought over two coffees and two muffins, I was feeling too sick to touch any of it. Ronnie tucked in. He looked and sounded for all the world as if nothing had happened. I hadn't been beaten up in a car park, and he hadn't taken down two big thugs like some kind of grey ninja. I was grateful that he wasn't being chatty because I was furiously working out what had just occurred and I had about a hundred questions I was trying to get straight in my head.

"Thanks for trying to help," he said after a while. "I didn't expect that."

I remembered running to Ronnie's aid and being swatted aside like an annoying fly. "It was nothing," I said drily.

"I suppose you're wondering how come I was in that car park at just the right moment," he said.

"No, I've worked that one out. You didn't have a single lead after Anning, so you had no way to move forward. But you knew I wouldn't really give it up, so you thought your best bet was to tail me and see where I went. Am I right?"

"Spot on. Nice little park that. The one with all the black swans."

I shook my head. He'd been watching me even there. "What I want to know is how you took down those two blokes. They were big and you're no spring chicken. No offence."

"Something I learned a long time ago. It's like riding a bike."

"In the Navy, I'm guessing."

"The Royal Navy." He had clearly decided he was going to tell me something about himself for a change. "The Special Boat Service. Heard of it?"

"Not really. They're like the British version of the American Navy Seals, hey?" I honestly didn't know if there was an Australian version. "So you were, like, special forces?"

He nodded. "I joined the Navy from school. Went into the Marines. Few years later the SBS recruited me."

"So you know all that stuff, like, fifty ways to kill a man with just your thumb and all that?"

He gave me his grim smile again, "It's only five ways but, yeah, stuff like that."

"And now you're like Mr. Miyagi, or something?" I don't know why I couldn't get my head around it. I'd always thought he looked tough enough to pull the heads off grizzlies but this special forces stuff was just too much to take in.

"If you mean the guy from *Karate Kid*, I suppose you could say that. Anyway, it's lucky for you I still keep up the training. Not like I used to, of course, but enough to keep myself fit."

"And how does that square with all the pictures of you at dog shows, grinning like a property developer on election night?"

"What? Trained killers can't have hobbies?"

I suppose he was trying to be funny but I wasn't laughing. "Do the cops know your background?"

"If they bothered reading my application form, they know I was in the Navy."

"So you're all 'Who Dares Wins' and notches on your machine gun?"

He looked at me darkly. "The motto was 'Not By Strength, By Guile' back when I was in the field. You are going to have to get past this."

He didn't mention the notches, I noticed. But he was right, however creeped out I was by Old Moocher suddenly transforming into James Bond's granddad, I needed to focus on the pressing matters – like the potential repercussions of our little dust-up.

"They were filming you, when you hammered those two blokes."

"Good. The police will see it was self-defence. It'll save us a lot of trouble. What made those two decide to give you a hiding and nick your phone?"

I'd almost forgotten. "I got a nice clear picture of them. I reckon they must have seen me taking it." The contrast between my attempts to stalk the bad guys and Ronnie's long surveillance of me, made me feel a bit pathetic.

"And what's the significance of Archerfield Enterprises, Limited?"

I told him the full story of my day's detective work. By the time I was finished, I could face my tepid coffee but not the muffin.

"That was good work, mate." I looked at him sharply but he didn't look like he was being sarcastic.

"They'll come for me now, won't they?" I asked, knowing the answer.

"You noticed the colours in the back of the car, then?"

"What colours?" I tried to remember the interior of the Holden but couldn't remember anything about the colour.

"There was a leather jacket on the back seat. It had gang colours on the back."

I felt my stomach falling. "What, you mean like the Hell's Angels or the Bandidos?"

"Yeah, mate. Like that. Only it wasn't either of those. I couldn't read the name but the logo was a red devil. It's not a gang I recognised. Maybe something new since I left the police. Anyway, it would make sense."

"Like anything makes sense any more."

"You know what I mean. I've thought for a while we were dealing with organised crime."

"And bikie gangs count as organised crime do they? I thought that was just godfathers in Armani suits and Donald Trump accents dropping people off the ends of piers in concrete overshoes."

He shook his head, despair in his eyes. "In 1920s Chicago, maybe. In twenty-first century Brisbane, it's guys in leather jackets and cycle boots who run most of the drugs and prostitutes."

"And illegal gambling?"

"Sure. And money laundering through otherwise legitimate businesses."

"And you think that's where Noah Lee and Archerfield come in?"

"Looks like it."

I stared at my uneaten muffin. I'd been in too deep from the very beginning but now I was beginning to realise just how far from shore I'd drifted. *Not waving but drowning*. The two heavies who killed Anning actually had me in their hands.

They might have beaten me, tortured me, even killed me. I'd walked into Archerfield like a complete idiot. No-one had known I was there. No-one would have even missed me for a long, long time. It was only because of Ronnie that I was sitting there with a few bruises instead of lying in a gulley out in the bush somewhere.

"Do you suppose they know who I am?" I asked. My guts were churning. I was in real, mortal danger.

"Maybe not yet, but they'll find out. The people at the shop reported our little scrap to the cops, remember. All the bikies have to do is ask one of their guys on the inside to look up the incident report and they'll know everything about you."

"Shit. Maybe I could get into one of those witness protection programmes or something."

"Maybe. What have you got to offer the police that is worth the State spending all that money to save your neck?"

I held up my phone, showing the photo of Hairy and Baldy driving out of Archerfield. "This is proof of their connection to Noah Lee, it verifies my story about Anning's death, and it has the rego of their car so they can be traced, See?" I pointed to the license plate.

Ronnie laughed. "The cops have got all that and more by now from all those shop assistants filming us. Besides, the bikies will have burnt their nice RS Cosworth by now – another reason for them to hate you – and it probably had false plates anyway. These blokes are not amateurs. So, what else have you got?"

"My testimony that those two killed Anning."

"Which is not to be sniffed at but you didn't actually witness the murder. A good lawyer – and they will have very good lawyers – will explain to the jury that your evidence is full of gaps, that you could have done it yourself, that your behaviour after the event was very strange and possibly evidence that you were a bit unhinged after your girlfriend's death, making your testimony pretty unreliable."

"But—" I wanted to argue but couldn't. He was right. I could almost imagine some bloke like Terry Marchant strutting up and down, sowing seeds of reasonable doubt in every mind.

"You need something a lot more solid than you've got now to convince the cops your life is worth protecting."

"Jesus. I should leave town, or something, go live in a little motel in Woop-Woop until it all blows over."

He looked at me with sad eyes. "Mate, do you know how easy it would be for someone to drop into your motel room in the small hours, slit your throat while you're sleeping, and disappear back into the night?"

I had a chilling suspicion that Ronnie had actually done things just like that, that he knew exactly how easy it would be.

"So what do I do? Where do I go?"

He took a long time to answer. He fixed me with his grey eyes as if he was looking into my soul. "You should come and stay with me," he said at last. "They don't know who I am and there's nothing much to connect us, just Reid and Bertolissio and a couple of other cops on the case. Unless the bikies are very lucky and their bent cops talk to exactly the right people, I don't suppose they'll connect us in a hurry."

"That's too dangerous," I said. I didn't want to bring all this trouble down on Ronnie too.

"No, it isn't. They'll connect us eventually, so it makes little difference. But we need to be able to work together until then because the only way we'll ever be clear of this, now, is to bring them down – totally and comprehensively."

The idea of running away and hiding held a lot more appeal than staying and fighting. I pushed my muffin away, thinking I might never eat again. Or sleep.

"You make it sound so simple."

"Yeah? Well don't be fooled. As of now, we—"

My phone rang and I jumped so much the table shook. It was Reid.

"So, you found our two persons of interest and, instead of coming to us, you decided to have a punch-up with them in a car park," he said, waiving the usual formalities, like saying hello. I put the phone on speaker so Ronnie could hear.

Wearily, I asked, "Can I help you, Detective Inspector?"

"Yes, you can get down here and report an assault with a deadly weapon. And you can tell bloody Jackie Chan to get down here with you." Ronnie grinned.

"Have you found their car?"

"That's none of your business but, for your information, we did find a burned out wreck that matches the description."

"And the rego?"

"Fake, of course. Listen, if you've got any idea of continuing your pursuit of these jokers, you should drop it right now. The Devil's Playthings are one of the most dangerous gangs in Brisbane and, trust me, they're very motivated right now to find you – and your geriatric ninja friend."

"Can you put me in witness protection?" I had to ask. Ronnie rolled his eyes.

Reid's voice became muffled and I assumed he'd put his hand over the phone so he could talk to someone else because I heard him say, "Now the stupid dick wants witness protection." A woman spoke in the background and Reid said, removing his hand from the phone, "We'll talk about that when you come in. When can we expect you?"

It was obvious that Ronnie had been right. I'd get no protection from the police until I had something to offer in exchange. "I'm sorry. The disturbance in the car park was a misunderstanding – a dispute over a parking space. I won't be pressing charges."

"Mister Kelly," he said, with an obvious effort to control himself. "We have the whole thing on film. It was a serious assault, probably attempted murder. We don't need you to press charges. It's a bloody slam dunk. All we need from you is a statement of the facts."

Ronnie leaned into the phone. "Trev? Hi, mate. Jackie Chan here. Look, mate, you know as well as I do that all the bikie gangs have got bent cops coming out their clackers and every one of them will be on high alert watching for us to turn up at the station. Now, I don't want to end up dead but, more importantly, I don't want to make more work for you by adding to the week's homicide figures."

"Just get in here you fuckwit."

Ronnie sighed loudly. "Oh dear, I hope this call isn't being recorded for quality purposes because, frankly, I foresee a refresher course in customer relations in your near future."

Reid fell silent. When he spoke again, his voice was low and angry. "Walker, you're obstructing my investigation. I'm asking you for the last time to come in here and make a statement."

Ronnie looked up at me and grinned, clearly enjoying himself. "Of course, Trevor. Just get in touch with my lawyer and arrange it. It's Terry Marchant, hey? The same one who's representing Luke. Nice talking to you."

He hung up before Reid could reply.

And then Ronnie took charge. He sent me to pay the bill while he wrapped my muffin in a napkin and put it in his pocket. We went into a little shopping mall nearby and he made me buy six cheap pre-paid phones – "burners" he called them – and a charger. He also made me buy a cheap laptop. "The one you have at home is gone," he said, ominously. "I know you're probably thinking your brilliant love poetry is worth risking your life for but you can't go back there."

Outside the shop, he took my old phone, took out the SIM card and handed the phone back to me. He did the same with his own phone. He broke both cards in half and dropped them in a bin. I didn't comment. I'd seen enough spy movies to know our phones could be traced.

We went grocery shopping in a nearby Woollies, buying enough to last for weeks, and clothes shopping in a couple of other shops, because Ronnie wouldn't even let me go home and pack a bag. Then we visited a branch of my bank where I withdrew four thousand dollars – my daily withdrawal limit. He grumbled about it being so little but, as I explained, I hadn't expected to be on the run from gangsters when I got up that morning. He wanted to break up my credit cards too and I had to promise on my life not to use any of them for any reason whatsoever before he stopped insisting.

Finally, we drove to Ronnie's house in Jindalee. It was a surprisingly large, well-kept place, detached, two-storey, with neat lawns and flower beds. Again, my expectations were completely confounded. I suppose I'd imagined him living in a dingy little unit, or, at best, one of those tiny two-room fibro houses with a yard knee-deep in weeds, tyres and old washing machines.

There was a bit of to-and-froing, getting his old Volvo out of the garage and putting mine in but, a few minutes later, we were inside, me and my car hidden from view and no electronic traces of where I was. I should have felt safe but, as I looked around his large, neat kitchen with all the shopping bags piled on the counter, I felt a vague unease. I was in hiding. My life literally depended on a man I'd known for just a few days and didn't like all that much. It all felt precarious. The bubble I was in could burst at any moment. Everything was strange and unknown. Even the clothes I had with me were new. I swallowed against the rising anxiety and looked out the kitchen window. Beyond the glass was hostile territory. That was where the enemy would come from when they finally found me.

"Lounge room's through there," Ronnie said, pointing. "Go sit down. I'll put this lot away and bring you a coffee."

I offered to help but he brushed it off with, "I've got a system. You'd only fuck it up." So I wandered off in the direction indicated. It really was a very nice home. Like many Aussie houses it was basically open plan, with rooms leading to other rooms through arches rather than doors. It looked like the downstairs rooms all connected through a wide hallway from which polished wood stairs led to the bedrooms upstairs. As well as the big kitchen/diner, there was a huge lounge room with doors that opened onto a patio and the garden beyond. There was also another room that must have been Ronnie's office. I drifted into it, taking in the photos all around the walls of dogs and people. There was only one picture of Ronnie in uniform, standing with a group of rugged-looking men, on a grassy, barren hillside, all grinning at the camera. Ronnie looked at least thirty years younger, maybe more. I wouldn't have guessed it was him if it hadn't been for the context. He looked fit and bursting with energy. They all did. He had black hair. Another surprise.

Right next to it was a picture of Ronnie, in a Hawaiian shirt, with his arm around a big brown dog with short, curly hair. Ronnie was holding up a rosette that had the words "Best in Show" on it. The dog looked pleased with itself and had a kind of goofy grin. Ronnie looked pretty pleased too. I scanned the walls but there was not a single picture of Ronnie with a wife or girlfriend. There were no pictures of him as a police officer, either, although there were a few framed newspaper clippings in a group. They each had headlines celebrating the capture of one killer or another. Although a quick look through them didn't reveal any mention of Ronnie, I was pretty sure these must have been cases he was particularly proud of cracking. I didn't recognise any of them and the dates made most of them ten to twenty years old – long before I started paying any attention to such things.

I heard water running in the kitchen and hurried out of Ronnie's office and into the lounge room, not wanting to be caught snooping. I stood in front of the patio doors and studied the garden. Should I be worried about standing, exposed, like that? Should I be checking lines of sight or something. There were neighbours' houses where a sniper could shoot from an upstairs window straight into this room. There were bushes and trees where a gunman could hide. Was that just me watching too much American TV, or was I really in that kind of danger? Ronnie would know, but I would be embarrassed to ask him.

As a precaution, I took a few steps back.

"NATO standard," Ronnie said, entering and putting a cup down on the coffee table. "White with two sugars."

I thanked him and took a seat on a cane sofa. He settled

into a big, overstuffed, leather recliner. It swallowed him up and made him look smaller.

"How safe are we here?" I asked, trying to sound sensible and professional, rather than like a frightened child.

"Don't worry about it. If they have the balls for a full-on assault, they'll turn up mob handed and there's not much we can do about it. But you know bikies, their MO is more the drive-by shooting sort of thing. My advice is to relax and focus on the investigation. They'll do whatever they do and we have no control over it."

I was a bit disappointed. I'd imagined he'd be running about laying booby traps and hiding guns so we could make a strategic retreat towards our last stand. But Ronnie Walker was not Rambo and I was not the willowy ingénue who shoots the bad guy in the final scene with trembling hands and tears rolling down her cheeks. In fact, I'd just noticed he'd changed into a pair of tartan slippers. No-one fights a heroic gun battle in tartan slippers.

"House rules," he said, briskly. "Don't make a mess. If you do make a mess, clean it up. Whatever kind of crap, modern music you like, I don't want to hear it. Simple enough?" I nodded, thinking, *Yes, Dad.* "Good. The guest room's got an *en suite*. Leave it as you find it. I'll get you fresh sheets and towels in a while. First, we plan our next move."

I picked up my coffee and took a mouthful. It was cheap instant and I winced before I could stop myself. He gave me a baleful stare, daring me to complain.

"This is very kind of you," I said. "I mean it. I wish I could have dropped by the unit to pick up the whiteboard." *And my cappuccino machine.*

"We'll muddle through, somehow." He sounded like he knew what I was really thinking. "OK, the way I see it is this.

Chelsea was doing business with Anning. She spotted something dodgy about his software and asked for a meeting to discuss it. What she didn't know was that Anning was in with some crooks and already knew all about it. When he told his gangster friends, they said she was his problem and he should deal with it. Permanently. My guess is he was into them for a lot of money, or they had something on him that could ruin him. Anyway, he comes to the conclusion it's his life or hers – which was probably true – so he puts her off with some excuse while he grows his disguise beard and makes his plans. Then he takes her to dinner and kills her. Like the sweet innocent she no doubt was, she kept the whole thing quiet, thinking she's protecting her old friend, who she probably thought was a victim in someone else's crime."

I nursed my coffee miserably. Why didn't she tell me about Anning? If she had, would I have advised caution? Would I have gone with her to the meeting? Probably not. I'd most likely have been as oblivious to the danger as she had been. Why would she even bother to talk about it with a man who was so completely useless he'd have had nothing sensible to say, nothing worthwhile to contribute? No, she'd have just dealt with it on her own: the way she dealt with all her problems.

"So, Anning gets on with his life, thinking his troubles are over. His plan worked brilliantly, or so it seemed to him. But someone else wasn't so confident. They knew Anning was a loose end and that the police might eventually get to him. They did a calculation and decided that, with Anning dead, there was virtually no chance anyone would connect him to their operation but, with Anning alive, he presented a long-term threat. So, they waited a decent interval, supposing the second murder would never be connected to the first, and then bumped him off. But they hadn't reckoned on you and me already being on their tails. Even then, if you hadn't made the connection to Archerfield, the trail would have died with Anning."

It was a compliment, I knew, but I also knew what a long shot I'd played. Lots of clutching at straws and very little deduction involved. "The police would have got there in the end," I said. "That Bertolissio woman. Don't you suppose she'd have worked it out?"

He shook his head. "Given all the time and resources in the world, maybe, but the cops are worked like dray horses. They don't have time to see things through. Besides, now there's a bikie gang in the picture, the Anning murder will have been shunted out of homicide into organised crime, where it will join a dozen others waiting for attention. Chelsea's murder might stay with Reid, or it might not, either way, since Anning is now the only real suspect and they can't prosecute him, they've probably been told to shut it down."

"Shut it down?" I was genuinely shocked. "They'd shut down a murder investigation?"

"Simple economics. Someone will do a cost-benefit analysis. Accountants rule the world these days."

"So why does Reid want to see us?"

Ronnie looked at the ceiling. "It's hard to let go. I've been there plenty of times. Even when you're spinning your wheels, even when you've lost jurisdiction, even when your eyes are bleeding from reading the same witness statements over and over again, you still think that with just a bit more effort, just one more interview, just another twenty-four hours, you'll find that piece of information that will lay the whole thing wide open." He closed his eyes, head still back.

"Is that why you followed me?"

Slowly, he lowered his head and opened his eyes. Looking straight into mine, he said, "People shouldn't get away with murder."

Chapter Seventeen

Ronnie's spare room was nice. It wasn't decorated with the sparse good taste that Chelsea had brought to our own home, but it had a comfortable feel, like my parents' house always had. When Ronnie brought me up to it, me carrying my bags of new clothes and toiletries, we passed another bedroom, full of gym equipment.

"Any time I'm not using it, feel free to have a go," he said, noticing me looking.

"Not really my thing," I said.

"Well, I'm afraid you'll find the library isn't exactly up to your standards, but I'll give you the wi-fi password and you can read what you like."

I'd noticed a couple of shelves in the lounge room full of memoirs and military histories, a few books on forensic science, a half-dozen books on dog breeds, and a handful of photo albums. He was right, that wasn't my idea of a good read at all.

I showered and changed. For I while, I tinkered with my new laptop, setting things up the way I liked them. I logged into my email and sent my parents a long message explaining that I couldn't contact them because I was in hiding. I was pretty sure my mother would have a fit when she read it but I needed to warn them. I gave them Alexandra Bertolissio's name and Terry Marchant's and suggested they talk to both of them about what to do. I also said they should take a holiday. There was a place on the coast – Lennox Head – that they liked to visit. It seemed to me like a good time to take a couple of weeks' vacation there. I didn't mention Ronnie, or where I was staying. If my parents' place was burgled, I didn't want the Devil's Playthings to find anything that could help them find me. Finally, I asked them not to contact me because I needed to lay low, possibly to move around a lot, and I might not be able to reply to any messages.

When I finished, I stared at it for a long time before hitting "Send". After that, I stared at the blank screen until Ronnie shouted up the stairs that dinner was ready.

* * * *

"Right-o," Ronnie said. "I've been thinking about it and these are the options."

We were in his garden, sitting on sun-loungers in the warm evening air, an esky full of cold stubbies between us and a sky full of dim stars above. I pulled one of the bottles out of the esky. Water dripped off it from the melting ice it had been sitting in. I put the lid back on and realised Ronnie was watching me, waiting.

"I'm listening," I protested.

"One," he said. "We get a confession from Mr Big."

"That's Noah Lee, right?"

"Nah, mate. Lee's not the one who sent two Devils enforcers round to shoot Anning. It doesn't work that way. For a start, he'd have his own goons to do jobs like that. For another thing, why would the Devils be interested in cleaning up Lee's messes?"

"Because they'd be implicated in Chelsea's murder somehow?"

He looked at me as if I was a complete moron. He obviously considered explaining it to me but then decided it would be too much work. "No. Mr Big is one of the Devils; either the top man, or one of his senior lieutenants. No-one else would have had the clout to order a hit like that. My guess is it's the top man himself. So we need to find out who that is. He's our prime suspect."

"OK." I wondered if he expected me to take notes.

"So, number one, we get a confession. That usually takes some undercover work and someone wearing a wire. You and me can't go into the Devils' clubhouse and strike up conversations because our friends from the car park would recognise us at once. We can't ask anyone else to do it, either, because it'd be too damn risky. The chances of pulling something like that off are pretty slim even with trained operatives and loads of backup. We'd just be setting someone up to die."

Again he went off into a deep reverie. Was he remembering past undercover ops? Was he thinking about people who'd died? People he knew? People he'd sent on such missions?

"Two," he said, snapping out of it. "We could force a confession. There's nothing I'd like more than to practice my old 'enhanced interrogation techniques' on a bastard like that. You might even enjoy it yourself." I doubted it. Somehow I even doubted that Ronnie would. "Trouble is, nothing he said would be admissible in court."

"Good. 'Cause I don't like option two."

He gave me a big, shit-eater grin. "Fucking pansy. All

right, option three: we go after his paper trail."

"What? You think he keeps records of all the people he's had murdered?"

"No but he might keep records of the money that's being laundered. We wouldn't get him for murder, but we might get him on some other rap. And he might only get five years instead of life but at least we get to fuck with him, right?"

It didn't sound much like justice to me. "And how would we do that?"

"Well, it wouldn't be easy. We'd have to break into their clubhouse, maybe a couple of homes, their accountant's place, their lawyer's… In the end we'd turn something up, I'm sure. It's just…"

"We'd probably end up in jail first."

"You probably won't like option four, either, then. It's the same as three, only we hack his computer and look for dirt on him."

"What? You can hack computers?" It occurred to me I hadn't even questioned the idea that he could do breaking and entering.

He shook his head. "No, but you know someone who can."

I held up a hand. "No way. Not again. Once was too much." I don't know why I was being so protective of Karen but the very idea of dragging that poor woman back into all this made me see red.

"O-kay," he said, slowly. "Not option four. Option five would be the most illegal of all. Namely, a bit of vigilante justice. It wouldn't be too hard to pick up Mr. Big, take him somewhere quiet, and put an end to his criminal career forever." He looked at me as if he was interested to see how I'd react. "Just spitballing, you understand."

"Of course." It was a crazy but tempting idea. A couple of days ago, it would have seemed utterly outrageous. Now, having witnessed a cold-blooded execution, having been attacked by the same killers and having had to flee for my life, knowing the cops could do nothing – weren't even interested in helping – my perspective had changed. Killing Mr. Big would solve a number of problems in one simple action. And yet…

"So, let's put option five aside for the moment," said Ronnie, as if he could see what I was thinking. "There's only one more possibility I can see, option six, we mount some kind of sting operation."

"A sting? Like some kind of con game?"

"Yeah. It's a bit like option one, going undercover, only more elaborate and more risk. And we have all the same problems; they know our faces, they'll be on high alert, and it could take a long time. Also, we'd need some brilliant plan to lure them in and get them hooked and, well, I suck at that kind of thing. I'm more a walk in there and shoot the bugger kind of bloke."

"What about 'Not By Strength, By Guile'?" I asked quoting his old SBS motto.

"Funny thing is, they changed that a few years back. Now it's 'By Strength *and* Guile'. Give it a few more years and it'll just be 'Kick Butt'." He took a thoughtful swig of beer. "Anyway, that's all I've got. We need to pick the best of that bad bunch and start planning."

He sounded quite morose. I was beginning to see he was a man who needed to keep moving forward. *Like a shark*, I thought, *that has to keep swimming to breathe.* And there was something distinctly shark-like about him, now that I knew him well enough to see past that old derelict façade of his. Or maybe he was more like an old galleon and needed wind in his sails because without it he was rudderless. Maybe a pirate ship. Shark? Pirate? Something dangerous, with strange vulnerabilities, but definitely a hunter. I remembered the first time I saw him, sitting in a bar, staring into a glass of rum, as if lost in some deep, empty place. Was that how he'd be if I cleared off and took my little adventure away from him? Was that why he followed me?

I saw the car park opposite Archerfield Enterprises Ltd., felt Hairy's fist clutching my shirtfront, bruising my chest, the hot car burning my back, saw Ronnie walking towards us. A miracle. A wonder.

If Ronnie hadn't been there for me, where would I be? How could I have done this, survived this, without him. If I lost Ronnie – or drove him away again – there would be nobody to replace him. The cops should have been there to step up for me but, even if they were willing, how could they ever replace Ronnie?

"I like the old motto better," I said, feeling the excitement of ideas forming.

"You would."

I put down my beer and swung round to face him. "Anning's dead."

"So?"

"So who replaces him? Who's next in line to take control of his business?" Ronnie's forehead crumpled into a frown of concentration, as if he was already seeing where I was going. "Do you suppose whoever it is knows about Anning's deal with Mr. Big? Or that Noah Lee is a crook? And what if they're only just now beginning to understand what the company is into? Even if they're still in the dark, even if this is all a side deal Anning set up and the company is fair dinkum, Mr. Big certainly knows he's lost whatever business he was doing with Anning. So what's he likely to do? He can't just approach the new CEO and offer them a deal. Well, he can, I suppose, but wouldn't that be really risky? What if the new guy goes running to the cops? No, he needs to abandon the whole thing – or look around for a new partner. It's got to piss him off. Yes, he needed to kill Anning and, yes, he thought it was worth it, in the scheme of things, but wouldn't it be great if he could have his cake and eat it?"

Ronnie also swung his feet off the lounger and turned to me, eyes alive. "Fuck me, I think you're onto something there, mate. This might be the good oil. We go to the new CEO and ask him to work with us."

"Or her."

"What?"

"Could be a woman. The new CEO."

"I don't care if he's a fucking Martian. We use it as our opening into Mr. Big's whole operation. We can film it, tape it. We'd have access to everything. We might even get a confession for the murder."

"If they'll do it."

"Why wouldn't they? He!"

"I can think of a dozen really good reasons – most of them to do with not getting killed by a bunch of gangsters."

"We'll just need to persuade him." He winked at me. "I can be very charming." He had actually begun to grow cheerful at the prospect of a way forward. There was a firmness to his jaw. His eyes were gazing through me into the far distance. The dogs had picked up the scent and the hunt was on again.

Chapter Eighteen

The Brisvegas Games Factory was in a converted woolstore by the river in the trendy suburb of Tenerife. It wasn't an area I visited often but, whenever I did, the atmosphere of monied yuppification reminded me why not. Without at least a designer hairdo, I felt out of place. With the shambolic Ronnie by my side, I could almost hear the locals sniffing in disdain.

There was a reception area consisting of a desk with a row of ceiling-high posters behind it proclaiming the thrills and wonders of the Fifth Annual East Coast Gamefest and, apparently its star attraction, the Silent Empire World eSports Final. A camp young man with pink-tinted hair sat behind the desk smiling hopefully at us. He wore a lapel badge that said, "Hi there! I'm Bobby." When we asked to see the Manager, he looked devastated.

"She's in meetings all day," he said. "Absolutely back to back. Even lunch is fully booked. Things are just crazy around here since... Well, you know. And then there's..." He pointed over his shoulder at the posters. As soon as Bobby said "she" I gave Ronnie a told-you-so smirk.

"We only need five minutes," Ronnie said. "And it's really important. I promise you she would want to see us if she knew why we were here."

"Oh, I'd love to help you," the young man said, looking like he might break into tears. "So many people want to see her. The police just won't leave her alone."

"Big fella?" I asked. "Trevor Reid?"

"Yes! That's the one! Scrummy but, like…" He pulled a stern face and mimed a sort of robot marching.

"I know," I said, not really knowing. "He's been bugging me ever since Chelsea died. That was my girlfriend. You probably read about it."

"O.M.G! That's the one that Simon… Oh my goodness!" He put a hand to his chest. "Oh you poor thing!" I nodded, sadly. The desk between us was probably all that saved me from a hug. "We had no idea," he said, wide eyed. "Who'd have thought Simon could…? Everybody was just shocked."

"We really need to see your boss about it," Ronnie said. "Something really important has come up that we need to talk to her about."

The internal struggle Bobby fought was all over his face. Finally, he jumped up and said, "I'm going to interrupt her. I'm sure this is more important than a silly project briefing. Just you wait here."

"You're not such a daft bugger as you look," Ronnie said, when we were alone. He said things like that, sometimes, slipping out of his Ocker Aussie accent into something more like Northern English. I supposed that's where he came from originally but he said so little about his life that I really didn't know. Of course, he'd tell me I should dig into it, check him out, ask a few questions, and maybe he was right. But my relationship with Ronnie wasn't one I wanted to develop and nurture. It was a collaboration of convenience and would be over soon enough, with any luck.

The young man with pink highlights came back after a minute or two looking very pleased with himself. "She'll see you now," he announced. "I'm to show you straight in."

The office beyond the obscuring posters was a big, open space with a high ceiling that showed off massive wooden beams and planks. But that was the only concession to industrial archaeology. The walls were painted black, with huge, abstract designs in neon colours. There was a small coffee bar and a billiard table. Brightly-coloured sofas and bean bags littered the floor and the randomly strewn desks were cluttered with inflated dinosaurs, plastic toys and pot plants. I'd thought Chelsea's office looked a bit anarchic but this one took things to a whole new level.

Our guide led us past a life-size Star Wars storm trooper dummy wearing a sombrero to a row of offices and meeting rooms. He left us there, promising to fetch coffee and "Debra", and left us to work out where to sit.

"Debra?" Ronnie said. "Do you suppose he means 'Deborah'?"

"Don't be a name snob."

But, as he dived into his phone, clicking frantically, I realised he was only asking so he could run searches.

"Nope," he said, putting his phone away. "It really is Debra. Debra Heinzer. Listed on the company website as 'Operations Manager'."

Bitterly, I said, "I suppose DI Reid thinks she shot Anning for the promotion."

He grinned but didn't comment because the door opened and a harried young woman rushed in, saying, "Sorry to keep you." Ronnie stood up and introduced himself, apologising smoothly for the unannounced visit. When I put out my hand, she said, "You must be Luke Kelly. Please accept my condolences."

She was a plump woman with a pleasant face and sharp eyes. She looked like she'd dressed in a hurry but was the sort who wouldn't notice.

"Sorry to interrupt your project meeting," I said.

"Me too," she said, smiling. "Project meetings are about the only thing I still do that don't give me the heebie-geebies since... Talk about out of my depth. Hopefully the recruitment consultants will find a new CEO soon and I can go back into my comfort zone. Now, what can I do for you?"

I looked at Ronnie. I had changed my mind. There was no way we could ask this pleasant, frazzled woman to front up a sting operation against an organised crime boss. But Ronnie just swung into the approach we'd prepared.

"Debra," he said. "Are you aware that Simon Anning was working with a local bikie gang? That your business partner Archerfield Enterprises is run by crooks who undertake money laundering operations for the Devil's Playthings? Are you aware that this bikie gang had Mr. Anning executed, after they first had him kill Chelsea Campbell, because she'd stumbled on Anning's illegal activities?"

I watched her face as Ronnie spoke. All I saw was shock and incredulity. No guilt, no shiftiness. This was good.

"What?" was all she said in reply.

"Debra," Ronnie said, with a sigh. "Anning was a crook. We're not sure quite what he was into but it was something big enough to have Chelsea killed for and it is what got him killed in turn."

"Simon was... He was..." She seemed to be trying to rally to his defence but something kept preventing her. Had she suspected something all along? Or was it just that she knew from the news that he had stabbed a woman fourteen times and left her to bleed to death in an alley? Tears welled in her eyes.

Ronnie looked at me. It was my cue to jump in with a plea for Debra's help. But I couldn't drag this poor woman into it. Planning our sting when it was all abstract and theoretical was one thing but seeing our star performer in the flesh and imagining her trying to bluff a hardened criminal was another thing altogether.

"We need your help," Ronnie said. "There's only one way to take down the man who ordered Simon's and Chelsea's deaths. We need to trick him into a confession. And, for that, we need you."

She shook her head. "No. This is crazy. If you know who killed Simon, you should go to the police. It's nothing to do with me."

"She's right," I said. "We should find another way."

Ronnie gave me a scowl under his brows that made me wish I hadn't spoken.

"Debra, there is no other way. I used to be a cop. I know how they work. They can't touch the kind of man we're after. He keeps his hands clean. He makes other people kill for him. He'll have ten loyal soldiers to swear he was with them for any time he needs an alibi. Unless we get someone on the inside, we will never reach him."

She shook her head again, beginning to panic. "I don't know what you mean. I'm not on the inside of anything. I think you should both go now."

"Debra, you could help us put a very bad man behind bars. No-one else can do it. It has to be you."

She stood up. "No. This is crazy. Please go."

I stood up too. "Ronnie?" He looked as if he would argue

but, in the end, pulled out his wallet and withdrew a business card. It looked like a Telstra card, with the front scribbled over and a number written by hand on the back. He pushed it across the table towards Debra.

"If you want to talk some more about it, give me a call."

Debra looked at the card as if it were poison and made no move to pick it up. With a sigh, Ronnie joined me on my feet and we let Debra see us out of the building. Standing outside in the busy street, offices and cafes along one side, apartment blocks and glimpses of the river on the other, we were the only still people in a bustling thoroughfare. I waited for Ronnie to explode and tell me I'd just blown our only chance. But he stayed ominously quiet. He looked up and down the street with a sneer. Finally, he said, "Come on, let's get out of this fucking kindergarten." In a flash, I saw what he was seeing. There was no-one in sight who was more than half Ronnie's age.

We walked about five minutes to where we'd parked Ronnie's old Volvo wagon, neither of us speaking. I tried to recall the various options Ronnie had outlined the previous evening. Hacking, breaking and entering, torture, murder... The more I turned them over in my head, the more I realised we really were at the end of the road. Debra Heinzer had been our last chance and she was a dead end. There was no way that frightened little woman was going to be of any use in an underworld sting operation.

The interior of the Volvo was hot and had that musty, old car smell. I wondered about why Ronnie had such a crappy car when he had such a nice house. Then I realised there was almost no computer tech in the car at all; no screens on the dashboard, no web of sensors, no clever algorithms watching to see if the driver was growing drowsy. It was a car from another era and Ronnie had chosen it quite deliberately. My companion obviously had a very strange relationship with technology. There were no smart devices in his home. He had one TV and it had no streaming services. He had an old hi-fi system with a tape deck and a turntable along with the CD player. There was nowhere on it to plug in a phone and no Bluetooth connection. And yet, he used his top-of-the-line smart phone with at least as much sophistication and skill as I'd ever seen, and his house had a state-of-the-art surveillance and security system that, in its complexity and functionality, left me baffled.

We sat in the car, not moving. I supposed Ronnie was going through his options again, as I had, and coming to his own conclusions.

"Don't do anything stupid," I said.

"What, like talk our only possible collaborator out of helping us?"

"I didn't—" I bit my tongue. He knew that as well as I did. "No, I mean like hurting someone."

He gritted his teeth. "Someone has to do something," he said.

My phone rang. It was Terry Marchant. I took the call.

"I'm here with Ronnie," I said. "You're on speaker."

"Excellent. Our good friend DI Reid has been bending my ear about you two. Seems you're not his favourite people. Even so, he's longing to talk with you both. I told him it would have to be at a neutral location and he agreed to see you in my office. How does that suit you?"

Ronnie was staring out of the window and didn't look like he wanted to talk. "Sounds great," I said. "When?"

"Can you get here in half an hour? Otherwise it will have to be tomorrow afternoon."

"Yeah, half an hour is no problem. We'll see you there."

I hung up and looked at Ronnie. He continued to stare out of the window.

"I think the best thing we can do now," I said, cautiously, "is to give everything we have to the cops and let them run with it." He said nothing, just sighed and started the engine "What do you think? Isn't that what we should do?"

He pulled away and into the traffic. "What I think is that they must give away doctorates of philosophy in cornflake packets. Because how a galah like you managed to get one is a bloody mystery otherwise." His voice was calm and measured but his driving was aggressive and erratic.

"I – I'm sorry. I just didn't think she—"

"Listen. We don't tell the police anything they don't already know. Do you understand?"

"No. I don't. Why shouldn't we? It's not like we've got any big leads or a new breakthrough."

"We've got Debra Heinzer."

"But she—"

"Doesn't want to help us? No, she doesn't. But she will."

"I don't see—"

"There's a lot you don't see. Debra's going to help us. Mark my words."

"But..."

"But nothing. Just keep your mouth shut about her. If she comes up, let me do the talking. All right?"

"But the cops have already interviewed her – more than once by the sound of it."

"Good."

"Good?"

What the hell was he planning to do? As we wound our way through the busy streets to the CBD, I imagined him digging up dirt to coerce her, threatening her family members, promising to sabotage her business rivals... I would not have put anything beyond Ronnie Walker. I stole a glance at his face. His expression was set and grim. Maybe I should have been more concerned about his mental stability. The man had been a special forces operative and a cop and, even by his own admission couldn't hold down a job. PTSD might be the very least of his mental health problems. What if he was prone to psychotic episodes? I'd seen what he was capable of when he took down those two bikies. Was he planning to hurt Debra Heinzer? Would he hurt me if I tried to stop him? And how did I end up living in the same house as a deranged killer?

My only conclusions, by the time we'd parked in a multi-storey car park by the river, were that I had to get out of Ronnie's house as soon as I could, that I'd take my chances with the bikies finding me in a motel in some little outback town, and that being a vigilante hero was definitely not the life I wanted to lead.

* * * *

Terry Marchant's prune-faced receptionist made us sit and wait in his cramped waiting room. It was something I would definitely not miss when all this was over.

"Ronnie!" the lawyer exclaimed, emerging from his office at last. He seemed genuinely pleased to see the old bugger and shook his hand, warmly. His smile dipped a little as he turned to shake my hand too. "Young Master Luke," he said, then, to Ronnie, with a grin, "The Force is keen to see this one." They both guffawed and we were ushered towards a meeting room with a polished wood table and uncomfortable-looking wooden chairs. The hatchet-faced lawyer was so cheerful, I wondered if he'd been drinking all morning.

"DI Reid will be here any moment," he said, as we sat. "Anything you need to tell me?"

"No, I think you're up to date," said Ronnie. "Luke's staying at my place until this is resolved."

"Sensible precaution." He grinned at me and winked. "Get him to tell you some of his dog show stories. You'll wet yourself."

I smiled politely, unable to imagine my gruff companion as a wit and raconteur.

"I'm thinking of moving on," I said. I saw Ronnie's head swivel my way but I didn't look. "It might be better if I lay low somewhere."

Marchant looked concerned. "But I thought—"

"Somewhere where the people out to get me don't know where to find me."

"I see. Well, you must do what you think is best." He didn't sound very convinced that it was a good idea. At least he didn't sound so cheerful now. That had been creeping me out.

A soft tap at the door and Ms. Pruneface came in with Reid and Bertolissio. We all stood and shook hands.

"Any progress?" I asked. Reid scowled at me as if I should only speak when spoken to.

"I'm afraid I can't discuss ongoing cases, Mr. Kelly."

"Even though it was my *de facto* who was killed?"

"Your partner's case has been closed, Luke," Bertolissio said, speaking rather more gently than her boss. "The man who killed her is dead and the investigation into Simon Anning's death has been moved into another department."

"Did you ever find out why he killed her?" I asked, coldly. Reid cut in. "Probably a sexual motive."

"What?" In amazement, I looked at Bertolissio but she was staring at the table.

"He thought it was a date," Reid said. "She thought it was a couple of old friends getting together. He tried it on. When she said no, it turned nasty."

"What a load of shite," Ronnie growled. He, too, turned to Bertolissio. "And you go along with this load of bollocks?"

"What I think the DI is trying to convey is that the motive is still uncertain and there are many possible scenarios." She said it smoothly, looking at Reid all the time. "However, it is possible we will never know what Anning's motive was because he's dead and the investigation is now closed."

"And what about the person who ordered him to kill her?" I asked. "Are you investigating that?"

"No," said Reid. "As DS Bertolissio just said, the investigation is closed."

"Then what the fuck are we all doing here?" Ronnie asked.

"A very good question, Detective Inspector," Marchant said.

Reid shook his head and sat back, looking like he'd had enough of the whole business. Taking her cue, Bertolissio spoke. "We've received a complaint that you two have been harassing a local businesswoman; a Ms Debra Heinzer."

"Bloody hell!" Ronnie said.

"What? We were just there thirty minutes ago," I said, confused. "It was the first time we'd ever seen her. We spoke for about ten minutes."

Reid jumped back in. "She says you wanted her to take part in some kind of illegal sting operation. She says you barged in uninvited and were behaving aggressively and tried to intimidate her into joining your little vigilante crusade."

"She's lying!" I cried. What the hell was going on?

"She doesn't want to press charges," Bertolissio said, watching me carefully, as always. "But she will if you try to approach her again."

Ronnie focused his scowl on Reid. "And whose name did she drop to get such prompt and enthusiastic service from our boys in blue?"

Bertolissio looked away. Reid looked like he might explode. Luckily, Marchant said, "Well, I'm sure my clients won't be speaking to…" He consulted a note he'd made. "…Ms Heinzer again. So, if there is no other business…"

"Walker?" Reid asked, still glaring at Ronnie.

"I'll talk to who I damned well please."

"You've been warned." He turned to me. "And you?"

I wanted to argue, just because the man was so very unpleasant, but I reminded myself I was getting away from it all as soon as I could. So I said, "Yeah, whatever."

And that appeared to be it. Reid and his sidekick left without goodbyes.

"Harassment?" I asked whoever cared to answer.

"Bullshit," Ronnie said.

"I think you're right," said Marchant. "Ms Heinzer obviously has friends in high places. I suspect DI Reid's gruffness was mostly a cover for his acute embarrassment."

"Couldn't we sue them or something?" I asked. "They've done nothing but harass us all along."

Marchant opened his mouth to answer me but Ronnie stood up, saying, "Come on. We're off."

The lawyer stood up too and they began saying their goodbyes. Reluctantly, I joined them.

Chapter Nineteen

Ronnie and I reclaimed the car and drove back to his place with hardly a word spoken. I watched him along the way, checking his mirror, slowing down, speeding up, taking abrupt turns.

"Are we being followed?" I asked, tightness growing in my stomach.

"Nah," he said. "Just being careful."

When he reached the house, he reversed into the drive – something he hadn't done before.

He sat on the patio most of the afternoon, cradling a stubbie, lost in thought. I didn't join him until early evening when I asked what kind of carry out meal he'd prefer. We settled on Chinese – it seemed to be his preference when he didn't actually care much what he ate – and I made the call. When it arrived, he joined me in the kitchen to eat it at the big wooden table.

"Here's some new rules," he said, half-way through his special fried rice. "One is, don't go near the front windows and don't go out the front of the house. I'm expecting bullets from a drive by or a Molotov cocktail through the window any day now – most likely in the evening."

I took the news in grim silence. He'd said as much before,

just not quite so definitely.

"Two. Keep a bag packed. I'll give you an old backpack. We might have to do a runner. When I say go, you bloody well go."

I swallowed a mouthful of rice that seemed to dry on my tongue. "Should I head for the car?"

"Depends. I'll tell you at the time. If I'm not about, just go, anyway. The keys will be in the ignition, just in case."

I didn't have to ask in case of what.

"Three. Ah, never mind. Two's enough, hey? Don't want to confuse you. Any questions?"

I studied my sweet and sour pork and its congealing sauce. "I meant what I said at the lawyers. I'm going to shoot through. Tomorrow, maybe."

He took a deep breath. "You know what I think about that."

"Yeah, I do."

"I won't follow you next time."

"I didn't expect you would."

"Yeah, well. Suit yourself, mate. It's your funeral."

"Will they still come after you when I'm gone?"

"I reckon."

It seemed grossly unfair that his life might be in danger just because he helped me. But thinking in terms of what was just or fair was an indulgence for old philosopher me, not something that made much sense for new fugitive me. What a bunch of ancient Greeks believed a virtuous man might do in a just society seemed a light year away from my present reality.

I watched Ronnie finish his meal and most of what I'd been unable to eat. Then I cleared up and went to my room. Ronnie appeared a few minutes later with a small backpack and said, "Do it now." I did. I'd want it tomorrow when I left. It took about a minute to put everything I had into the bag. I didn't want to join Ronnie as he resumed his brooding by the pool, so I lay on the bed and did some brooding of my own.

The fact that my new partner seemed unreasonably angry with me, made it easier to disregard his advice and clear off. I knew I owed him a lot – maybe even my life – but we weren't going anywhere with the investigation. The only thing I could think of to do was to bugger off for a while and let things settle down. The past couple of weeks had been insane. I really needed somewhere quiet where I could focus on what my life meant without Chelsea. Like most Australians, I'd lived all my life in the city but I had vague romantic longings for the bush. Now, it seemed, the Red Centre was calling to me. I wanted red dirt and rocks, big skies and solitude. Maybe that would help me grieve. Anyway, I'd find out in a couple of days' drive. I spent a while looking at maps and planning routes and, as night closed in, I fell asleep on top of the bed.

I woke at three AM, cold and uncomfortable but too sleepy to make the effort to get up, get undressed and go back to bed. So I lay with my eyes closed and tried to make myself sleep again. It might have worked except that Guilt, my constant companion since Chelsea's death, crept up onto my pillow and started whispering in my ear. "You've done nothing but let her down," it said. "You're about as useless as a detective as you were as a boyfriend. And now look, you're planning a road trip when you should be trying to get justice for her."

I sat up in the dark. My phone charger had a little green LED that gave the bedroom an eerie, underwater glow. If the bikies found me and dropped my weighted body in the

Brisbane River, my last living moments might look something like this. Only a hell of a lot murkier. But they must know where I was by now, so why hadn't they come for me? What were they thinking? What was Mr. Big planning? Why wouldn't Debra help us? Why had she set the cops on us? What was the scam Anning had been involved in? It couldn't have been money laundering. People who gambled online used credit cards or cryptocurrencies. Archerfield Enterprises, yes, they had plenty of access to cash through ordinary gambling outlets, but not Brisvegas Games, their whole business would be cashless.

I meandered through various ways they might exploit cryptocurrencies – embedding bitcoin mining apps with their games, for example, so that all their customers were haplessly generating money for them every time they played – but I didn't know enough about how it all worked and I quickly ran out of ideas. Besides, it would only take a single customer to notice and the whole scam would be exposed. But if it wasn't money laundering and it wasn't cryptocurrencies, what on earth could it be? Skimming credit cards? Identity theft?

I was like an engine running on fumes. I needed to go back to the evidence. That was what got Chelsea killed and it was what would expose her killer. Anning's company was doing something odd with its database. Something to do with online gambling. So how did a crook make money through gambling?

I sat bolt upright. The answer was so obvious! You fix the match. You put all your money on an outsider at good odds, and then you make sure they win. And the only sporting fixture that Anning had total control over was the Fifth Annual East Coast Gamefest. And the big game there was going to be the Silent Empire World eSports Final. That's the game they planned to rig. I had no idea how, but that was it for sure.

I bounced off the bed and ran to the hallway. I grabbed the handle of the door to Ronnie's room. I had to tell him. It was a new lead, maybe the big breakthrough we needed.

On the other hand... What the hell was I doing? Did I want to start it all up again? I had my trip planned. I was getting out, lying low, getting clear of this nightmare. Anning was dead. Justice had been served. Bikie gangs and organised crime were the cops' problem, not mine.

I hesitated, hand still on the knob. Ronnie wouldn't stop. He was the bloody Terminator. He'd go on working the case till he put Mr. Big away, or – much more likely – ended up dead. If I didn't tell him about what I'd just worked out, he might not make the connection himself. He might miss the vital clues or whatever and it would all be my fault. I should tell him. It wasn't fair not to.

But right now? At three in the morning? Well, I was wide awake and I couldn't see myself going to sleep again that night. So I'd probably take advantage of that and get an early start. If I didn't tell Ronnie now, when was I going to do it?

I turned the handle and pushed open the door. His room was at the front of the house and, in the light from the street lamps outside, I could see him lying peacefully asleep. I felt a sudden affection for the old bastard. Sure, he was bad tempered, rude, obsessive and not a little bit morally suspect but, in his strange, aggressive way, he had actually been very good to me. Even so, I wasn't going to hang around to be part of his pointless suicide mission.

"Ronnie?" I said, softly. "Shit!"

He moved incredibly fast. One moment he was the picture of quiet repose, the next, he had swung round into a half sitting position, both arms straight out in front of him and a big, scary handgun in both hands pointing straight at me. I sort of screamed and tried to hide behind my arms and legs.

"You fucking dill!" Ronnie bellowed. He threw the gun down on the bed and clutched his ribs. "Fuck!"

I straightened up, slowly, making sure the danger was over. "I just wanted—"

"I nearly shot you, you boofhead. And I've fucking pulled a muscle. Damn! I hate getting old. What's the bloody idea, sneaking around in the night?"

"I was just going to—"

"Shee-it!" This as he swung his feet out of the bed and sat up, still clutching his side. "I should fucking shoot you just so you never have the chance to breed." He put on his hideous tartan slippers and walked past me, apparently not caring whether he bulldozed me into the wall or not. "Well?"

I followed him down the hall to the kitchen.

My shock and embarrassment were starting to wear off and I found myself cataloguing a few interesting facts. One, Ronnie slept like a cat. Two, he slept with a bloody great big gun in bed with him. Three, in the face of imminent death, my reaction was to turn into a squealing, cringing wuss. All of which were very unsettling.

I watched Ronnie from the doorway as he made two cups of coffee and carried them to the table. He sat down heavily, wincing as he did so.

"Well?" he asked, not looking at me. "What was so bloody important it was worth getting shot for?"

I walked over to the table and sat down. There seemed to be no point sulking about my harsh usage at his hands. And, in hindsight, maybe I had been a bit of a dill.

"I worked out the scam Anning was running." Ronnie

didn't react, just watched me as he sipped his coffee. "It's the big e-sports thing at Gamefest. He'd planned to fix the match."

Ronnie nodded. "Go on."

I was confused. "Er... That's it. That's how they were going to make their money."

Ronnie shook his head, sadly. "Congratulations, you cracked the case. Where would I be without you?"

"What? What do you mean? You already knew?"

"Of course I already knew. And I know two other things as well. One is that the Gamefest starts in ten days' time."

How did he...? But he could have just looked it up online. I felt acutely embarrassed that I hadn't thought to do that. Then I remembered the big, floor-to-ceiling posters in the Brisvegas Games Factory, they would have had the dates all over them but it just hadn't sunk in at the time. And that made me feel even more embarrassed.

"The other is that Debra Heinzer is in on it."

"What?" How could he possibly know that? And why would he even think it? If there was anyone we'd met lately who didn't look the part of a crook engaged in a major fraud, it was Debra Heinzer. She was practically the epitome of the innocent bystander. "How...? Why?"

He squinted at me, as if looking for signs of intelligent life. "Because the racket they were all engaged in starts in ten days' time. Don't you remember the reason you gave for why Mr. Big wouldn't try to recruit Debra for the sting?"

"I – I said it would be too risky."

"And it would have been if they'd had all the time in the world to set up something else. But they don't. The scam is already in progress. They've probably already laid their bets, told other dangerous people to lay bets, invested too much money in it to be able to back out, put their reputation on the line with the kind of people who wouldn't forgive or forget if it all went wrong."

"So they had to recruit Debra. But…"

"But she'd be too scared? Too honest?" He shrugged. "Maybe she's got relatives they can get to. A mother. A child… Maybe she's got her own money troubles. Maybe they've got some leverage on her. She's a closet dominatrix. She turned tricks to get through uni. Could be anything. Maybe they just threatened to kill her and move on to the next in line. You know how gangsters work. They make you an offer you can't refuse."

My stomach turned. Maybe I should call my own parents, check that they were OK.

"So, when we talked to her…" I was slowly catching up.

"She'd already had a visit from Kurt Opperman."

"Who?"

"Mr. Big. That's his name. I made some calls. He's a very nasty piece of work. Suspected of involvement in three murders. He's done time for aggravated assault and assault with a deadly weapon. But that's just the tip of the iceberg. Do not find yourself alone in an alley with this bloke."

It all seemed so much more real now that our mystery villain had a name, was an actual person who hurt people, had visited someone I'd met and scared her into helping him. That this monster was the man who ordered the deaths of Chelsea and Anning was suddenly horrifying. This was the man I'd been chasing. This was the man I had been trying to confront. And what if I'd found him? What could someone like me have done? A big tough guy like Reid might have been capable of bringing a man like that to justice. And Reid had the full authority of the cops behind him. People like

Kurt Opperman were the reason we had cops – to counterbalance his unfathomable willingness to hurt people with their own unfathomable willingness to oppose him.

I had a quick flash of memory – Alexandra Bertolissio when she visited me in my unit, small, pretty, petite… It was confusing and uncomfortable to think she too was on the front line in this subterranean war of monstrous forces.

"Why didn't Debra just go to the cops?" I asked, weakly. But I knew the answer. No, I had a better question. "Why did she set the cops on us? We were offering to help."

"We were offering to set her up as a Judas goat to get a confession out of Opperman."

"Yes. Yes, of course. It's no wonder she was so scared."

"I think, after our visit, she called Opperman – probably to tell him she couldn't be part of it any more, that people were starting to work it out. He would have told her what to do. He probably gave her the name of a high-ranking cop she could drop to get DI Reid all hot and bothered."

I tried to think, to follow through the implications, but my stomach was in a knot and my thoughts were all over the place. "So that's why you said we could expect Opperman's people to attack soon. Once he heard we were still on his tail, he would have been furious, right? He'd have issued orders. Oh shit." I could feel panic rising up to choke me. "I should go now. Right now. You should go too. We should get out of here. Come on." I stood up, ready to go. Ronnie didn't move. He just sat there like a rock, like a heavy anchor I was tethered to.

"Come on," I said, raising my voice. "They're coming for us." It was infuriating that I couldn't just turn away and go.

"You've got it all arse about face, mate," he said, quite calmly. "They're not coming for us. We're coming for them."

I don't know why I stayed to argue with him. "You're going bloody senile, mate. There's, what, fifty of them? A hundred? All armed bloody psychopaths. And we've got what? Me? An old man with a gun and his memories of his glory days in the Navy Seals?"

"It was the SBS."

"Yeah, well, to me, all the SBS means is a TV channel that shows foreign films and the news in Chinese. What the hell have we got to go up against that lot with? Nothing. That's what."

"We've got what we know. We've got Debra. And we've got the police."

"You're joking, right? We know bugger all. It's some kind of gambling scam at Gamefest. It's being done with Brisvegas Game Factory software. Debra Heinzer knows about it. Kurt Opperman is organising it. Archerfield is probably in the mix somehow." Now that I said it out loud, maybe we did know quite a lot. We certainly knew all the major players, even some of the mechanics of how it would be done. We knew it was all being run out of the Brisvegas offices and we knew exactly when it would all be going down. "All right, maybe we do know some stuff but Debra's not going to help us and neither are the cops."

"We'll see," he said and something about the look he gave me made me stop panicking for a moment.

"You've got some kind of half-arsed plan, haven't you?"

"Maybe. Why do you care?"

I ignored his jab. "You've been talking to..." Not Debra. Not Reid. "...Bertolissio. You've cooked up something between you. What? Why would a cop risk her job to help you? And why do you think Debra's going to risk whatever she's got on the line?"

He stood up, his pale eyes fixed on mine. "Yeah, dumb, hey? Why would all of us do something so stupid, when the only person who has a real motive to put Opperman behind bars is running away like a scared chook."

I was getting angry. "Don't you try to guilt trip me. All I care about is Chelsea and we got the bloke who killed her. That is, Opperman got him and saved us the trouble."

He took a step towards me. "Just be bloody honest with yourself for once. You know as well as I do that the man who really killed Chelsea is Kurt Opperman and the only reason you're not going after him is because you're scared shitless."

"Of course I'm scared shitless. Anybody in their right mind would be. If you're so keen on honesty, maybe you could try explaining what the hell you think you're doing chasing these crooks around Brisbane. None of these people are anything to you. I'm nothing to you. Yet there you are putting your life on the line. Why? You've got a nice home. You've got your dog club. You've got your mates, your beers on the verandah. There are plenty of people who'd give their right arm for what you've got here. Why would you throw that away to take down some evil scumbag whose name you didn't even know yesterday?"

He looked like he was ready to knock my teeth out but I saw a tiny waver in his eyes, a minute hint that he was actually thinking about my question. So I stood my ground and waited. I waited so long it became awkward. Eventually, he turned away.

"Go on then, bugger off," he said with his back to me.

I should have, I suppose. Right then. I should have grabbed my bag and hit the road. But I didn't. For some crazy reason, I didn't want to leave it like that. And there was something in his tone, when he told me to go. Somewhere beneath the belligerence, he sounded hurt.

Hesitantly, I said, "I appreciate that you've been helping me. I really do. Mate, I'd probably be in jail now on some bullshit charge and Anning would be dead but I'd never know who he was or what he'd done. But, shit, don't you think that's enough? What's the point of going on? I know you and Bertolissio have got some kind of co-operation going but, for Christ's sake, you're going to get killed, your house is going to get burned down and she's going to get sacked. And, if you drag Debra into it, she's going to suffer too. Just tell me what the point is."

He kept his back to me. In a low angry voice, he said, "So we just give up? It's all too hard so we just let bastards like Opperman get away with murder?" He turned to face me, angry but controlled. "Do you know what life is? You're the fucking philosopher. Do you know what life is worth? Is it so cheap that anyone who feels like it can just fuck up someone's life, or, if it becomes convenient, take it away?"

He seemed to be waiting for an answer so I started talking about ideas I'd read about why we think life has intrinsic value, why we each might consider our own lives the most valuable, why the only true value you can place on a life is the value the living creature gives to its own life, and so on. He cut me off with, "Oh, for fuck's sake, don't say another fucking word!"

"I – I thought you wanted—"

"I wanted to know if you, personally, had any comprehension at all of what the issues are here. I think I got my answer loud and clear. I don't need to listen to any more of that drivel to know you've never really asked yourself the question at all. And you know why? Because you've never had to look into the eyes of someone you're about to kill and ask whether there could be a good enough reason in the whole fucking universe to do what you're about to do."

He turned away again, abruptly, leaving me staring in shock at his broad shoulders. It was like he'd pulled the curtain away for the briefest moment and given me a glimpse into the awful depths of his soul. Compared to what he'd just shown me, everything I'd said was, indeed, complete drivel, abstract word-play, a house of sticks and straw, built by a child, blown away by the first winds of raw emotion and terrible experience.

"I'm sorry," I began.

But he snapped back, "Are you still here?"

I had no answer. I found I had nothing to say. I'd prodded him to tell me. I'd pushed. And, when he gave me just the slightest clue as to what his motives were, I was overcome with embarrassment and shame. I left him without another word and went back to my room. I sat on the edge of the bed with the light off, staring at the floor. The first grey light of dawn was already giving the room some form and, as my eyes adjusted, I could see the tufts of the carpet and a small, black spider moving against the skirting board in short, anxious spurts.

Chelsea would never let me throw spiders out of the house. They were "spider friends" to her – just little creatures she shared her life with, fellow travellers on our incredible journey. She should have been a Buddhist. She knew the value of life, not because she'd calculated it like an insurance company, not because she'd stared down the barrel of a gun at a pleading victim, but by simple empathy. By fellow feeling. By love, you might say.

I found myself crying again. Big, fat tears rolled down my cheeks and dropped onto my thighs. Hers was a life that was worth something. Mine, not so much. And Ronnie was right. Some random bloke, working his little scams, running his little gang of thugs, had given the order that had stopped Chelsea's precious, precious life. And had all but destroyed mine, too – for what that was worth. It wasn't right. It wasn't right that such a thing should be tolerated. It wasn't right that he be allowed ever to do such a thing again.

I had no idea what a life was worth. I knew mine was a complete waste of oxygen. So what was the price of avenging one and saving more? Pretty damned little. So why was I running away? Why was I hiding? To protect a life even I didn't value?

I got to my feet, marched over to the kitchen to tell Ronnie I was with him. He wasn't there. I marched to his bedroom and found the door closed. I tapped on it. "It's me. Don't shoot."

"Why not?"

I opened the door and went in. He was sitting up in bed, reading, a pair of reading glasses perched on his nose. He didn't look up. "Because I want to tell you something."

"Another earth-shattering revelation about the case?"

"Not quite. More about myself, really."

He laid the book down and took off his glasses. "Christ, mate, I'm not your shrink."

"I just wanted to say—"

He held up a hand. "Be a good boy and tell me in the morning, hey?"

"No, you irritating old bastard. I just wanted to say you're right. Running away isn't the answer. This is more my fight than anybody's. So, if you and the cops have got a plan, I want to be in on it. OK?" I held up both hands and backed out of the doorway. He eyed me speculatively. "That's all I wanted to say. Now you can go back to drinking the blood of first-born babes, or plucking the legs off spiders, or whatever you do keep yourself amused when you're not pointing guns at your house guests." I closed the door on a slowly expanding grin.

Chapter Twenty

Right in the middle of Brisbane, there is a concrete lake with a sandy, artificial beach. Whenever the weather is warm – which is most of the time – the place is filled with families playing and relaxing. Mostly it's mothers and their bubs. There's a lot of laughing and screaming as you'd expect but, for all the noise and splashing, it's a joyful, heartening place. The kind of place that makes you feel good about your fellow humans and happy to be part of the great river of life.

Ronnie and I met Detective Sergeant Alexandra Bertolissio there at nine AM the next morning. We got takeaway coffees from one of the stalls there and sat together at a white-painted steel table. I've always had a stereotype of what a female cop is like; biggish, a bit mannish, trying a little too hard to be one of the boys, acting a bit too tough, hard-faced, and humourless. It's an impression I must have got from watching TV cop shows because I don't remember ever meeting a policewoman in real life. DS Bertolissio was the exact opposite of my preconceptions. What was even more amazing was that she showed a keen and well-informed interest in my philosophical studies. Predictably, my explanation of the Gettier problem and the relationship between justified belief and knowledge, drove Ronnie nuts.

"All right," he snapped, cutting across me as I was in full flow. "No-one cares how many coins are in whose pocket. Especially not me. So, can we get back to reality now?" Bertolissio's smile of acquiescence was indulgent and amused. "Right. So. Before we got sidetracked into the realms of fantasy..." He glared at me, then turned back to the cop. "...you were telling us you're willing to help us – on the QT – but no-one else at police HQ is going to lift a finger."

"That's right. DI Reid is off the case. So am I. We're all working on other matters now. Chelsea's murder is officially closed and Simon Anning's is with State Crime Command."

"Where it will fester and die," Ronnie said.

She began to give some bullshit defence of her friends in organised crime but cut herself short. "Yes, probably."

"But you don't want to let it go," said Ronnie.

She looked at him for a long moment, choosing her words. "I think you understand what it's like when a case starts to open up in interesting ways and then the grown-ups tell you to put all your toys away and get ready for dinner."

"Oh yeah, that used to get right up my fucking nose. But, if you don't mind me saying, you don't strike me as the rebellious kind. You're what, thirty-five? A Detective Sergeant. You're not exactly streaking up through the ranks but you're doing OK. Probably a combination of doing your job better than every man around you, keeping your nose clean and tucking yourself tightly under DI Reid's protective wing."

She pursed her lips. "Something like that."

"And the levels above Reid, and most of your peers and subordinates, would just love to take you down a peg or two. Nobody likes an uppity woman, hey?"

"Or a tall poppy," she said, taking it all in good part.

"So why risk everything by going rogue over this case? Anning was a lowlife and Kurt Opperman has a whole department trying to bury him."

She shrugged. "Look, I'm not going to be copying police files for you or getting you weapons out of evidence. All I said I'd do was talk it through with you and help where I can." Ronnie's face sort of closed up. He physically pulled back a little. He did not like her answer. "All right," she said, seeing it. "I've run into the Devil's Playthings before and I don't like them. You two seem to have a way of bumbling your way through to the answers we've been missing and I just have the feeling that, with a little bit of support, you might actually get somewhere."

"Big of you," said Ronnie, scowling.

"If you don't want my help, I can—"

"We do," I said. "We definitely do." I looked pointedly at Ronnie. "Don't we?"

Bertolissio didn't wait for Ronnie's answer. "All right, we've all had fun kicking the tyres of this little collaboration. I assume we're going to buy, regardless of the state of the bodywork."

I hooked a thumb at Ronnie. "And the mileage."

"I need to go soon," Bertolissio continued, all business. She addressed Ronnie. "You're going to contact Debra Heinzer. You're going to persuade her that she's better off with us than with Opperman. Can you do that?" Ronnie gave her a shrug and she frowned.

"He can be very charming," I said.

She looked doubtful but went on. "I'm going to spend a bit of time with a friend from State Crime Command and get up to speed with what the Devil's Playthings are up to these days, who's who in the zoo, that kind of thing. I'll let you know if I find anything useful." She looked sideways at Ronnie. "You're sure you wouldn't rather I approached Heinzer? If she calls her lawyer, she'll almost certainly get a restraining order against you."

"She'll be right," Ronnie said. "We'll be extra nice. Besides, if you went and she called Reid, you'd be back in uniform doing crowd control at footy matches."

She left us to finish our coffees and enjoy the morning sunshine.

"So, how do we get in to see Debra?" I asked. "The kid on reception's going to throw a fit if we go anywhere near the place."

"We hijack her."

"Right." I laughed. Ronnie didn't. "All right," I said, slowly.

"Tonight, when she goes home."

"We're just going to talk to her, yeah?"

He furrowed his brows. "You have some pretty strange ideas about me. The first one you need to get rid of is that I'm an idiot. Of course we'll just bloody talk to her." Then he grinned. "We're going to kidnap someone else entirely."

* * * *

My unit was in a block of four, purpose-built apartments on a very quiet little street in Indooroopilly. I walked along the quaintly broken pavement, looking around anxiously. Ronnie had told me to look nervous but, honestly, I didn't need any coaching. Like most of the other blocks of units on my street, mine had a group of four post boxes built into a low wall at the front. Like all the other post boxes, mine was stuffed to overflowing with junk mail. There were plastic-wrapped magazines and other rubbish no-one wanted or felt responsibility for, piled on top. I glanced up and down the street and unlocked my post box. By the time I'd heaved out an armload of envelopes and flyers, a car horn sounded from the road to my right. I stuffed everything back in, relocked the box and ran towards the sound.

Ronnie was leaning on the door of a small van, grinning at me. In the driver and passenger seats were two men in grey overalls. They seemed to be sleeping. Ronnie had been dead right. Two of Opperman's soldiers had been staking out my unit and my appearance at the post boxes had held their attention enough that he could sneak up on them and do whatever he'd just done.

"They're not...?"

"Dead? Nah." He seemed to be enjoying himself. "Come on. Give me a hand."

He went round the back of the van and climbed in. I opened the driver's door and, leaning inside, helped him drag the unconscious men into the back of the van. He busied himself tying and gagging them for a while, then joined me in the front. I drove the van, as we had agreed, into my parking space under the unit.

"Eenie, meenie, minie, mo," he said, gazing at the two men. They were both still out cold and I tried not to think about what he must have done to them. "That scar-faced bastard gave me the most trouble," he said, pointing. "Let's have the other one." Scar-face was burly, with long, black hair. The other one was slighter, blonde and looked about my age.

"You're sure this is a good idea?" I asked as we manhandled the blonde out of the van.

Moving him seemed to bring him round. His lolling head

lifted and he groaned. Then he looked around wildly and began thrashing and trying to yell. Ronnie hit him in the stomach and snarled, "Shut the fuck up, or I'll gut you," into his ear. The man stopped struggling and seemed to refocus his energy into glaring at Ronnie with pure hatred in his eyes.

"Here." Ronnie handed me our prisoner and I held him from behind. I looked at Ronnie desperately over the man's shoulder. He wasn't a big bruiser, like Scarface, but he was plenty big enough to scare the crap out of me. "Here," he said again, joining me behind the man. He poked out a thumb and pressed it into Blondie's ribs. The bikie went stiff and still. "Take this knife. Just there, between the third and fourth ribs. If he gives you any trouble, push hard. It'll be quick. We can always take the other one." I copied what he showed me, pressing the end of my thumb into Blondie's back. To my relief, he stayed still and didn't call my bluff.

Seeing I had him, Ronnie went back into the van. He put on a pair of those thin plastic gloves like surgeon's wear. I wondered where he got them but it didn't surprise me too much that he had them in his pocket. Inside the van, he laid Scarface on his belly and tied the man's ankles to a slip-knot around his neck. Even I could see that, if the bloke was stupid enough to struggle, he would strangle himself. Then Ronnie searched the van and both prisoners. He was quick, efficient and thorough. He came away with a load of stuff that included a bunch of phones, a couple of envelopes, a bag of crisps, two handguns and a shotgun.

"OK, let's get him upstairs." He put a gun in my hand and pushed the muzzle into Blondie's back. "Use the gun," he said. "Keep the muzzle against his back to keep the noise down if you have to use it."

Incredibly, Blondie didn't struggle or shout all the way up

to my unit. I didn't think there'd be anyone around in the middle of the day but, if anyone had opened their door, we'd have been in serious trouble. I unlocked the door and we took our prisoner inside. Ronnie dumped the guns and the other bits and pieces on the kitchen worktop, dragged a chair out from the kitchen area and tied Blondie to it.

As soon as Ronnie took off the man's gag, he began yelling for help. The noise set my heart thumping in my chest but it was cut off almost immediately by a sickening wet thud as Ronnie smashed his fist into Blondie's face. He stood over the seated man, fists balled.

"Go on," he said, softly. "Shout again."

Blondie looked like he wanted to tear Ronnie apart with his teeth, but he kept silent, perhaps understanding, as I was finally beginning to, that he was dealing with a bloke who would not hesitate to hurt him very badly.

"Maybe this wasn't such a good idea," I said. Even to myself, I sounded like a scared little wuss.

"Shut the fuck up or get out," Ronnie snapped, not looking at me. "Go through that junk on the worktop and see if there's anything useful. Use these."

He pulled out another pair of surgical gloves and handed them to me. I tried not to look at Blondie – who was now bleeding from a cut on his lip – and hurried away, glad to be able to turn my back on whatever was coming. I could hear Ronnie asking questions – "What's your name? Who sent you? Why?" – that kind of thing. He didn't seem to like the answers much because he started doing things that made Blondie cry out in pain. I tried to tune it out and focus on the miscellany in front of me.

The guns, I didn't touch. The phones were all locked. The letters were both addressed to Matthew Pruitt at an address in

Chermside. One was a demand for unpaid road tolls, the other was a demand for unpaid child support. I took a photo of the name and address and put them aside. There were two, small ziplock bags. One contained a half-dozen smaller paper bags. The other contained about twenty little white pills.

"What've you got?" Ronnie said, walking over. I glanced past him at the man he'd been torturing. His face was starting to look bruised and puffy. He looked back at me with sullen, hate-filled eyes. I showed Ronnie the letters and the two bags of drugs.

"OK," he said. "We're finished here. Grab what you want from your stuff. Get your passport and anything else important – insurance docco, keepsakes, anything valuable. You won't be coming back. Don't argue. Just do it."

I did what he said. I grabbed a holdall and stuffed it with everything I could think of that I might miss if I never saw it again. I was shaken and angry. I was mad at Ronnie for the savagery of what I'd seen him do. I was more mad at myself for becoming his accomplice in all this. I was trembling as I packed, sickening tremors in all my muscles. I'd never seen a man tied up and beaten, never thought I ever would. I'd seen it on the telly, of course – who hasn't? – but the reality of seeing it happen right in front of you was so very much worse.

By the time I was done, Ronnie had bagged up the stuff from the worktop and had Blondie on his feet with a gun in the small of his back. Without a word, we went back down to the van. Ronnie pushed Blondie into the back and tied his feet to his neck, just like the other bloke. We got in and he drove us out onto the street and down to where his car was parked. He gave me the keys and told me to take his car and follow him. I obeyed, mechanically, just glad to be out of the van and away from Ronnie.

He drove out of the city and into the bush. On a dirt road in a National Park to the north, he pulled off the road and I pulled up behind him. My stomach was in a knot again. There was only one reason he'd bring those men out here: he was going to kill them. I could see the logic of it. They knew who we were. If we let them go, they'd go straight back to Opperman and tell him what had happened. After what we'd done, it would be all out war. They'd come for us and we'd die. The only way to avoid it was to make sure neither of these men could talk to the cops.

Even though it made sense, I couldn't let it happen. I had sleepwalked into kidnap and torture, but I wouldn't let myself be a party to murder. Yet I had no idea how I was going to stop it. Old as he was, I was no match for Ronnie in a fight. All I had on my side was my brain. I was trained in philosophy. I had studied rhetoric. If I couldn't talk him out of committing this most terrible of crimes, what use had all that been? I began marshalling my arguments, trying to find appeals to his honour, to natural justice, to authorities he might respect, as I climbed out of the car. He was already opening the back.

"The true guide to life is to do what is right," I said. He turned to look at me. The two men in the back of the van turned to look at me.

"The fuck are you talking about?" he asked.

"That was – that was Winston Churchill," I stammered, aware that I was already making a mess of it.

"What, that murderous old bastard?" he said. He had the bag that had all the contents of the van and was looking inside it. "You know he ordered the police to shoot at striking miners in Cornwall once?"

"What? I – I thought you might be a fan."

"Yeah, right!" He pulled out the two bags of drugs. I noticed he was still wearing his plastic gloves. "One for you," he said, stuffing the bag of pills in Blondie's trouser pocket. "And one for you," slipping the bag of baggies into Scarface's shirt pocket.

"You can't kill them," I said. Three pairs of eyes turned to me in surprise. "It's not right."

"OK," said Ronnie, pleasantly. The two in the van seemed to sag with relief.

"I – What?"

"OK, I won't kill them." He pulled one of the burner phones out of his pocket and dialled triple-zero. I must have looked as nonplussed as I felt. "Oh, hello," he said into the phone. "I have a message for Detective Inspector Trevor Reid. I am a concerned citizen and I have captured two evil druggies and tied them up in their van. They are members of the Devil's Playthings Motorcycle Club and they are implicated in the murder of Simon Anning and Chelsea Campbell. There are weapons and drugs in their van too." He gave the precise location and hung up.

I was still gaping at him in astonishment.

"You really thought I was going to kill them?"

"I – Maybe."

He shook his head, sadly and went to talk to his prisoners. "OK, guys, listen up. The police will be along to arrest you soon." As he spoke, he took the ammunition out of the two handguns. "Gee, I hope these guns haven't been used in any crimes or anything because I'm sure the cops are going to be all over them. Same with the van, of course. Not stolen, I hope. You'll be doing a bit of time, anyway, for the drugs, I reckon, so the rest is just icing on the cake, hey?" He pushed a gun into each man's trouser belt. "There, now, just one last thing. You probably won't get a chance to talk to Kurt Opperman directly, but you'll be seeing one of his pet lawyers pretty soon, so you can pass on a message for me. Tell the miserable coward I'm coming for him. Tell him I know where he goes, I know where he lives, I know who his friends are, his relatives and his loved ones. Tell him I know the scams he's running and the people involved. Tell him he fucked with the wrong bloke when he had Chelsea Campbell killed. Tell him he's going to regret it."

He stepped back and slammed the van doors shut. "Come on. The cops'll be here soon. Wouldn't do if we were still standing around chatting." He got into the driver's side of his Volvo and I, snapping out of my amazement, got into the passenger side. He grumpily adjusted the driver's seat position and the mirrors, muttering, "Lanky bastard." and drove off in a cloud of lose dirt.

"What the hell was that?" I demanded when we were on the road and well on our way. "The cops are going to crucify us for this. Not to mention the bloody bikies."

"Don't worry about the cops," he said. "Those two won't snitch."

"What? You mean it's like the gangster code of honour? They'll keep their mouth shut because the Devil's Playthings clean up their own messes? That kind of crap?"

"Something like that."

He said no more and I subsided. Truth be told, the relief I'd briefly felt that we weren't going to be burying two bodies in the bush, had quickly been replaced by a dread of being dragged off to jail in my underwear by a SWAT team. For some idiotic reason, I believed Ronnie when he said our victims wouldn't involve the police – even though what we'd done would send them to jail, possibly for years. Instead, they'd convey Ronnie's message to Opperman and he'd give them the revenge they wanted.

"So, I ask again, what the hell was all that? You deliberately provoked them. You didn't want to question those blokes, you just wanted to annoy them." And, through them, Kurt Opperman. "Aren't we in enough trouble?"

"You really thought I was going to kill them, didn't you?"

"Don't change the subject. Why did you decide to poke the two hundred pound gorilla with a sharp stick? What good could that possibly do us?"

"You really thought I was going to execute two blokes who hadn't done anything except spy on us."

"I don't know. Maybe. Look, I don't know you at all. I don't know what you might do. One minute you're drinking coffee like a normal bloke, the next you're torturing people in my lounge room. You hang around in bars like an old derelict, then I find out you're a central figure in some creepy old people's dog cult. You put me up and help me out and the next thing I know I'm aiding and abetting you in a kidnap plot. Yes, I thought you were going to kill them. I wouldn't put anything past you at this point."

He nodded to himself as if I'd confirmed something for him.

We drove on in silence. I wanted to keep pressing him for an answer but I was getting to the point where none of it mattered any more. For better or worse, I'd hitched my fortunes to those of a crazy man and I might just as well accept it.

"What do you think Opperman knows about us?" Ronnie asked.

I sighed. We were off on a new tangent. Right-o. Why should I care?

"Probably a fair bit. Our names, where we live, my relationship to Chelsea, the fact we know about Archerfield and that you beat up two of his guys there… Loads of stuff."

"And he probably thinks we're the usual kind of people he pushes around and threatens."

"And aren't we? I mean, I probably am. I know you're bloody Rambo-in-Retirement, but isn't it just being a normal, non-crazy person to cross the road when there's two hundred bikies on the path ahead, looking for trouble?"

"Maybe but now Opperman knows we're not the road crossing type. Now he knows we're hunting him down and he doesn't scare us one little bit."

"Speak for yourself."

"How do you think he feels about that? The first two guys he probably put down to incompetence, me surprising them, maybe, or me getting lucky. But now we've done two more, trussed them up like Christmas turkeys and delivered them to the cops. Now he knows it's not luck. Now he knows he's in danger. How do you think he feels?"

"I don't know. Angry? Furious? Vengeful? Mad as a cut snake?"

"Oh, for sure. But underneath all that? Don't you see how scared he's going to be? Don't you think he'll be the one sleeping with a gun under his pillow tonight?"

Despite all the crazy talk, he sounded perfectly calm. "So all this kidnap and torture was just to mess with Opperman's head? Are you out of your fucking mind?" He grinned and I looked away in frustration. That's when I realised we were winding our way through the streets of Tenerife. He'd brought us back to see Debra Heinzer, carrying on with his little plan as if we hadn't just been involved in a major crime.

"Did Bertolissio know you were planning to beat up Opperman's men? She didn't, did she? What do you think she'll say when she finds out? She's not going to play along with your little psyops adventure. She's better than that."

He found a parking spot and pulled over. "You underestimate her. Didn't you notice the steel in that woman's eyes. I did. I recognised it. When it comes right down to it, she'll do whatever it takes."

"Oh great, I'm suddenly in a Jack Reacher novel and all the good guys are autistic sociopaths."

He looked at me for the first time since we'd left the forest. "Shut the fuck up. I'm sick of your endless whining, you bloody sook."

He got out before I could answer and slammed his door shut. Not that I had any answer to give him. I was sick of hearing myself whine too. I was sick of feeling trapped in that nightmare, sick of being scared all the time and sick to my very core of feeling helpless and incompetent.

Ronnie banged on the roof and I jumped like a startled roo. I got out of the car.

"Are you ready for this?" he asked. His tone was belligerent, challenging.

"Ready for what, exactly? I told you she won't see us. She'll just call the cops."

"Oh, she'll fucking see us," he snarled and set off, head down, jaw set, fists clenched, like he was planning to walk straight through the wall of the building. I thought about leaving him to it, getting a cab and getting as far away from there as possible. But I knew I couldn't. I'd made my decision to stick with it, no matter what, and that's all I could do now.

I ran down the street to catch up with him and we walked in silence to Debra's office.

Chapter Twenty-One

"Hey! You can't— Hey!" was all the young man on reception had time to say as Ronnie marched straight past him into the body of the building.

Hurrying along behind, I held up placatory hands and said things like, "We'll only be a minute. It's cool." I followed behind Ronnie and the young man followed behind me. Everybody looked up and stared, even the two women playing pool.

Ronnie burst into Debra's office, making the door crash against a filing cabinet. Debra was there behind her desk. There were two other people with her – young employees, at a guess. All three stood up in alarm.

"You two, out," Ronnie told the employees. "We need to talk," he said to Debra.

"Oh Debra, I'm so sorry," the receptionist said in genuine anguish. "But you can see what they're like."

Debra, who had been startled at first, was now composed. To the receptionist, she said, "Bobby, call the police."

"I wouldn't do that," Ronnie said, speaking to Debra as the young man fumbled for his phone. "We know about you and Kurt Opperman."

The whole room seemed to wait for Debra's reaction to

this cryptic announcement. Even young Bobby waited, phone in hand. I saw Debra's nostrils flare but she showed very little emotion otherwise. She turned to the two employees and said, "Would you mind if we did this later. I'll just deal with these gentlemen." To the receptionist, she added, "Bobby, thank you. Everything's fine."

"The police?" he asked, holding up his phone.

"I overreacted. Everything's fine." She gave him an encouraging smile.

Everyone left and we were alone with Debra. I closed the door.

"Just what do you think you know?" she asked Ronnie. She sounded angry but I was sure I could hear an underlying fear in her voice.

"I know he's threatened you," Ronnie said. "You, or someone you love. He's making you work with him to pull off a gambling fraud during Gamefest."

She turned her back to us abruptly. She stood in silence for several seconds. Ronnie and I exchanged glances. "Debra?" I said. "We don't want to put you, or anybody, in any danger but we can't let him get away with this."

"Can't you?" she asked.

Again I looked at Ronnie, urging him to say something, but my companion, so dynamic when it came to barging into people's lives, seemed to have no clue what to do now to bring this woman around.

"He's killed two people already," I said. "He's coercing you. He plans to rip off hundreds or thousands of people. He's a thug and a bully. He leads a criminal organisation that runs protection rackets, prostitution and drugs. The bloke is a monster. Someone has to take him down. Someone has to draw a line in the sand."

"And that's you?"

I don't know how I expected Debra to react. How does a woman react when two strangers turn up to tell you they know your guilty secret and creating the possibility that something dreadful will now happen to you? Angry? Pleading? Despairing? These long silences and quiet questions didn't fit any of my expectations.

"It's us," said Ronnie. "And you're going to help us."

Finally, she turned back to face us. She still looked angry but the underlying fear seemed to have vanished. "They turned up at my home," she said, glaring at Ronnie. "Opperman and two of his standover men. They had photos of my mum and dad with Opperman in the background, grinning. They wanted to show me how easy it was to get close to them. Then they told me about Simon and what he'd got himself mixed up in. They said it was too late to back out and that I had to go on helping them." Her lip curled in a snarl as she said, "What would you have done?"

Ronnie met her anger with tight lipped contempt. "Gone to the police."

"The police? Have you ever met DI Reid? I'm not going to risk them hurting my mother and father. I'm certainly not going to put my parent's lives in the hands of an idiot like that. Besides, it's only money. They can have as much as they like if it keeps my parents safe."

I was inclined to agree but Ronnie was unmoved. "But it's not, is it? It's not just money, it's lives. Some of them innocent lives. People killed, people corrupted, people ruined. Scum like Opperman depend on people like you telling yourself it doesn't matter. The fear and cowardice that makes you justify your actions is simply part of their business model."

I saw Debra's face turn white. "Jeez, mate, she's just—"

Ronnie turned on me. "She's just what? Scared for her poor mummy and daddy? Doing the best she can in an impossible situation? Or is she condoning murder and extortion for her own personal benefit?" He returned to his assault on Debra. "Because that's what it looks like from here. You get what you want. Opperman gets what he wants. And, if a few people get hurt or killed along the way, at least it wasn't your people. Isn't that the calculation in your selfish little head?"

Debra looked ready to explode. "You bastard," she said through clenched teeth. "If it was your parents—"

"If some lowlife piece of shit was threatening my parents, I'd want him behind bars. I'd do everything in my power to make that happen. And, if he ever hurt them, I'd want him dead. If I couldn't make it happen any other way, I'd walk into his home carrying a hand grenade."

"You're – you're completely insane." She looked shocked, as I was, at Ronnie's vehemence. Possibly, like me, she could see he meant every word.

He took a step towards her and she, nervously, took a step back.

"We're taking him down, Debra. And you're going to help us."

She seemed mesmerised, staring into his eyes like he was a cobra about to strike.

"Have you told the cops all this?" she asked.

"The cops will be on board when we make our move," he said.

"But have you told them yet?"

"Don't worry about the coppers. They'll know what they need to know when they need to know it."

I couldn't understand why he was being so deliberately obscure. It seemed to me that just saying "Yes," would have been more reassuring but maybe Ronnie knew better because Debra seemed to relax a little.

"You have some kind of a plan?"

My heart skipped a beat. It was the breakthrough we'd been hoping for. Ronnie began running through his plans – in far more detail than he'd shared with me – and Debra listened. She listened carefully, considering what he said and asking relevant questions. Her anger and rejection gradually evaporated. Ten minutes later, she was on board. She still kept asking questions like, "Are you sure?", "Can you really do that?" and "Won't he suspect something?" but I had the impression they were increasingly half-hearted, as if she felt she ought to sound sceptical and uncertain but really she was completely sold on the plan.

When we left, Ronnie handed her one of our burner phones, saying, "It's got my number in it. Don't call me on any other phone and don't call anybody else on this one. Use it to call me when you've got the meeting with Opperman sorted out. We won't see you again until that happens."

She took the phone and looked at it uncertainly.

"This is the right thing to do," he said. "And it's the only way you'll ever get out from under his thumb. Or ours. You're an accessory to a major crime, right now. This is how you get clear of that."

Debra nodded in silence and we left.

* * * *

"All I'm saying is you came on a bit strong."

We were sitting in the Botanic Gardens, eating burgers and

chips under a massive tree. The river was brown and slow. The day was hot and still.

"It worked," was all Ronnie had to say on the matter. He'd said it twice already.

It was very frustrating. "The means don't justify the ends," I said. Every first year ethics student learned that. It should have been bloody obvious. But Ronnie was another kind of animal: a Pragmatist to the bone: a true blue, dinky-di utilitarian. His moral calculus was something I would never grasp.

I gazed at the pathetic, desiccated beds of roses. The climate was changing. Chelsea had said that hotter and hotter summers meant that, one day, councils would have to stop trying to put on displays of flowers from temperate regions. Only Aussie natives would survive the droughts and the heatwaves. I suddenly felt it. The brown grass that crunched when you walked on it, the endless water restrictions, the trees, dying on their feet. It was the new normal. Children born today would never know anything else but, to me, the world was slowly turning post-apocalyptic.

Or maybe it was just post-Chelsea. That's why everything seemed so much bleaker now.

I turned to Ronnie. "OK Mad Max, what do we do now? A little trip out to the Thunderdome?"

"The fuck are you talking about?"

"Just… It was just a joke. But, seriously, what's next?"

"Next, is waiting. Are you going to finish those chips?" I handed him the bag. "The way I see it, Debra is going to take some time plucking up the courage to do what we asked. She might still bottle out. If we're lucky, she'll call Opperman this arvo for a meeting. If she hasn't called him by tomorrow lunchtime, we'll need to go see her again."

"Maybe we could tie her up and throw her in the van?"

"How come you've got such a hard on for little Debra, hey?"

"I haven't got a— I just don't like how we're treating her. She's getting bullied and threatened from all sides. She's scared. I feel sorry for her. It's called empathy. If I had my crayons with me, I'd draw some pictures and explain it for you."

"You're a sarcastic little sod. Don't forget she was quite happy to go along with a gambling fraud."

"To save her parents!"

"Yeah, whatever."

There was no point arguing. "So we wait?"

"It takes a while but you get there in the end."

"OK, here's a question, where do we wait? You've already said I can't go back to my place and, this morning, we left your house with our bags packed, so I reckon you don't plan to go back there tonight. We can't stay in the gardens all night, so…?"

"Don't worry. I know a place."

"Like a hotel?"

"Like a mate."

Great, it had come to couch surfing on strangers' sofas. I felt hard done by. I stared at the sludgy river in a self-pitying sulk. None of this was my fault. I didn't ask for Chelsea to die. I didn't ask to be mixed up with a load of gangsters. I didn't ask to be saddled with Ronnie. Well, actually, I suppose I did ask for that, sort of. But I didn't ask for him to get them all so riled up I couldn't even go home any more. I ran through my list of grievances over and over again, each time adding one or two more. I'd just added that I didn't ask to be sitting in a drought-blasted park in the middle of the day, sweating like a pig, when my phone rang.

"Mr. Kelly," said a voice I didn't recognise.

"Doctor."

"What?"

"It's Doctor Kelly. How can I help you?" I had never insisted on my title before but winding up the cops was a matter of duty and this guy had "cop" stamped into every syllable he uttered.

"Doctor Kelly," he said. For some reason he didn't seem as pissed off as he should be. "I'm Inspector Tim Pearce with the Queensland Police. I've got some bad news, I'm afraid."

My breath caught. My mum and dad. I'd told them they needed to get out of town but I should have checked. I should have been more forceful, made sure they'd left.

"I'm investigating a fire at your unit in Indooroopilly."

"What?" I was so ready for really bad news that this hardly seemed worth him calling me about.

"Your unit has been deliberately set alight. The fire department tells me the place reeks of accelerant. Where are you now, Doctor Kelly?"

"I'm – I'm in the Botanic Gardens."

"This was arson, sir, possibly attempted murder. I'd like you to come into Indooroopilly station as soon as you can."

I looked at Ronnie, suddenly certain he'd known this was going to happen.

"I – Look, I know who's responsible. Have you spoken to DI Reid or DS Bertolissio from homicide? They've been on the case for a while now. There's probably someone in organised crime – what do you call it?"

"State Crime Command," he said.

"Yeah, that. There's probably someone there who needs to know about it too. You need to type my name into your computer or something. Better still, type Chelsea Campbell or Simon Anning."

He went quiet. Then he said, "Would you mind holding on for a moment, sir?"

"Sure." I put the phone on speaker. "They've burned down my unit," I said to Ronnie.

"Well," he said. "It's taught us one thing; Kurt Opperman has impulse control issues."

"You bloody knew they were going to do that. I remember when you told me to pack, you said to pick up my insurance documents. It seemed weird at the time but I thought you were just being funny."

"But you picked them up anyway, right?"

"No I bloody didn't!"

He shrugged. "She'll be right, mate. It'll just make the claim a little bit harder, that's all."

"They burned down my home! All because you wanted to prove how bloody macho you are."

"Yeah, well, it had to be done. If it's any consolation, they're probably over at my place, burning that down too."

His complete insouciance left me gasping. "You are a real piece of work. I suppose you packed your insurance docco this morning, hey?"

"Too bloody true, mate. Have you ever had to deal with an insurance company?"

I shook my head, speechless.

"Look mate," he said. "It's only stuff. You won't even notice ninety per cent of it has gone."

"Luke?" It was DI Reid's voice. "Are you there?"

I wasn't quite sure how to answer that. I was somewhere but it wasn't a world I recognised any more.

"Yes, I'm here. I've got Ronnie with me. You're on speaker."

"And I've got DS Grogan from SCC here. Listen, Luke, I'm sending a couple of uniforms over to Ronnie's house. It's probably next on their list. Tell me where you are and I'll get a car to pick you up."

Ronnie shook his head vehemently but I told Reid anyway. Police protection sounded pretty good to me just then.

"Good," said Reid. He sounded relieved. "Don't go anywhere. Just identify yourselves to the officers when they get there. I'll see you when they bring you in."

We hung up and Ronnie got to his feet. "I'm off," he said. "Say hello to Trevor for me when you see him."

"Ronnie, the bikies are running around town burning our lives to the ground. Don't you think it's a good idea just to talk to the police?"

"Nope," he said. He picked up the rubbish from our meal and headed towards a waste bin. I walked alongside him.

"But why not. They might be able to catch the people who did it?"

"They'll just get in the way."

"Look, I know you think you've got it all under control but this is getting way out of hand."

He dumped the rubbish and turned to me. "This was way out of hand the day they decided to kill Chelsea. Putting a couple of footsoldiers away for arson isn't going to make any difference at all. Do you know how much money is involved in Debra's silly little video game thing?"

I didn't. It hadn't occurred to me to ask. Thousands, I supposed, maybe tens of thousands.

"Well I do," he said. "I called some bookies and asked around. The game isn't just Australian, it's global. So is the betting. Companies like Archerfield organise the gambling through offshore jurisdictions where the rules are very gambler-friendly. My contacts estimate that there might easily be tens of millions in the pot for a game like this. It's not horse racing or boxing but it's big, Really big. Big enough that Opperman and his partners are going to do whatever it takes to get their hands on all that money."

"But surely we'd be safest with the police?"

He'd been reasonably calm until that moment but what I said seemed to trigger an explosion.

"Are you fucking kidding me? Do you know how many deaths in custody happen every fucking year? How man people die in police vans on their way to the station? Do you think they're all bloody accidents?"

Again, I had to ask myself what he'd seen. What he'd done. The strength of his conviction that some in the police might be working for the crooks, shook me. He seemed to see the surprise in my face and sneered as he turned away.

"Stay if you like," he said over his shoulder. Again I hurried to keep up with him. "We're being hunted. And, if there's one thing I've learned from being on the other side of this game, it's that if the prey keeps moving, keeps its options open, keeps away from traps and tight corners, it might just survive long enough to escape."

I looked around the gardens. There was still no sign of any cops. For some reason, in that moment, I felt safer walking beside Ronnie than waiting for my rescuers. *Folie a deux*, I thought. *His paranoia is rubbing off on me.* But I also thought, *Better safe than sorry.*

Chapter Twenty-Two

We found a motel near Breakfast Creek. It was a little pricey, according to Ronnie, but I was happy to go a bit upmarket. I got two rooms – again, against Ronnie's wishes.

"It's just bloody extravagance," he complained.

"Yeah, well, I'm not sharing a room with you and that's that."

"It would be safer, it would be cheaper and I wouldn't have to worry about you being garrotted in the night."

"Honestly, mate, if I don't get some personal space soon, I'm garrotting myself."

He shook his head in despair and went into his room. I closed the door on my own with such a sense of relief that I leaned against it with my eyes closed for a moment, just to savour the sensation. For days I'd had dark forces pressing in on me from all sides – including Ronnie – but, just for that moment, I could breathe again.

It lasted about ten minutes before my phone rang. It was DS Bertolissio.

"Trevor wants me to take you to task for not coming in," she said. She sounded friendly and relaxed.

"Ronnie's being all paranoid about bent cops giving us up to the bikies. He's got me jumping at every shadow." I tried to make it sound light but I'm sure she could tell how scared I was.

"Yes, I've just been talking to him. I want to check that you're fully on board with his decision."

"Do you think he's crazy?"

She was silent for a moment. "I think you're in real danger and that we'd be hard pressed to give you the kind of protection you need."

"So, he's not crazy?"

"I wouldn't go that far." I could hear the smile in her voice. "The fact is, any course you take has its risks. I've been asking around about Ronnie. Some of the older cops here remember him. From what I can tell, they all think he's a miserable old bastard but they all said he was a great cop and definitely someone they'd want on their side in a fight. It seems to me that you're probably safer with Ronnie than you would be with a couple of uniforms sitting outside your house."

"If I had a house."

"Good point."

I thought about what she'd said. "So, I reckon I'll stay where I am then."

"It might be for the best. And, if Trevor calls, tell him I gave you a thorough bollocking, OK?"

I laughed. "Did Ronnie tell you what we did today?"

"I told him I'd rather not know – especially if it had something to do with two Devil's Plaything members found beaten and tied up in a van, surrounded by drugs and unlicensed firearms. Their story is that they were attacked by six masked men who then fitted them up. Ronnie thought that was hilarious."

"Did he mention Debra Heinzer?"

"He said you had persuaded her to join the cause."

That was one way of putting it. "I guess you're up to speed, then."

"We're meeting again in the morning."

"Yeah?"

"Just trying to keep you two on a short leash. You seem to have the knack of aggravating some very dangerous people."

We said goodbye and almost immediately, Ronnie was at the door.

"Pub," he said and walked away. I shrugged and followed him.

We found a little place smart enough to make the pokie machines seem out of place and took our drinks to a table with a beaten copper top.

"Bit of a dump but it'll do," was Ronnie's verdict. I got the impression he'd have preferred sawdust on the floor and tobacco stains on the ceiling. But I wasn't really concentrating on the décor.

"What do you make of Bertolissio?" I asked. He looked at me as if my question itself was a puzzle to him. "I mean, I had her pegged for a straight-laced, by-the-book type. You know, the way she dresses, like she was on her way to some posh church on a Sunday." He grinned. "And the way she talks, too. Kind of formal. Like she's reading something she prepared earlier. Who talks like that? Yet, here she is, helping us out. You reckon she's really good and, with blokes like Reid in charge, it must be a real struggle for her. But she's putting it all at risk. I just don't get it. Do you?"

"She should be DI by now," Ronnie said. "Why do you think she's not?"

"I don't know. Sexism? Glass ceiling? Tall poppy syndrome?"

"Bollocks. With a clear-up rate like hers, she should have blown past dinosaurs like Reid, male, female and all points in between. Nah, it's because she cares enough about collaring villains to stick her neck out but she doesn't care enough what the brass thinks to play their games. I've heard some stories about her that you wouldn't believe. There was one time she slipped the leash and pulled off an unauthorised undercover op on a jewel thief. Nearly got herself killed. It was only because she got the bastard and Reid covered for her that she kept her job."

"Are she and Reid... you know?"

"Buggered if I know. Every female cop in the service is having it away with half the blokes they meet – especially their bosses – if you believe the rumours. Somehow, I don't see it in her case. I'm pretty sure Reid wouldn't say no but I don't see it."

I nodded. "Too good for him."

"Mate, you should know by now that all women are too good for the men they hook up with."

I felt it as a personal attack. If there was ever a woman too good for the loser she'd taken up with, it was Chelsea. I looked into his eyes for the judgement I knew would be there but he was staring into his beer, lost in some other thought.

"So, some kind of closet maverick, then?" I said, to bring him back.

He looked at me as if he knew exactly what I was doing. "We need to talk about our plan."

"You mean your plan."

"The plan. As soon as Debra calls Opperman, we need to be ready to move."

"You mean, if she calls him."

"She will. They'll arrange a meet, somewhere quiet. I can't

make her wear a wire. If he sees it on her, she's dead. So we're going to use a parabolic mic."

"A what now? I mean, I know what a parabola is but... Oh, right, it's got a parabolic reflector to focus the sound, right? So we can listen from a long way away. But won't that need line of sight?" I felt proud of myself for working it out and spotting the drawback. "How big are they?"

"Will you shut up? I've got a bloke coming here to lend us one. You can measure it if you like. The thing is, we need to get to the meeting place first and set up before Opperman arrives. It might not be somewhere we can easily hide and there might not be much time, so I'm going alone. I want you—"

"What? No. That's not right."

He closed his eyes, the very picture of long-suffering patience. "Which bit isn't right, Luke?"

"Well, all of it actually. One, it's a stupid plan. You have no idea if he'll meet somewhere where you can eavesdrop on him. What if he picks somewhere indoors, like his own house or something? What if he picks a forest, so there's no line of sight and some bloke with a load of electronic gear would stand out like a vegan at a barbie? What if he picks a public place but has twenty of his thugs patrolling the area?"

"She'll be right. This is not my first rodeo."

I ignored that. "Two, this is my show as much as it's yours. More, even. If anyone is risking their neck, it should be me. And what if you have to climb a tree, or squeeze into some tight space? What then?"

"Mate, I'm as fit as a Mallee bull. If a limp piece of lettuce like you can climb it, I'm bloody certain I can."

"Three, if you're going, I'm going too. And that's final."

He looked ready to argue for a moment, then capitulated.

"It's your funeral. But, if you trip over your feet or drop the mic or whatever, you could get all three of us killed."

It was a sobering thought but I stubbornly clung to my victory. I was going too and that was that.

We ate, we had a couple more. At about nine PM, a guy turned up with a holdall and sat with us for a while. He looked like an ageing hippie, the kind you still see hanging around Byron Bay – and practically every little coastal town, come to think of it. He had blond hair, full of grey streaks and wore wooden beads round his neck and wrist, with leather thongs on his feet. He showed Ronnie the audio equipment in his bag, holding it open while Ronnie poked around inside. It was so blatantly clandestine, I expected someone to call the cops for sure.

When he left, we went back to the motel. I was nervous and restless. Maybe tonight, maybe tomorrow, we were going to see Kurt Opperman for the first time. The man who had had Chelsea murdered. The man who commanded an army of over two hundred thugs and killers. The man who wanted Ronnie and me dead. And we were going to try to trick him into recording a confession. I knew Ronnie's plan was terrible. I knew a thousand things might go wrong. But I knew we had no better plan and that I would be there to do my bit.

* * * *

I don't know how but I fell asleep and didn't wake until my phone rang at about six-thirty the next morning. It was Detective Sergeant Alexandra Bertolissio.

"Is Ronnie there with you?" she asked.

"We've got separate rooms," I said, not quite awake. Then

I realised what was going on. "You've already tried his phone, haven't you?" I was already getting dressed.

"It goes to voicemail. Would you—?"

"Already on my way."

I ran barefoot to the room next door and knocked. Then I knocked louder. I looked around the car park. His car was gone.

"He's not here. He's gone."

"Is there a note? A phone message?"

I'd have noticed something pushed under my door but I went back to look, anyway. My phone had no messages at all.

"Debra must have called him," I said. "You can maybe check that, can you? She must have called last night or first thing and the arsehole has gone off on his own to bug the meeting."

"To do what?"

"The plan."

"What plan?"

"Shit! I told him it was a stupid plan." I explained what we'd talked about in the pub.

"That is a very stupid plan," she said. She seemed a lot calmer than I was feeling.

"What are we going to do?"

"*We* are not going to do anything. You are going to wait right there and call me if Ronnie turns up. *I* am going to try to find your idiot friend – hopefully before he gets himself or anyone else killed. Stay there. Keep your phone with you. He might come back. He might call. Understand?"

"You don't know where to look."

"No, I don't. Do you?"

"No."

"Then stay there."

She hung up. I went back into my room and sat on the bed. It was all my fault, as usual. I should have kept an eye on him. I shouldn't have believed him. I shouldn't have gone to sleep. I shouldn't have insisted on separate rooms. God, what a mess! I got dressed properly. I went outside and stood in the car park, watching for his car coming back. I didn't even have my own car. I wanted to go out searching for him. If he'd gone out last night and wasn't back yet, it could only mean his plan had gone badly wrong. Was he dead? Were they both dead?

Debra! I should phone her. She might know something. She might not even have called him. He might just be out getting breakfast the miserable, inconsiderate, old…

Debra's phone rang. She picked up on the second ring.

"Debra, where are you? Is Ronnie there?"

"Luke, I wanted to call you but I only had Ronnie's number. Something terrible has happened. I called Kurt like you asked. He wanted to meet. We arranged to go to Roma Street Gardens at midnight. I called Ronnie. He said I should just go, get Kurt talking, that he'd be nearby in case anything happened. So I went. I met Kurt. It was all OK until one of Kurt's men found Ronnie hiding nearby. He had headphones and all kinds of gear and it was obvious he was trying to get a recording. Kurt went ballistic. I thought he'd kill us both but he didn't. Ronnie told him I had nothing to do with it. He said he'd been following me for days. He saved my life, Luke."

She sobbed and seemed unable to speak for a while.

"What did they do to Ronnie?" I asked. "Is he alive?"

"Yes, yes I think so."

"You think so?"

"They beat him up. Right there in public. He was a mess.

Then they took him away. I – I don't know what they did with him or where they took him."

"Jesus. Did you call the police?" She didn't answer but I heard her sobbing again. "Debra, did you call the police?"

"I was scared. I'm all mixed up in this. You were supposed to get Kurt and help me get clear of it. Now I don't know what to do." She was full-on crying after that. I listened to her with nothing but anger at first. She'd let Ronnie lie for her and save her life and then she'd just abandoned him to those thugs, watched him get beaten up and taken away and not done a damned thing to save him. But the longer I listened to her crying, the more I relented. She'd been scared, terrified. She still was. We'd talked her into this. We'd told her it would all be fine.

"Have the police called you this morning?"

She pulled herself together, sniffling. "I think so. The woman with the Italian name. I didn't pick up. I didn't know what to say. I don't want to say I was there in case it implicates me. You and Ronnie were supposed to sort this out. You were supposed to put an end to this. Now what am I going to do? I'm all alone again now."

I felt sorry for her but Ronnie was a far more urgent problem.

"You have to find out where they took him. They still think you're with them, right? So you need to find out from them if he's all right."

"I can't! These men are not my friends. We don't just meet socially and have drinks and stuff. They're blackmailing me, forcing me to help them. If I upset them too much they… You know what they might do."

It was frustrating beyond all reason. I wanted to yell at her and force her to help me but, at the same time, I understood her fear and her reluctance to make things worse for herself and her parents. I was marching up and own my motel room, every muscle tense and straining. I wanted to scream and smash things. But I forced myself to calm down enough to speak.

"How did you leave it with them? What did Opperman say?"

"Once they discovered Ronnie, that was the end of it. Kurt told me to go home and wait for his call. He told me not to talk to the police or anyone."

"All right," I said, although nothing was even approximately right. "All right. We wait for his call. You let me know the minute you hear something. Will you do that?"

She said she would and I hung up. I started dialling Bertolissio but stopped half-way. She'd just tell me to stay out of it and let her do her job or something. But she ought to know about Ronnie. So I sent her a text explaining that Opperman had him and might have killed him by now. I didn't go into the details and didn't mention Debra. The last thing Ronnie needed, if he was still alive, was for Opperman to think Debra was talking to the cops.

No, I had to find Ronnie and I didn't have much time.

I called an Uber with no plan in mind but, by the time it arrived, I had one. The driver was a big, bubbly woman in her mid-forties who called herself Mimi and, although she was white, had a mass of black dreadlocks tumbling down her back. I told her to take me to Chelsea's office.

"Mimi," I said, as we drove along. "How much do you make in a day?"

"Good day or bad day?"

"Good day."

"Including tips?"

"Including everything."

"Before or after the company takes its cut?"

"Please, just tell me."

She thought for a moment. "One day, last Christmas, I made over four hundred bucks. It was a twelve hour shift, mind but, you know, you get it while the going's good, hey?"

It didn't seem much for such a long day's work but it was a lot more than I'd ever earned doing gig work. I was relieved she hadn't said it was more.

"I'll give you twelve hundred if you'll be my driver for the rest of the day." Three times a good day's pay seemed like it should buy me an eager and willing driver. Yet she didn't seem hugely impressed with her good fortune.

"What's the end of the day? Nightfall? Midnight?"

"Midnight."

"I'll need breaks."

"I'll be reasonable. Meals are on me."

"You know you could hire a self-drive car for the day for a couple of hundred? Nice one, too."

"Do we have a deal?"

"You doing something illegal?"

"Absolutely not but I might need you to drive fast if I ask you to."

She shook her head, dreadlocks dancing. "No way. I need a clean licence."

So, not so eager and willing. "OK, just this trip then and I'll work something else out."

She was silent for a minute. I'd just about decided I'd have to rent a car after all, leave a trail for the cops, waste all the time going to a rental place and filling in forms, when she spoke again.

"I know someone."

"Who?"

"My nephew. He's not a rideshare driver or anything but he's got a car and he doesn't care about his licence. Same deal, hey?"

"Sure. No worries."

"OK. We're here." She pulled up outside the office. "Will you be in there long?"

"I don't know. Maybe."

"It doesn't matter. When you come out, Dicko will be waiting."

"Dicko?"

"Yeah. My brother married a moron. She named him. But he's a good boy."

I pointed to the parking spaces under the office. "Tell him to wait in there."

So now I was going to be driven around by Mimi's nephew, Dicko. It might have been something I'd have worried about a few days ago, in that other life I used to lead.

* * * *

Chelsea's office was already starting to feel familiar. When I walked in, people didn't stop to stare at me – just glanced my way and carried on. I recognised a couple of faces. Kazima didn't rush over to greet me. In fact, she was sitting beside a young man at his desk, engrossed in whatever he was showing her. I walked over and they both looked up. Surprised, she jumped to her feet and greeted me with a smile that barely disguised her desire to ask, "What are you doing here?"

"Can we talk?" I asked and she showed me to her office. The name on the desk had been changed, I noticed. She'd also put up a couple of wall hangings – a hide shield and a tribal mask.

"Family heirlooms?" I asked, studying them.

"Nah, tourist junk from the last time I went to visit my family back home."

As dismissive as this was, I could sense that she was asserting herself. I could hear the confidence in her voice. Her new role had been good for her. It was odd to think that she had been working here, getting the company back on its feet, establishing her leadership, dealing with her loss and building a new life for herself and the people here, while I had been running around in a state of constant fear and confusion, fighting and struggling and sinking deeper into the quicksand. I could almost feel the invisible barrier that had been growing up between my dark life and the bright, normal world around me.

"How can I help you?"

"I need to borrow Karen again."

She pursed her lips and nodded. "You said it would just be the once."

"I'm in a hurry, so let me just apologise now and take her."

Her brows descended over her large, clear eyes. "What's going on?"

"I have a friend in grave and imminent danger. I need to find him. Karen can help me."

"You're still chasing Chelsea's killer?"

"Yes, I am."

"But they caught him. I mean, they found him dead. It was Simon Anning. I gave you his name." Her eyes widened. "You didn't…?"

"Kill him? No. Not me. But the man who had him killed is

the same man who ordered Chelsea's death."

Her mouth fell open. She pressed a hand against her chest. "Dear Lord, what are you doing?"

"I'm going to get justice for Chelsea."

She looked at me with concern in her eyes. "My family fled from wars and violence. I have seen horrible things. I know what evil looks like, what it does. You should not be chasing it. You should be running from it. And you should not be involving that little girl out there."

"Karen is not a child. She's old enough to make up her own mind."

She shook her head, rejecting my premise. "From a position of ignorance, no-one can make a good choice."

"Tell me about it! I haven't had the luxury of enough information since this all started. But I also don't have the luxury of doing nothing. A friend of mine is in trouble. Serious trouble. They might kill him. They are definitely torturing him. If I don't—"

My phone rang. I snatched it out of my pocket, thinking it must be Debra. But it wasn't, the number was Ronnie's.

"Ronnie?"

"Well, if it isn't Luke fucking Skywalker."

I didn't know the voice but I knew who it was. "Opperman!"

"Listen, my young Jedi, I've got your old Obi Wan here, mate." I heard a roar in the background but, if it was Ronnie, he was gagged. Opperman laughed. "Fuck me but the Force is strong with that old cunt. What do you feed him on? Tell you what, you know that old gag about his blood being worth bottling? Well, I could arrange that. What do you reckon?"

"I don't – What do you mean?" There was a racket in the background. In my mind's eye, it was Ronnie trying to shout something and someone else beating the crap out of him. Whatever, Opperman was saying, I couldn't concentrate on it.

"What you mean, little Lukie, is 'What do you want?' Go on, ask me."

My stomach felt like it was full of ice. "What do you want?"

"Nothing. Well, nothing much. All I want is for you to keep your fucking trap shut and keep your nose out of my business for the next nine days. That's not much, is it? And, in return, I won't kill Obi Wan, here. But I'll hang onto him, hey? Put him up somewhere nice, see to his every need, keep him comfy. What's he like best, boys or girls? Never mind, I'll ask him. So, are we all square, Padawan? You're going to be a good little soldier, hey? Because, if you're not, if I get a sniff of the cops or any more fucking snooping about from you, the old geezer is going to be taking a swim with an engine block tied round his wrinkly old neck."

"I understand."

"I hope you fucking do."

The line went dead. For what must have been ages, I just stood there with my phone in my hand staring at the wall. *I know what evil looks like, what it does. You should not be chasing it. You should be running from it.*

"Who was that?" Kazima asked. She sounded worried.

"A Star Wars fan."

"Luke?"

I snapped out of it and turned to face her. I noticed her eyes widen a little as if she'd seen something shocking in my face.

"So, can I borrow Karen for a while? No-one will know she was involved."

She studied me for a long, long time. "If you can persuade her," she said, at last. I set off at once but she caught my arm as I passed. "You keep her safe. Do you hear me?"

"Of course," I said. I could see Karen at her desk, so pretty and delicate. She was looking back at me. "She'll be all right."

I walked out into the open plan area. Karen was still watching me. I tilted my head towards the door and went out. A moment later, she joined me.

"You want me to do something else," she said. I nodded. "It's just like before, at home. First one little thing, then another, then another."

"I'm not trying to rip anybody off, or hurt anybody. I just need you to help me find a friend who is in grave danger."

"How?"

"I – I don't know. I thought you might be able to find his phone." I realised she had brought her oversized laptop out with her. "You don't have to do this. You can say no."

She looked at me stone-faced. "Even though you're my boss?"

I was appalled. "I own the company. I don't own you. I can't make you do anything you don't want to do." She just kept on looking at me with the same blank expression. After a while, she looked away. "My friend's life is in danger. He was helping me find the man who ordered Chelsea's murder. Now they've got him and they're holding him to force me to stop looking into it."

She looked at me sharply. "So why don't you stop, then?"

"Because I don't trust them. I think they'll kill him anyway. And maybe me too. And… another person who's involved."

"And what about me?"

"No-one knows you have anything to do with this."

"Maybe," she said.

It hadn't occurred to me that they could possibly know but she was right, there were ways. The Brisbane tech community wasn't that large. All it would take was an arrogant prick like that database guy I called to tell someone at Archerfield or The Brizvegas Games Factory that Karen had been doing secret jobs for me and Opperman might get to hear about it. Then she'd be a target, too.

"All right. It was a stupid idea. I'm sorry." I put my hands up in a gesture of capitulation and started to leave.

"What's his number?" she asked. I stopped dead. "Does he have location services turned on?"

"I really don't think…"

"I'll need somewhere to work."

Chapter Twenty-Three

"Aren't we going back to your apartment?"

"The bad guys burned it down."

"Oh my god! Was anybody hurt?"

I blinked at her. I hadn't even asked. Fortunately, I was spared the embarrassment of a confession by Dicko, who called back from the driver's seat, "Here we are, mate."

Mimi's nephew, the reckless driver, turned out to be a skinny bloke in boardies and a mullet hairdo, barely old enough to have grown a little facial fuzz and a bunch of zits. Perhaps to compensate, his car was an ancient Holden Torana, painted in bright yellow and red. From the noise it made, I'd say its exhaust needed replacing. And from the smell of the interior, I'd say new upholstery and carpets wouldn't have hurt either. Karen had looked rather distressed when we found it in the office car park, but not quite as distressed as I had been.

"Bright, isn't it?" I said, when Dicko proudly showed it to me.

"Chicks dig that," he told me, with a broad wink and a nod towards Karen.

Of all the "chicks" in the world who were unlikely to "dig"

that dayglo monstrosity, I'd have put the tasteful and refined Karen close to the top of the list.

We pulled into the car park of a small hotel in Highgate Hill. We left Dicko in the car and went inside to the bar. We got a couple of soft drinks and went out to sit beside a small pool. I waited while Karen checked that the wi-fi was OK and, when she gave me the nod, went back in to order some food. Karen was sitting back, sipping her drink when I returned. I felt a little irritated that she wasn't hard at work but I tried not to show it, forcing myself to remember she was doing me a big favour.

"Why don't you just let the police find your friend?" she asked.

"Because if the cops show up, bad things might happen to him."

"But what can you do, even if you find him?"

"I really don't know. But he's an old man. I can't let them just torture and kill him without trying to do something."

She nodded to herself and took another sip. "Very brave, or very foolish."

"Definitely the latter. I'm scared to death all the time. I thought grief was bad but I didn't know then what it was like to live with constant, gut-wrenching fear." I smiled, as if I were joking. "And, of course, the grief doesn't go away; the fear just insinuates itself into whatever space there is left in your tormented soul."

"A poet," she said as if she were remarking that I was right-handed.

"Oh, worse than that; I'm a philosopher."

She smiled. It was surprisingly impish. "Like Confucius."

"Only without the wisdom."

She smiled again. "'By three methods we may learn

wisdom: first, by reflection, which is noblest; second, by imitation, which is easiest; and third by experience, which is the bitterest.' I had a rather old-fashioned education. I acquired all my wisdom by imitation."

Despite everything, I found myself smiling, too, and felt a pang of guilt because of it – and of regret that I couldn't just sit there in this woman's pleasant company all day.

"We need to press on," I said as the food arrived.

"I've already tracked your friend's phone. I know where he is. At least, I know where he was an hour ago."

The last scraps of my mellow mood were washed away by a wave of irritation. "Then why are we sitting around chatting? This is really urgent. I'm not kidding. His life is in danger."

She nodded. "I believe you. I just wanted to know you a bit better. If I told you and you went and killed someone, that would be on me."

"More Confucius?" I asked, bitterly.

"Don't be cross. What if I told you and you went and got yourself killed? That would be on me too."

"I'm not your responsibility. My decisions are my own to make."

"And so are mine."

It was outrageous. I felt my anger building. "Are you saying you won't tell me?"

She pursed her lips and furrowed her brows. It was very cute, like a child making a very grown-up decision. "No. I will tell you. Just don't go rushing off like a crazy man. Eat your – what is that?"

"A club sandwich."

"Eat that, finish your drink, and then go."

I looked at the sandwich. It might as well have been a pile

of sand for all the appeal it had. "I won't do anything crazy, I promise."

"No, I think you will. I think maybe you think your friend's predicament is your fault."

"It is!"

"He is not your responsibility. His decisions are his own to make."

"*Touché,*" I said grudgingly, annoyed to have been so easily hoist by my own petard. "But it doesn't matter whose fault it is. I need to get him out of this mess, somehow."

She took a forkful of the salad she'd ordered and chewed on it. She ate with her mouth open, little fragments of green leaves adhering to her teeth. I looked away, oddly disturbed.

"Eat your sandwich," she said. "A few more minutes won't hurt."

"I don't want it." Even to myself, it sounded petulant. "Why don't you just tell me?"

She carried on eating. It was infuriating. "How did you manage to trace him so quickly? I was only gone a couple of minutes."

She waved a dismissive fork. "There are apps. Besides, with his number I was able to hack into his location history. If you look for his phone, you won't see it. Someone keeps taking the SIM card out. But his history is all stored in the cloud. They took it out when they got where they were going last night. Then they put it back in to make a call about an hour ago. Then they took it out again. But the location last night and when they made the call were the same, so I assume he's no longer on the move and he'll probably still be there when you send the police for him."

"I can't call the cops. There are cops in the pay of the people who are holding him. If I tell them, the bad guys might find out and then they'll just move him." I brooded for a moment on the mess Ronnie was in. Then a thought occurred to me. "Can the cops do what you just did? Hack his history?"

"Of course, but they won't. To do anything like that they need a warrant. Finding out where his phone is would be easy and they'd get the warrant without any problem but the SIM card is out, so they either need to do what I did – which is illegal and involves hacking a foreign corporation, so no warrant unless they can persuade the US to cooperate – or they get a warrant to review his phone's metadata. That would give them all they need but it will take time. Do they know he's missing?"

"Since early this morning."

"So it's probably still grinding around in the bureaucracy. It could be a long time before they find out what they need."

"So you should tell me and I should get going, hey?"

She put down her fork and sat back, her salad barely touched. She picked up her drink, crossed her legs and studied me. I realised, a little late, that her looks were deceptive. She looked like a teenage girl and she acted so sweet and deferential, that I could forgive myself for being fooled. She wasn't at all like that, really. Beneath the meek appearance was a quiet strength, a self-confidence that only revealed itself in the occasional glance or gesture. I found myself wondering about her family. She had the self-assuredness of a young woman who came from money. Lots of it.

She asked, "Aren't there any cops you trust?"

I dragged my thoughts back to the problem at hand. Bertolissio was clearly sympathetic but, while it was one thing passing information to us, it was another running a raid on a bikie stronghold. She would need to get other people involved, probably get permission from Reid. Once other cops were involved, Opperman's people would be all over it and Ronnie would be dead. I shook my head.

With a start, I noticed the sandwich in my hand with at least two bites out of it. I hadn't even been aware I'd picked it up. Jeez, I was losing it. I took another bite. I might as well finish it now.

"There's one," I said after a while, realising that Karen had the trick of sitting quietly and letting me take my time. "She's a bit brighter than the rest and kinda cool, but I don't know if she'd be willing to risk her life and keep the rest of them in the dark."

"You could ask her."

"I don't know how, not without putting her job at risk." I had no idea if the police monitored their officers' phones but, if they did, and there were recordings, or records of text messages, an enquiry afterwards would find that I'd asked her and she'd be an accomplice to whatever shit went down. As much as I could use her help, I didn't want to do that to her.

"You like her."

I smiled, remembering Ronnie's teasing on the subject. "I do. So would you, I think."

"Send her a coded message," she said.

"Yeah." I was dismissive but it wouldn't have been a bad idea for us to have arranged a few secret signals beforehand. It would certainly be handy about now. "Look, it's just me. Can I have that address now."

She read it off her phone for me. I looked it up and it turned out to be a place in a strip of shops in Chermside. It was a suburb I knew only because of the huge shopping complex there and because I'd passed through it a few times driving north on vacations. It wasn't an up-market area and I imagined any shops in the shadow of that mega-mall would be doing it tough. I called up a street view of the address and it all made sense. The building was a two-storey shop, with its windows bricked up and the front painted black. The two dozen motorbikes parked in front of the building would have given it away even without the red devil logo stencilled above the door.

"What's wrong?" Karen asked.

"Nothing," I said, putting my phone away. "I should get you back to work now, if you've finished."

"You saw something."

"Yes, I did. But that's not your problem." I stood up. We exchanged phone numbers – just in case. "Thank you for… helping out. And for…" She stood up, too, moving with a natural elegance. Or was it something she'd learned at a fancy private school? "You may not believe this but this chat we've just had, is probably the nicest time I've spent in the past three weeks."

She gave me a sad look. "I believe it."

I had Dicko drive her back to the office while I finished my sandwich and had another lemon, lime and bitters by the pool. The phrase *lull before the storm* came into my head and wouldn't go away. When Dicko got back I got into his hideous car and we headed north in heavy traffic. We stopped at a Hungry Jack's burger place in Lutwych, just short of where we were headed, and sat in the car park. The windows were all down but it was stinking hot inside the car. Dicko apologised for his useless aircon.

"You should go in," I told him. "Grab some food, enjoy the cool. I need a few minutes."

"Was that your girlfriend then, the Asian chick?"

"Nah. My girlfriend is dead." His grin turned into a frown, as if he couldn't tell if I was joking. "Karen is my employee." That seemed to resolve his doubts. The grin came back.

"Right-o, mate. No need to explain. I'll be off then. Catch you later."

I watched him go. He walked with a carefree swagger that made me feel old.

I got out my phone. I was going to send a message to Bertolissio. When she'd visited me at my unit, I'd noticed a newspaper in her handbag, folded back so she could do the crossword. I distinctly remember the word "Cryptic" in black letters above the grid. I wasn't a cryptic crossword puzzler myself but I'd struggled with enough of them to have a fair idea how to construct a cryptic clue. So this would be the code I could use to communicate with her. And my guess was that none of the DI Reid types she worked with would have any idea what the solution would be, even if they saw it. All the way out here, I'd been working on it in my head. Now I just needed to get the wording right.

I started composing a text message. "DS Bertolissio, as a fellow crossword enthusiast, I wonder if you could help with a couple of clues that have been bugging me? The first goes: Beat with pipe and sounds like you inside a gathering place (9). The second goes: Di and schemer all tangled up in the suburb (9). You alone are my best hope for a very quick solution."

I read it over half-a-dozen times, each time feeling more stupid. I should just call her. I was probably being paranoid about the cops recoding calls. Yet how could I know, in these days of total state surveillance? I didn't trust the government not to be spying on its own cops. The clues were probably awful and really easy for someone who did lots of crosswords. But that was a good thing, right? I didn't want her not to solve them, just not anyone else.

I hit the send button.

Agitated, I got out of the car and went into the burger joint. Dicko was at a table with a trayful of debris flicking and clicking at his phone. It was blissfully cool and I stood for a moment appreciating it. Dicko spotted me and waved me over.

"Hey man. You gonna get something?" I shook my head. He picked up a giant beaker, half full of dark, fizzy liquid and waved it at me. "Sit down. I've nearly finished."

I nodded towards the phone. "You haven't told anyone what you're doing, or where you are, have you?"

He looked a bit shifty or, should I say, a bit more shifty. "Nah, mate. Just, you know, chatting."

"Only, if things go badly today, there are some real heavy types who might think that you driving me around is a good enough reason to break your legs. Do you know what I'm saying?"

He nodded. "Yeah." Then shook his head. "Nah. Hey, no-one told me this would be, like, dangerous or something. Maybe I should be getting paid more, hey?"

"You're getting paid plenty. There's no danger for you as long as you don't go telling the world who you're with and what you're doing. I did ask you not to."

"Yeah, well…" He looked at his phone doubtfully. "Just a sec." He spent the next two minutes scrolling up and down his Facebook timeline, deleting posts. When he'd finished, he looked up and grinned at me. "No harm, no foul, hey?"

"I need to get going."

"Yeah, right-o." He gulped down his drink and we set off. We got in the garish car and he drove us on up Gympie

Road. I navigated to the address Karen had given me using my phone. When we reached the strip of shops, I got Dicko to drive slowly past the Devils' clubhouse. There were a few bikies in the street outside, between the crowd of gleaming motorbikes and the black shopfront: big, bearded men in denim jeans and black boots with tattooed arms and necks. My stomach clenched at the sight of them. The door was closed, which seemed ominous but probably meant nothing more than that they had the air on inside. I'd have liked to have lingered or gone round again but Dicko's car was so distinctive any odd behaviour would be noticed.

We took the first turning past the clubhouse and then the next. According to the map on my phone, we were directly behind the repurposed shop. It was a quiet suburban street filled with smart-looking houses all crammed together on tiny blocks. I told Dicko to stop. The clubhouse had a concrete drive at the side of it. I had no idea what went on in a bikie's clubhouse but in my mind it was like a gentleman's club for degenerates – with a bar and maybe even food. My guess was that it took deliveries round the back. If I could sneak through one of these houses, I'd come to some kind of a yard behind the building – probably with a fence, probably also with a dog. If I wanted to get in there to take a look, it would not be easy. I identified the house that backed onto the clubhouse, the one I needed to get through, and checked it out for fences, gates and dogs. It didn't seem to have any of these.

"OK, Dicko, let's go. Take me to the Westfield mall."

When he parked, we walked together into the massive shopping complex.

"What's going on?" he asked.

"Just getting a few things. Fancy a coffee?"

"Sure. But what are you doing? I saw you scoping out the bikie place. Then we went round back like you was casing the joint."

"Just taking a look."

"Only those blokes is nasty fuckers, so, if you're thinking of robbing 'em or something, you'd probably want to rethink that."

I stopped walking. I didn't want to tell Dicko anything but it was looking like I'd have to. We were close to a coffee shop – when are you not, in a shopping mall? – so I went in and ordered a cappuccino for me and a flat white for Dicko. We tool our drinks to a quiet spot.

"Look, mate," I said, leaning in. "It's best you don't know anything about what's going on. It's safer for you. Do you see?"

He shook his head. "I don't want to do nothing illegal."

"I won't do anything bad. A bit of trespass, maybe. A friend of mine is in trouble and I need to help him. You know what I mean?"

He nodded, unconvinced. "Yeah but, like, that's the Devil's Playthings, hey? You don't want to fuck with them."

"I'll be all right."

"Maybe you should get a few blokes, hey? I know someone I could call. Even the odds, like."

I noticed he didn't suggest the cops. "Thanks but I'm not thinking of starting a war. I'm just going to take a bit of a look, see where he is and try to work out how to get him out of there with no fuss." From the sour face he pulled, I reckoned he was still unconvinced. I took another tack. "You'll be OK. You can park well away from the clubhouse. I'll go in alone. If anything happens to me, you can just drive away. No-one will know you were even there."

He squinted at me. "I'm not worried about me. No offence, mate, but you don't look like you could win a fight with a girl guide if she was feeling a bit crook and had one arm in a cast."

I gave him a level stare. "Which arm?"

It took him a few seconds but he finally got it. He laughed then put up his hands in surrender. "Fair goes. It's your funeral. Just don't say I didn't try to tell you."

"Thanks, but I'll be all right."

He nodded as if he'd heard it all before. He leaned in closer. "I could maybe get you a gun. I know a fella might be able to arrange it."

I pulled back. "I wouldn't know which end to hold. Besides, my friend had a gun and it didn't do him any good. I tell you, I'm not planning to fight anybody, just get in, get out, see how the land lies."

With a flick of the eyebrows he dismissed me as the fool I obviously seemed. He leaned back in his seat, conversation over. When my coffee was gone, I asked him to wait and went shopping.

On my way back to collect Dicko, I felt my phone vibrate – the ambient noise was way too high to hear it ring. It was a call from DS Bertolissio.

"Interesting message," she said.

"Did you solve the clues?"

"I did but I'm still having trouble understanding what on earth is going on in that head of yours."

"It's – it's the location," I said, confused.

"Of what? Where they're holding Ronnie?"

"I was trying to be discreet."

"You want me to turn up on my own and help you free Ronnie from a bikie gang?"

"Should you say that on the phone?"

"Do you have some reason to believe your phone is being tapped?"

"No. I thought, maybe, yours…"

There was a long silence.

"How do you know where Ronnie is?"

"I'd rather not say."

"Well that makes it rather hard to get a warrant to search the place. In fact it makes it impossible. Your hunch is not probable cause."

"I don't want you to search the place. I don't want you to tell anyone. Bent cops, right? They're only keeping Ronnie alive so I don't go to the cops. If a mob of you turns up at the clubhouse, they won't have that reason any more."

Again there was a silence. When she spoke again, her tone had just a hint of humouring the lunatic about it. "Look, Luke, I understand how upset you must be. They've burnt your unit, kidnapped your friend, the police can't help you… You feel like you're on your own and desperate to do something. And all this after your loss. It would make anybody behave rashly."

It was far more irritating than soothing. "Have you ever spoken to Kurt Opperman?"

"The leader of the Devil's Playthings? No."

"Well I have. He called me today. He sounded…" I remembered his voice, casual and playful as he told me about Ronnie's plight, like none of it meant anything to him. Like all that mattered was what he wanted and to hell with anyone who got in his way. "He sounded evil."

"That's all the more reason not to go and put yourself in his hands."

"That's not my plan."

She was silent again. "I can't help you, Luke. Even if I had enough justification to get a warrant for a raid – which I don't – you've said it yourself; it wouldn't work to get Ronnie free. It would tip them off. It would only make things worse. Your cute little crossword clues have only served to make me an accomplice."

"Only if you managed to solve them."

"It's kind of you to leave me a way out but I don't think pretending they're too hard will convince anybody."

She didn't sound scornful, exactly, but my pride definitely took a hit. It made me a little bit belligerent. "So, what are you going to do?"

"Nothing. And neither are you. There's no way to get Ronnie out that doesn't end up in a shoot-out and a hostage situation – at the very best. The most likely scenario is Ronnie ends up dead and you with him. Look, DS Grogan and his team have got this. He's a good officer and he knows what he's doing. I've told him everything I know – including where Ronnie is being held – and they'll do their best to make sure he comes out of this unharmed."

"You told them?"

"You left me no choice. I can't sit on information like that."

"I thought you were supposed to be on our side."

I was getting angry but so was she. "Luke, you need to grow up. This isn't some kind of game. Running you two as informants was one thing but the minute they snatched Ronnie, things moved to a whole new level. Do you understand?"

"Running us?"

I heard her sigh.

"You need to stay away from the clubhouse. I can't tell

you more plainly than that. If DS Grogan's team catch you hanging around there, they will arrest you for obstructing the police."

"They've got the place under observation?"

"You don't need to know any more than I've told you. Do I have your promise you'll stay away from Opperman and the clubhouse?"

"Are you going to raid the place anyway? Is Grogan? They can't just let him get away with this, can they?"

"You're not listening to me."

"You're going to – what? – call in a SWAT team, kick down the doors, shoot everyone?"

"Don't be silly, Luke. This isn't a TV show. Right now, the only evidence we have that Ronnie has been kidnapped is you saying so. The only evidence we have of his location is from you."

"But it's true. You know it is."

"I'm talking about evidence. The stuff we need before we can do anything at all. Do you want to tell me where you got your information?" I said nothing. I couldn't tell her about Karen. "So, it's just your word, then?"

"What about Debra? She was supposed to be there when Ronnie was grabbed."

"DS Grogan's team interviewed her this afternoon. It seems she turned up to the meeting place and nobody was there. She hasn't heard from Opperman since. My guess is that Ronnie was spotted by Opperman's crew setting up his surveillance and they grabbed him and cleared out."

"That's not what she told me. She's lying." Of course she was lying. For some reason, she didn't want to say she'd met Opperman. "Look, she's scared. They've threatened her. You know Opperman will think she had something to do with it, right? You know he'll think she set them up? He needs her now, but…"

"Of course. She'll get twenty-four hour protection."

"And her parents?"

"Yes. She should have come straight to us."

"Should she?"

Another silence. "I'm still waiting for your promise."

"All right, but first tell me how you plan to get Ronnie out."

"You know I can't do that."

"I know you just told me you don't have any evidence so you can't do anything."

"We're working on that."

"Not impressed."

"It's not my job to impress you, Luke, only to keep you safe. Do you promise not to go to the clubhouse, or do I have to send a couple of uniforms out to bring you in?"

"Do what you like," I snapped and hung up. I'm not exactly good with confrontations. My hands were actually trembling as I fiddled with the phone to pull the SIM card out.

* * * *

"Bit of a blue?" Dicko asked as I collected him from the café.

"What do you mean?"

"I could see you over there talking on your phone. Looked like you was spewing with someone."

"It was the cops. We need to get going."

He got up and we made our way back to the car.

"Nothing illegal, you said."

"I'm not doing anything illegal," I said, trying to sound

convincing. "They want to put me in protective custody."

He pursed his lips. "Might not be a bad idea. Better than going up against all them bikies, hey?"

"I've told you. I'm not going up against anyone."

"So what's in all them bags?" We reached the car and I slung my purchases in the back. There was a loud, metallic clunk. "Fuck, that's not a shooter, is it?"

"No! It's bolt cutters. In case I need to get through a fence."

"Yeah? Well that, right there, sounds bloody dodgy to me."

"Like I said, you can go and be miles away while I'm... bending the rules a bit. You'll be OK if I get caught."

He sat behind the wheel, frowning as he pondered this. I checked my watch. It was late afternoon, just a couple of hours before nightfall. I'd been rushing to get to Ronnie but now it struck me that, if there was any chance of finding him, it would be better at night.

"Fancy a trip to the beach?" I asked. Dicko looked at me as if I'd gone crazy. "Come on, drive us to Sandgate. I fancy a walk on the foreshore." With a shrug, he started the engine and we threaded our way out of the car park, leaving just as two police cars came hurrying in by a different entrance. They had their lights flashing and I congratulated myself on disabling my phone. However, it wouldn't be long before Bertolissio arrived and she'd take a look at the mall security cameras to find out what car I was driving. She'd see Dicko, she'd get the car's rego, and she'd have every cop in Brisbane looking out for us. It was frustrating that I didn't know the law. Could she just put me in prison because she thought I was in danger? It seemed improbable. I desperately wanted to reassemble my phone so I could call Terry Marchant, the lawyer, and get his expert opinion, but I dare not. I borrowed Dicko's phone and had to look up the number because it was in my phone's memory and not my own.

To my surprise, Marchant was a bit vague on the matter. Having gone round the houses a couple of time, he said, "The bottom line is, if they want to put you in custody for a while, there are plenty of ways they can do it. They don't even have to be very creative. Conspiring to commit an offence is always handy. If you've spoken to a criminal lately… Have you, by the way?"

I was about to give an emphatic no but then I remembered the call from Kurt Opperman. I told Marchant about it and he chuckled.

"What an exciting life you and Ronnie lead. Anyway, that's enough for them to trump up some kind of conspiracy charge. It won't stick, of course, but they could deny you bail and hold you for several days, if they're being bloody minded. On the other hand, if they can pin a terrorism charge on you, the sky's the limit."

I didn't think Bertolissio would go that far. She just wanted to help me, not destroy me "What if they don't charge me?"

"Eight hours, max. Look, I'm in the middle of something. Give me a bell if they nab you."

Eight hours was too much. I had to get Ronnie free that very night. If I didn't, some crazy police raid by DS Grogan and his people would put Ronnie right out of reach and might even get him killed. My stomach clenched at the thought that I might soon be creeping through some criminal-infested death-trap, looking for Ronnie in the dark.

Chapter Twenty-Four

When we reached Sandgate, I told Dicko to avoid the public car parks and find a spot off the main streets. I didn't want a prowling cop car to spot us. I felt the need to be alone but Dicko didn't take the hints I dropped and followed me to the main parade. We didn't talk, which was something, and, pretty soon we had the ocean roaring in our ears to deter conversation. A wind blew in from the east, whipping up low waves. The ocean was grey and immense and shrouded in haze. I spotted a fish and chip shop and bought us a couple of fish dinners. I led us down to the beach where we ate from the cardboard trays as we walked along.

"Bloody ace, hey?" Dicko announced, holding up a piece of battered fish.

"Yeah, always tastes better at the beach."

"Bloody oath!" he agreed, warmly.

We walked on in silence.

"So, I was thinking," he said around a mouthful of chips. "If you go to that bikie place tonight and you don't come out again…"

"How am I going to pay you?"

"Yeah."

"I have no idea. I haven't got that much cash and there's no way to get it at this time of day. You'll just have to hope I make it."

He stared at the sand as we trudged along. "You could, like, pay me up to the time you go in and then I wouldn't be so out of pocket if... you know."

"And I could trust you to still be there waiting when I got out? You wouldn't just bugger off?"

"Nah, mate. Scouts honour."

Oh why not? I thought. He was probably right to worry about me disappearing. In fact, I'd just pay him the full amount and have done with it. "You got a PayPal account?"

"Sure."

I reached for my phone and remembered. "Bugger! I can't pay you now 'cause I can't turn my phone on without the cops finding us."

He held out his phone. "Do it on mine."

"I can't, I don't know my password."

"What? Come on!"

"Seriously. I use a password manager. It runs on my phone. All I know is the master password – which is useless on its own. Mate, you're just going to have to trust me to come back."

"Fuck!"

His disappointment was clear evidence that he did not expect me to survive the night. "Thanks for the vote of confidence."

To his credit, he looked a little guilty – but only a little.

I spotted a pub up on the road. "Fancy a coldie? My shout."

He nodded, dismally, as if to let me know that a beer wasn't much compensation for all the money he expected to lose. When we were settled in a quiet corner of the pub with condensation beading on our glasses, he said, "Tell me again what all this is about."

I hadn't really told him much at all but his tone of voice said he needed some reassurance that his wasted day and prospective loss was all in a good cause. So I told him the whole story, from the beginning. When I'd finished, he frowned at his beer.

"What's the matter?" I asked. I'd expected him to now understand everything and to be completely on-side. It was irritating that he looked as if I'd been speaking in a foreign language.

"You went after your girlfriend's killer, right. I get that. And you found him. So that's case closed, hey? So what the fuck are you doing messing about with these bikie fuckers? What's that all about?"

I tried explaining again but he wasn't having it.

"Nah, mate. I reckon you've just got a death wish. And as for this mate of yours you want to rescue, sounds to me like he's got kangaroos loose in the top paddock." He tapped his temple for emphasis.

I gave up. "Time to go." He looked meaningfully at his half-finished beer. "You'll drive better without it." He was clearly annoyed but so was I. I stood up. Angrily, he downed the rest of his drink in one swallow and followed me out to the street. It was almost dark. I should have waited a little longer but maybe waiting was a bad idea. God knows what they were doing to Ronnie while I sat around chatting to Dicko.

As we walked up the road, a police car drove past. I watched it carry on up the road until it came to the pub. It turned into the car park.

"Fuck!"

"What?"

"They're tracking us. Shit! It's your phone."

"What?"

"Take the chip out."

"What?"

We had to get off the main road. I broke into a trot, urging Dicko along with me until I found a turning and took it.

"Give me your phone," I said, walking fast, holding out my hand.

"What? No."

"I won't damage it. The cops know who you are. They got your rego from the surveillance cameras in the mall car park. So now they've got your phone number and they're using it to track us. You need to take the chip out so they can't." I should have thought of it. It was a stupid mistake. I watched comprehension slowly dawn on his pimply face. He pulled out his phone. It was an old model iPhone. The SIM card was in a little drawer and we needed to insert a pin into a tiny hole to make the drawer open. I pulled him off the street behind a bush. We had to sort this out before we went any farther.

Of course, he didn't have a pin and neither did I. I scanned the area for something, anything we could use. But there was nothing.

"You need to get rid of your phone. Or smash it."

"Fuck off."

"I'm serious. Getting it onto a moving vehicle would be best." But the chances were slim. There was no traffic on the side-street and I didn't want to go back to the main road. "Or we could hide it somewhere." But they'd know where it was and find it easily. "Or smash it. That's the safest option."

He put his phone behind his back as if I might try to snatch it.

"No, wait." I had spotted the letter box for the house whose drive we were hiding in. It was one of those little metal boxes on a pole, with a slot at the front and a flap at the back. I called Dicko to me. "Hold your phone in there and see if it's got a signal."

"What?"

"For God's sake, just do it. The cops will be cruising back this way in a minute."

Looking dubious, he did as I asked.

"Does it have a signal?"

"What?"

I clenched my jaw to stop myself screaming at him. "Have a look at the screen and tell me if it has a signal."

He squatted and peered into the post box for a few seconds. "Nah."

"GPS?"

It took him a while longer. "I don't think so."

"Good enough. Leave it in there. You can pick it up again later."

"It'll get nicked."

"It won't. Look, if it does, I'll buy you a new one. A better one. All right?"

He stood up, leaving the phone inside the box. I breathed a sigh of relief. As far as the cops were concerned, the phone had just disappeared. I hustled Dicko back into motion. We went farther down the side street and turned into another. No-one from the main road could see us now and no-one knew where we were going. I imagined Bertolissio getting cross and calling up maps of the area. They'd try the car parks first. I smirked at my cleverness in not parking in one. Now all we had to do was get back to the clubhouse without being seen.

We reached the car without incident and I made Dicko drive through the tiny suburban backstreets, heading roughly south and west until we were completely lost. After a while, we came across a servo and, while Dicko filled his tank, I went inside and bought a new pre-paid SIM card for my burner phone. If the police found we'd been to this place, all they'd have is a random point indicating a random direction.

Armed once more with Google Maps, I could now direct Dicko on a complex late-evening trip through Brisbane's northern suburbs, avoiding all major roads and ending up at the back of the Devil's Playthings' clubhouse without spotting a single cop car or, I hoped, passing a single traffic camera. I got in the back of the car and ratted through the bags of stuff I'd bought. We'd wasted so much time dodging the cops that it was properly dark and there was no-one about. In an hour or two, people would be going to bed but I couldn't wait that long.

I stuffed a roll of gaffer tape, a torch, a selfie stick, a plastic bag full of meat, and a long-bladed pocket knife into a small backpack. I pocketed a pair of leather gloves and hefted the bolt cutters. I took off my T-shirt and put on the black, long-sleeved polo-neck sweater I'd bought. Then I rubbed black shoe polish on my face and hands.

"Fucking hell," Dicko said, watching me.

I already felt like a dill and didn't need him to comment. "I don't want to be seen," I said, defensively.

"You're stinking the car out. They won't have to see you. They'll smell you a mile off. Do not get any of that shit on the seats."

It was a bit late for that, I realised, but I assured him I'd be careful.

I spent a couple of minutes familiarising myself with the phone. I needed to be able to take photos – with the flash off! – and maybe record conversations without having to work out how to do it all while hiding in a bush. It was all pretty straightforward except I managed to smear black shoe polish all over the screen and had to use my discarded T-shirt as a rag to clean it up.

"You're sure you want to do this?" Dicko asked. He sounded concerned.

"I'm sure I don't want to do this," I said, honestly. "But it has to be done. I know if I was in there, Ronnie would move heaven and earth to get me out."

"You two are good mates, hey?"

"No, not really. In fact, I don't even like him that much. We just, sort of, got tangled up in this." I looked at my assembled equipment and my polish-smeared hands. "I should go."

"I'll be up the road there and parked just around that corner, If I hear running feet, I start the engine. If it's you, I pick you up and we shoot through. If it's a bunch of bikies with hammers, I floor it and you're on your own. Fair goes?"

I nodded, feeling glum, and got out of the car. I had a horrible feeling I wouldn't be seeing it again.

* * * *

The house behind the clubhouse had a big shiny four-wheel in the drive that I had to squeeze past on the fence side. It was a tight fit and I cursed the mentality that makes city dwellers buy these big metal monsters. With the bolt cutters in one hand and the torch in the other, I could barely move without knocking into it with one or the other. I promised myself I would slip some money in the owner's post box one day to pay for the scratches I must be making. If I had to come back this way at a run, I'd be able to go round the other side where there would be loads of space but, right at that moment, it was better to avoid being seen from the house. Some fat old guy waving a golf club at me would be the end of my whole plan.

I slid past the car, out the back of the car port and carefully opened the gate in the garden fence. It creaked like a castle door in a horror movie but I stood inside the back yard, holding my breath, until I was sure no-one was coming. My heart was already racing and I'd started sweating. *This is the easy part*, I told myself. *Get a grip*. Steadying my breathing I moved down the garden. I'd gone about three paces when everything was flooded in dazzling white light.

I stood frozen, completely exposed on a small lawn strewn with kiddies' toys. They had a security light with a motion detector. Why hadn't I thought of that possibility?

"Jesus fucking Christ!" My stomach leapt into my throat. It was a woman's voice and I spun to face it. But all I saw was empty garden and a wooden fence. "If that fucking light comes on one more time I'm calling the cops," the woman said, loudly. "That is not how you treat your neighbours. It's just bloody rude." A man's voice could be heard, low and placating. It was the couple next door. My heart started beating again. "No, you should bloody go round there and tell him," the woman said, still loudly. "If you don't, I will." The man carried on trying to soothe her but by then I'd got my wits back, at least to the extent that I could sprint to the end of the garden and hide myself in the bushes that lined the boundary fence. It wasn't much cover – especially with that security light going full blast – but it was better than standing around like a garden ornament, waiting for the neighbours to come round to start a punch up. I hunkered down in the foliage and looked back at the house. The woman was still shouting and now her partner seemed to be shouting back at her. The lights were on at the back of the house and there were no curtains, so I could clearly see inside. No-one came to see what had triggered the light, or what the shouting was about next door. I felt light-headed and was trembling from the scare I'd had but it looked as if I could have strolled in, whistling, kicked some of the brightly-coloured plastic junk around on the lawn and not worried about it.

I turned to the fence. It was, as I had seen from the road, a steel, chain link fence about two metres high that ran all the way around the bikie's property. Through it, I could see a concrete yard with a big shed, beyond which was the clubhouse itself – a two-storey brick building with few windows and ugly pipework. There were a couple of cars parked in the yard – one might well have been the Jeep I'd seen at Anning's house, the other was some kind of fancy sports car – as well as a couple of big motorbikes. I could hear a low, thumping bass rhythm coming from the clubhouse. Lights were on in all the windows on both levels. The yard, too, was lit up by lights on the wall of the house and the side of the shed. At least I didn't have to worry about motion sensors and floodlights.

I lifted the bolt cutters and got to work on the fence. I'd never used such a tool before and found, to my dismay, that it was incredibly fiddly. The jaws barely opened enough to get the wire between them, they were so heavy, it was hard to hold them by the hand-grips and still put the tiny jaws around the wire, and then they needed all my strength to close the jaws and cut the wire. By the time I'd made three cuts, I was sweating profusely and cursing the idiot who'd designed such a ridiculous tool. When they did it in films, it always looked so easy. It certainly didn't reduce the hero almost to tears as he struggled with aching arms and stinging sweat in his eyes. Manfully, I refrained from counting how many more cuts there would be and calculating how long this would take me.

On the fourth cut, a dog exploded into furious barking. I looked across the yard and saw it immediately – a huge, shaggy German shepherd, straining towards me on a long chain attached to the wall near the back door. It was snarling and bellowing at me as if I'd personally insulted it. I swallowed hard, pulled back into the shadows and hoped the brute was well secured. I don't have any particular fear of dogs. I've always quite liked them. But this one turned my blood to ice, not because it was the biggest or most aggressive dog I'd ever seen – although it might well have been – but because I had to get past it somehow, without being eaten.

I was still staring at the Hell Hound when the back door of the clubhouse burst open and a big, hairy man stormed out bellowing, "Shut the fuck up, you useless bloody mongrel. Quiet, or I'll beat the fucking snot out of you." To back up his threat, he waved a massive stick at it. The dog immediately stopped barking and cringed away from him with a whine of submission. My fear transformed instantly to pity – and anger at the thug with the stick.

"So, what is it this time?" the dog-beater asked, turning towards where I was hiding. My breath caught. I wanted to dive back into the garden but daren't move. "Another cat? A possum?" He took a couple of steps towards me, peering into the dark shrubbery. How he couldn't see me, I didn't understand. I felt lit up like a Christmas tree. But he didn't. I thanked the god of reckless idiots that the security light behind me had gone out. I must have been just one dark shape among many. The man turned away, cursing the dog and went back inside.

The dog lay on the ground, watching me, growling with sullen resentment but not daring to bark again. Gradually, my heart slowed and my breathing steadied. I put down the bolt cutters and used my polo-neck to wipe the sweat from my eyes. Watching the dog, I picked the cutters up again and continued the slow process of snipping my way through the fence. The dog continued to growl from time to time but, each time it did, looked anxiously over its shoulder as if expecting retribution.

I pushed the fence apart, pushed my bag through and crawled after it. I left the bolt cutters behind. Emerging through the fence was too much for the dog. It leapt to its feet and went wild, barking and snarling and leaping against its chain. But I'd already planned what I'd do. Rising to a crouching run, I cut across the yard to the Jeep and ducked down behind it. Lying on my belly I saw the door fly open again and the man with the stick reappear. As before, he yelled at the dog. This time, it ran, tail between its legs, back to its spot by the door and grovelled in fear as the dog beater cursed and threatened it. It was sickening to see an animal so cowed. If I could have taken the man's stick and beaten him to the ground with it, I would.

I waited, full of anger, for him to go back inside, then I opened my backpack and pulled out the plastic bag. Inside, wrapped in paper, was two kilograms of diced beef. Crawling to the end of the sports car to be nearer the dog, I picked up a piece and threw it to where it was sitting. Eyeing me suspiciously, it went to the lump of meat and sniffed it, cautiously. After what seemed a very long time, it picked the meat up in its teeth and gobbled it down. It looked up at me with a quick, sharp movement as if it had suddenly understood that its miserable life was about to take a turn for the better. I stood up and threw it another chunk of beef. This time, it caught the piece in mid-air and waited, alert and eager for the next. I moved closer, tossing another morsel. Then another. Soon, I was standing beside the dog, feeding it pieces of meat by hand and stroking its shaggy head. I put what was left on the ground and, while the dog ate, I unfastened its thick, leather collar.

"You're free," I told it. "Even if I don't get Ronnie out, I did one good thing tonight." It was an irresponsible thing to do. I could see that. For all I knew, the dog would go and eat someone's kid, or it would be caught and put down within the week. But at least it had a chance now of finding a new home, one where it wouldn't be beaten and chained up all the time.

I left the dog eating and went to look through the windows. There were four on the ground floor at the back and they all had bars on them. I took a picture with my phone. My idea was to build up a layout of the building so I could find my way around at some later date if necessary. I crept to the first window and peered in. It seemed to be some sort of junk room. Its light was off but the door was open and light came in from a hallway. I held my phone to the glass and took another picture.

I realised that the music I was hearing was coming from upstairs. It confused me because I'd fully expected the main room and bar to be on the ground floor but, clearly, it wasn't. So, downstairs would be just ordinary rooms – offices, store rooms, that kind of stuff. Upstairs would be where everybody hung out. This was good. It meant Ronnie might be downstairs and I wouldn't have to creep past dozens of people or climb a wall to get to him.

I moved to the next window. It had frosted glass and was obviously a toilet. The next one was an office. That is, it had a desk and a computer, a filing cabinet and a bookshelf, but it also had a gun cabinet, a badly-chipped department store mannequin with its head missing, a dartboard and a wheel from a motorbike. On one wall was a huge whiteboard with what looked like an organisation chart. I took my picture then studied the chart. I couldn't make out much but I quickly realised this was not the Devil's Playthings' corporate structure. It was the Queensland Police's. Specifically, it was the State Crime Command. The only name on it I recognised was Grogan. It sent a chill through me that, while the police were collecting intelligence on the criminals, they were, in turn, collecting intelligence on the police. There were notes and symbols against each name. Many, like Grogan, had photographs.

I stepped back. It was disturbing. It was an image I didn't want in my head but it was too late. I looked around the yard. The dog had gone. I heard laughter from upstairs. I wanted to go, too, but there was still work to do. I moved to the last window and peered in.

It was a small room with little furniture – a bed, a wooden chair, a bucket by the door, a roll of toilet paper beside it. There was old lino on the floor and the single light in the ceiling had no shade. I felt a twitch of irrational irritation that it was an old-style incandescent bulb, not a low-wattage energy-saver. I raised my phone for a shot and froze.

Someone was in the room. There was a second chair

beneath the window and someone was sitting in it. I hardly dared move. Slowly, I turned my head and looked down at a man's head and shoulders. He was just centimetres away on the other side of the wall. He was wearing a white vest that exposed beefy shoulders, covered in curly grey hair. The stubbly hair on his head was grey too. I blinked. In one of those sudden twists of perception, the dangerous bikie transformed into Ronnie.

I almost cried out. I did a quiet dance of triumph. I'd found him. It was unbelievable. I realised I hadn't really expected to get anywhere near him, let alone find myself standing just an arm's length away. I put my face up against the window and tapped, hissing, "Ronnie! Ronnie!"

My partner jumped out of his seat and spun to face me. He gaped at me with wide eyes and an open mouth. My exultation drained out of me as I took in the blood on his vest that had run down his neck from cuts on his face. The bastards had beaten him. His lip was cut, his nose had bled. One eye was badly swollen, both cheeks were puffy and inflamed. My nostrils flared as I breathed stertorously through my nose, rage building in me. I caught the bars of his window in my hands and gripped them hard. He moved quickly to the window, shoving the chair aside.

"Fuck off you stupid bell end!" he snarled, his voice barely audible. "You'll get us both killed you idiot."

I looked around at the bars. They were firmly anchored into the brick wall. I had a crowbar in my pack but I was pretty sure it would take more than that. Ronnie knocked on the window to make me look at him but I was thinking. If I could get the dog chain off the wall, tie it to the bars, tie the other end to the Jeep and, somehow, get that started, I could pull the bars out, Ronnie could climb through the window and we could get away in their own vehicle.

"You fucking moron!" Ronnie hissed. "Get out of here."

The look of horror on his face when I turned to him, grinning and gave him a thumbs up sign, was priceless. I scuttled over to the wall by the door where the chain was fixed and almost whooped in triumph when I saw it was only tied on to a staple in the wall. I began working at it to get the chain untangled.

"Here you are, darl," a woman's voice said, behind me.

I spun around, falling backwards onto my arse. A woman stood in the doorway, one hand on the handle and the other holding a bowl of dog food. We stared at one another like stunned mullets for several seconds before she threw down the dog bowl and took a step towards me.

"What the fuck do you think you're doing?" she asked.

I tried to scrabble away, backwards but in a couple of paces, she was standing right over me. She looked down at me with her expression hard. She wore denim jeans, a tight top and a denim waistcoat. *Bikie chick*, I thought, stupidly.

"What the hell have you done with Simba?"

I had to get out of there. I turned over to get my feet under me but she gave a push with her booted foot on my backside and I went sprawling on the concrete.

"Butch! Get out here," she yelled, placing a foot in the small of my back to hold me down. "We've got a prowler."

I rolled over to get free of her weight on my spine but that just left me lying on my back with her standing astride me. I tried to get my elbows under me so I could get up but she calmly bent forward and punched me in the face. Lights exploded in my head as her fist connected, then again as the back of my skull hit the concrete. Dazed, I unscrewed my eyes just in time to see the big hairy dog-beater turn up, stick in hand, to stare down at me with an expression of purest puzzlement.

Chapter Twenty-Five

They sat me in a swivel chair in the office I'd seen through the window. The gun case and the battered mannequin took on a new, sinister aspect now that I was so close to them. The dog-beater and the Amazon who'd almost cracked my skull handed me over to a couple of blokes they called down from upstairs. My stomach fell as I recognised Hairy and Baldy from my previous encounters with them. They recognised me, too, judging by the grins they exchanged.

"Wallet and phone," Baldy said. He held out his hand and I passed them to him. He took them and held them but didn't look at either. "Everything else on the desk." I pulled out a handful of coins from my pocket and dumped them, as ordered. Too late, I remembered the SIM card from my phone was among them. Baldy noticed it immediately and picked it out from among the coins.

"The police know I'm here," I lied. It didn't seem to affect them in the slightest. Probably everybody said that when they ended up in that chair.

We waited for at least a couple of minutes before I heard quick footsteps on the stairs. A man strode into the room. He wasn't a big man but he was lean and hard. He looked to be in his late thirties, with short black hair and a short, neat beard. Unlike the others, his clothes were smart and formal, with polished black shoes, a white shirt, open at the neck and a pair of charcoal grey trousers with a crease in them that were probably part of a business suit. I wondered if maybe he'd been in court that day. He was so obviously in charge that it had to be Kurt Opperman.

He walked around me and sat at his desk. Baldy handed him the wallet and phone without a word as if they'd rehearsed this a dozen times. Opperman flipped open the wallet and pulled my cards and driver's licence out onto his desk. I bit down on my objections. Hairy and Baldy were standing right beside me and looked like they were hoping for any excuse to hurt me. So I tried not to give them one.

Opperman looked from my licence to me and grinned. To Baldy, he said, "Is it true Sharon beat him up and dragged him in here?"

Baldy grinned. "Fucking poofter."

"Now, now. You know Sharon can be very physical." They all laughed.

Opperman turned his attention to my phone. "So you're Luke Skywalker," he said, not looking up. "You know all that blackface shit is supposed to be offensive to our coloured friends?"

I remembered the polish on my face and hands and felt ridiculous.

His eyes lifted from the phone to meet mine. "What's the password on this?"

For a moment, I considered not telling him. In that moment, Hairy and Baldy each grabbed one of my arms and held them against the arms of the chair I was on. Baldy pulled a hunting knife out of nowhere and pressed it down against the knuckle of my middle finger. Blood welled around the blade and a shock of pain shot up my arm. "Fucking hell!" I shouted. "112358! It's 112358!"

They let go of my arms and I grabbed my hand to me, studying the finger. I still had all of it. The cut wasn't even very deep. I sucked it miserably.

"What's that, your dad's birthday?"

"Fibonacci series," I said.

"I should have guessed," Opperman said, happily, poking at my phone again. "Some fucking nerd shit. Ah, here we go." For a while, he poked and flicked at the screen. Then he put the phone down and sat back. He grinned at me. "Let's try again shall we?" He pulled out the SIM and tossed it in the bin. Then he replaced it with the other one. He didn't even bother to ask the password this time, just tapped it in. "That's better." For a while, he was lost in browsing through my call logs and whatever else he felt like. He finally put down the phone, rested his hands on the desk and regarded me calmly.

"I warned you about dicking around in my business, didn't I Master Luke?" He frowned, puzzled. "What were you planning to do? Sneak in and get Obi Wan out? Are you a fucking retard?" I sucked my finger miserably and didn't answer, assuming it was a rhetorical question. When he slapped the top of the desk with the flat of his hand I jumped so much I almost bit my finger off. "Well?"

I had to swallow to make my voice work. "I was just… taking a look."

"He nicked Simba," Baldy said.

Opperman looked annoyed for the first time. "What?"

"The dog's gone. He took it."

Opperman scowled at his henchman. "Shut the fuck up."

"The police know I'm here," I said again. I had to say

something and it was the only thing I could think of that might worry this cocky bastard. But it didn't. He just shook his head, sadly, and tapped my phone.

"No, they don't. You haven't spoken to the cops since you called DS Bertolissio at 4:32. Nah, mate, you're here all on your lonesome. No-one knows. No-one cares. And no-one is coming to your rescue. So, the only question now is, what the fuck do I do with you?"

"You're wrong. People know I'm here. I told people."

His eyes instantly locked onto mine. "Who?"

As soon as he asked, his two thugs grabbed my arms again and Baldy pulled out his knife.

"All right! All right! I lied. No-one knows."

"Are you sure?"

Baldy pressed the knife into my knuckle again. I felt bile rising in my throat, imagining that blade sliding between the bones of my finger.

"I'm sure. No-one knows. The police don't want to know. They said they needed evidence to get a warrant. I thought... I thought I could..." They say the best lie is mostly to tell the truth. I hoped I'd told enough truth to keep them from suspecting Dicko was out there waiting for me. The tear that rolled down my cheek probably helped convince them.

Opperman stared at me for a long, uncomfortable time. In the end, he said, "Put him in with the old man. I need to think this through."

"Do you want me to rough him up a bit?" Baldy asked.

Opperman snapped back at him. "Just do what I fucking tell you, hey? For once? Can you do that?"

Baldy's face fell into a sullen mask of repressed anger. He muttered, "Yeah, sure," and dragged me to my feet.

Outside in the hall, Hairy slapped Baldy on the shoulder. In an angry whisper he said, "You need to keep your mouth shut. We're in enough shit for getting beat up on video. What do you wanna bring up the fucking dog for? Who gives a fuck?"

We stopped just one door down from the office. Baldy snarled past me at his friend.

"I give a fuck." He pushed me up against the wall, banging the back of my head where it was already sore from Sharon bouncing it off the concrete yard. He grabbed me by the shirt front and pushed his fist up under my chin. "What did you do with the bloody dog, cunt?"

"I let it go."

"You fucking what? Are you some sort of fucking greenie or something?"

"A what? Oh, like an animal liberationist or something? No. No, I – I don't know why I did it. It just seemed…" I swallowed. "…sad."

"See?" Hairy said. "He's a retard like Kurt said."

Baldy looked at me as if I disgusted him. He pulled away from me, letting me breathe again. To Hairy, he said. "I hate fucking retards. Are you gonna open the fucking door or what?"

Scowling, Hairy fished in his jeans for a key and opened the door. Baldy threw me inside and they slammed it and locked it after me.

"Well, well, well," Ronnie said. I picked myself up off the floor and looked around. He was sitting in the chair by the window wearing nothing but his bloody singlet and a pair of boxer shorts. He had his arms crossed and was shaking his head. "You, my friend, are dumber than a bag of fucking hammers."

I opened my mouth to defend myself but I couldn't help agreeing with him. I went to sit on the bed, staring at the dusty floor.

"Please tell me you had more of a plan than stumbling around disguised as a black and white minstrel until someone found you."

It was sort of accurate but it felt grossly unfair. "So tell me how well your plan worked out, then? Where does sitting around in your jocks fit into the master plan?"

He didn't seem keen to answer. I squinted at him sideways, wondering if I should maybe a bit more sympathetic. He looked pretty battered and he seemed to have aged ten years.

"It was a set-up," he said. "That little bitch Debra led me right into Opperman's hands."

"No way!"

"Way!" he said, mocking me.

"But…"

"She seemed so nice? So sweet? So helpless?" He turned away, looking like he could spit nails. "Yeah, well, she took us both for fucking wood ducks. That woman should get a bloody Oscar. Turns out the whole bloody thing was her plan from the start. She took it to Opperman – and guess who he is, by the way."

This was terrible. "Her boyfriend?"

"Her brother – half brother from a different mother. She almost fell on her arse laughing, telling me about it. It was Debra's idea to involve Anning – up to his bloody arse in debt and embezzling from the company to stay afloat. Anning brought in Archerfield, who were already laundering money for the bikies as well as providing software for the Gamefest. 'It was just meant to be,' as Debra put it. I think she really believes a benevolent God dropped this into her sticky little fingers."

"And then Chelsea worked out what was going on," I felt sick. If she'd just gone to the police instead of taking it to Anning first.

Ronnie seemed to sense what I was thinking. "Anning was just a puppet. They had him in their pocket. But they knew he was too weak to rely on once they'd made him kill Chelsea. Knocking him off was Opperman's idea. Just to keep things tidy."

And then we turned up. "Are they going to kill us? Opperman said he needed time to think about what to do next."

Ronnie looked tired. "If you'd stayed away, I'd have said no. As long as they could intimidate you into silence, there was no need. Now, I'm not so sure. It depends who else knows you're here."

"There's someone. Just some rando, really. He might go to the cops. Or he might not." My guess was that Dicko would keep his head down and try to avoid being involved. "Bertolissio might work it out. I think organised crime have the place under surveillance since you got snatched but…" But I'd sneaked in and been grabbed without them apparently noticing, so their surveillance was probably a car parked up the street, watching the front door.

"So we're on our own. I reckon Opperman will wait a day or so, to see if any cops come sniffing around, then you and me are going on a one-way drive out to the bush."

"What if the cops do come?"

"Unless they bring a search warrant, all the good it will do is to give Opperman a chance to find out how much they know. If I was him, I'd kill us tonight, stick the bodies in a big box and get it far away from here, despite the risk of the cops noticing. But he's the cautious type and completely up himself. He thinks he's a criminal mastermind. He'll play it cool. Try to impress his mates. Play chicken with the cops. And, frankly, he'll get away with it. Unless your rando goes to the cops with a convincing story, there's no chance they'll get a warrant. Opperman knows that."

The words, *So, what are we going to do?* were forming in my mind when a commotion broke out in the room next door. It was a man and a woman in Opperman's office having an argument at ever-increasing volume.

"Me?" the man yelled. "This was all your bloody idea!"

"Oh, forgive me for trying to make us both rich," the woman shouted back.

"Kurt and Debra?" I asked Ronnie in a low voice. He shushed me, listening.

"Anyway, I delivered the old bastard, like I said I would. It's not my fault if the other one's so bloody stupid he comes sneaking round."

"Isn't it? Really?"

"What do you mean by that? How is it my fault?"

"We wouldn't have had to kill his bloody girlfriend if you hadn't stuffed up and let her find out what we're doing."

"Oh, right, it's my fault she was a nosy bitch."

"Too bloody true. And it was your fault your bloody boyfriend went off the rails."

"Simon was not my bloody boyfriend. It was your job to keep him in line and look what a dog's breakfast you made of it."

The recriminations went back and forth for quite a while. So long, in fact, that I got bored. And depressed. If they'd only let me keep my phone so I could have recorded it all, there was more than enough to convict the pair of them ten times over. As it was, as the argument went on and on, I began to realise that Opperman was working himself up to murder Ronnie and me and, at the rate he was going, it would be sooner rather than later. Ronnie seemed to have come to the same conclusion.

"Listen," he said, softly. "When this blue is over, Opperman, is going to send his goons in here to finish us off. They'll probably tie us up, stick us in a van or something, and drive us far away. Then they'll kill us, hide the bodies and come home."

"This is all my fault," I said, feeling miserable. If I'd just stayed away, they'd probably have kept Ronnie alive.

"Yeah. Thank you Captain Bleedin' Obvious. Look, the point is, we have one chance to get free and that's before they tie us up. After that, it will be nearly impossible. Do you understand?"

My heart began to quicken. "Won't they be armed or something? What chance would we have?"

"A better chance than if we just let the bastards take us."

"Right. Yes, of course. It's just... I suppose it's just natural to cling to life as long as you possibly can, you know? Spin it out, like. Not rush to meet death. I'd never thought about why people let themselves be taken to death camps or whatever, but maybe that's it. If both courses of action – you know, fight or be taken – obviously lead to the same outcome, you pick the one that gives you more time."

He scowled angrily. "That's so profound. You should write a bloody thesis about it when we get out of here. Now, are you going to listen to my plan, or are you going to spout crap all night?"

As it was, we had another half hour before there were heavy footsteps in the hallway and a key rattled in the lock.

Chapter Twenty-Six

Baldy pushed open the door without entering. He was holding a gun. I'd never seen a sawn-off shotgun before – or even an intact one – but I was pretty sure this evil-looking device must be one. There were two other blokes behind him in the corridor: Hairy and some other guy. He glanced around the room then fixed his eyes and the gun on me.

"Where's the other one?"

I pointed to a space behind the door and grimaced. "He's… er… you know… using the bucket."

From behind the door, Ronnie said, "How about some fucking privacy?"

Baldy rolled his eyes and lowered the gun. He stepped into the room and pulled the door back. Ronnie, who had been standing there waiting, grabbed the barrel of the shotgun and punched hard and fast at the bikie's throat. Choking and obviously unable to breathe, our would-be executioner let go of the gun and fell to his knees, clutching his throat.

Ronnie pushed the door shut and moved to stand facing it. I leapt up and went to stand beside the door clutching a leg from one of the wooden chairs "Help!" Ronnie shouted in a strangled voice. The door burst open and Hairy rushed straight in at Ronnie. My partner didn't flinch, even though the younger man was huge by comparison. He hit the bikie in the face with the stock of the shotgun and Hairy reeled back. The third bikie had to stop his inward rush because Hairy was sinking to his knees in front of him. As he did, I swung the chair leg with all my force at the man's head. It struck with a sickening crack and the third man went down like a puppet with its strings cut.

Ronnie's plan called for me to run at that point but I didn't move. I stared at the man I'd hit, shocked by the violence of it and the real possibility the man was dead. Ronnie grabbed my upper arm and pushed me towards the door, almost sending me flying through it.

"Move!" he hissed.

It snapped me out of my frozen state and I lurched down the corridor towards the front door. The door to Kurt's office opened as I passed. I heard him curse but that was cut short as Ronnie went past and poked him in the stomach with the shotgun barrel. I'd barely gone a couple more steps when Opperman's cursing started up again, this time very much louder and mixed with bellowed demands that everybody "get down here now and kill these fuckers." Feet began pounding on the wooden floor above us and then on the staircase.

I saw the front door ahead of me. It was a double door with no windows. I'd stupidly imagined some kind of push-bar emergency exit, not something I'd have to stop at and pull inwards. From the sound of feet in the hallway behind me, it was absolutely certain we wouldn't have the two or three seconds it would take to get the door open and start running again but I didn't dare look. I slammed into the door, my hand on the knob and looked back just as the whole building shook to the sound of a massive explosion. Ronnie was standing facing the oncoming mob, pointing the gun straight at them. There was a pall of smoke through which I could see a big hole in the ceiling and a wall of angry bikies standing still, dusted in plaster and snarling like caged animals.

"One more step," Ronnie said.

Kurt Opperman pushed to the front of the mob and said, over his shoulder, "Someone go to my office and fetch the guns."

Without taking his eyes off the bikies, Ronnie said, "Take your time with the door, Luke. No rush, mate."

"Right," I said, snapping out of yet another daze. I twisted the knob and pulled. The door opened and I almost sobbed with relief that it wasn't locked. *Run!* I told myself. That was the plan. Run like hell to the nearest house with its lights on. So I ran.

Straight into a black-clad bikie in a crash helmet. He was carrying something like a big, heavy pipe and it hit me in the ribs as I smashed into him, sending us both sprawling across the concrete forecourt. Immediately, there was a racket of shouting, bellowing men. Cutting across the shouts was a woman's voice.

"Don't shoot!" it said.

I rolled into a crouch, gasping at the pain in my ribs, and peered back at the clubhouse, expecting to see Debra. I had to blink hard and shake my head before I actually understood what I was seeing. Ronnie was outside, on his knees with the shotgun on the ground and his hands behind his head. Armed police in black armour and helmets had machine guns pointed at him. A woman was running towards me. It was Alexandra Bertolissio, wearing a bullet-proof vest. Loads more armed cops were surging into the clubhouse, bellowing at people to get down on the ground. Nearby, the cop I had thought was a bikie picked himself up off the ground and, with a scowl directed at me, picked up the battering ram I'd knocked out of his hands in our collision.

"Are you OK?" Bertolissio asked, squinting at my face, offering me a small, delicate hand.

I let her help me up. "Yeah, just about."

She turned her attention to Ronnie. "Let him up," she told the cops. "He's one of the victims."

Ronnie was grinning. "Pretty good timing," he said.

"We need to find where they put your clothes," she told him. He looked down at himself and his grin broadened. An ambulance pulled into the forecourt. "OK, that one's for you two."

Ronnie waved dismissively. "Nah, I'll be right."

"Maybe, but I think Luke might have a cracked rib, the way he's nursing it."

"Nah, he's a wimp. It's probably nothing."

"You'll both get checked out." Her tone left no room for argument. Not that I was arguing in the slightest. "Are there any more in there the paramedics should be attending to?"

Ronnie nodded. "Three. All in worse condition than the Little Princess, here. Not that I care."

Even as we spoke, a couple of police vans pulled up and a second ambulance.

"You were right on the verge of raiding the place," I said. "What made you change your mind?"

Bertolissio smiled. It was a happy smile but there was also something feral about it. "New evidence," she said. "Enough to put Opperman and his accomplices away for nice long stretches."

I wanted to ask more but the paramedics arrived with

blankets and sympathy and took Ronnie and me in hand, letting Bertolissio stride away toward the clubhouse to claim her prize.

Chapter Twenty-Seven

Two weeks after that night, my ribs still hurt but I was out and about again and the painkillers had actually started helping – which I was very pleased about. This was the first time I'd ventured out on my own. Ronnie had been looking after me like a chook with a retarded chick – which was fun for about the first ten minutes. Even when I went out, he came with me, "To open doors and shit," as he put it. He complained constantly about what a wimp I was and how he'd known blokes run twenty kilometres with half their leg blown off, and so on, but he did seem genuinely concerned for me and I tried to keep my own complaining to a minimum.

I was at the cemetery again, on the bench near where Chelsea was buried. I was waiting to meet somebody but, more than that, I wanted to talk to Chelsea. I always wanted to talk to her. Every time I heard a joke, or saw something interesting, or had an idea, my first instinct was to share it with her. And every single time, the pain would stab at me or squeeze my throat. Because she wasn't there any more. She never would be. Ever.

I'd thought a lot about her during my convalescence, wondering what she'd have made of my big adventure and my new friend, Ronnie. She'd probably have liked him. She managed to like all kinds of people. I couldn't see her approving of me running around playing detective and putting myself in so much danger, though. And that was really what I wanted to talk to her about.

Look, don't get me wrong. She was dead. I knew she was dead. She wasn't sitting up on a cloud with a harp, or haunting the tombstones and vaults as a restless spirit. But there was a real sense in which she lived on – inside me. I could talk to her and I could imagine her replies. Sitting there in the cemetery just provided a focus. And it gave me a socially acceptable way to conduct my imaginary conversations, so people wouldn't think I was mad.

It was late February and the heat of the summer was finally starting to ease off a little. I was looking forward to the autumn and – my favourite season in Brisbane – the winter. People in the northern hemisphere might think it odd that, while they enjoyed a verdant summer with sunny days in the low twenties, I was enjoying a winter that was pretty much the same down here in my subtropical paradise. Brisbane was a good city, sprawling, beautiful, relaxed and full of good people. It had always been my home and I loved it. And yet, after Chelsea's death, I'd seen another side of it, a dark, disturbing shadow-world. Even in the brilliant sunlight of a Brisbane summer, soulless creatures moved through my city's streets like cancer cells in its bloodstream, looking for the chance to settle among the good and decent, to steal their lives, to corrupt and fester and grow.

Now, when I looked at the city, I couldn't help but wonder how that home was paid for, how that man could drive a Mercedes, what that woman's designer dress cost in human misery. Ronnie said, "Welcome to the real world,

Philosophy Boy." He seemed to think it was all just a normal coming-of-age, loss-of-innocence story. I felt it more as an emotional bindi seed in my sock that I needed to scratch very badly. I felt I had been taken by the scruff and pushed down and down into the city's sewers. By a miracle, I'd survived, but the stench still clung to me and I needed to do something about that.

"Hello."

I glanced around to find Karen Cha standing beside me. She looked cool and pretty and younger than ever. I stood up and reached out a hand.

"Hey, how are you?"

She shook my hand and I asked her to sit. She sat primly, knees together, hands in her lap, perched at the edge of the seat, her back straight. With that quiet serenity of hers, she waited patiently for me to speak.

"Thanks for coming," I said. "I wanted to thank you for saving my life."

She looked at me with a polite, quizzical expression.

"I know what you did," I said. "Don't worry, I will never tell the cops it was you who sent them everything they needed to raid the Devil's Playthings' clubhouse. They really don't have any idea who it could have been. You're quite safe. Only, I'd love to know how you did it and why you did it."

She pressed her lips together, thinking. "OK," she said, at last. "It was quite easy. After your friend drove me away from the hotel that day, I was worried. I was sure you were going to get into trouble and I thought I should do something. The least I could do was track your phone, to keep tabs on you. But then I realised that I knew some other things that might help. I was there when Kurt Opperman phoned you, you remember. So I could get his number from your phone and track that as well. I didn't know at the time he'd called you from your friend's phone but that didn't matter. I searched that phone for other numbers and there were only two. One was a cop – DS Bertolissiso – the other was Debra Heinzer. So I tracked Heinzer too.

"Eventually, you all ended up in the same place. I looked it up and found it was that bikie place, so I guessed you were probably in trouble. I had your phone, Opperman's and Heinzer's all in the same place and I was dying to know what you were all saying. So I turned on the microphones and cameras on all three phones. Opperman and Heinzer must have had theirs in their pockets but yours was lying on the desk in Opperman's office so I could see them and hear them shouting at one another."

A small frown creased her smooth features. "It was shocking stuff. They were arguing about killing your girlfriend and that man, Anning. And it sounded like you and your friend, Ronnie, would be next.

"I'd recorded all of it, of course, so I packaged it up with a note for the detective lady and sent it all anonymously." She smiled. "I'm glad they took it seriously. I'm glad they got to you in time."

I nodded. "Not as glad as I was. If you'd sent it to anyone but Bertolissio, there might have been a fatal delay. I don't think I would have survived that night if you hadn't given the police a reason to be there."

For a moment, I found myself reliving the rush for the door, turning back to see Ronnie holding back all those angry blokes with his gun, my heart pounding like a frenzied dance song, my mind all fear and desperation.

I shook it off. No doubt I'd revisit it all again in the night, as I had done every night since it happened.

"Anyway, I wanted to thank you again." She began to make deprecating sounds. "No, seriously. I know you didn't want to get involved. I know it reminds you of things in your past. And that's why I'm even more grateful that you did what you did. If there is ever anything, anything at all, no matter how big or small, that I can do for you, just ask. It will be my privilege. It will be my duty."

Sadly, I seemed to have embarrassed her. She gave a small, stiff bow. "Thank you," was all she said.

After a long silence, she said, "This is Chelsea's grave?" It was a change of subject, moving the conversation on. I pointed to where Chelsea was buried. I wondered what kind of spiritual beliefs about the dead Karen might have but felt it best not to pry.

"What will you do now?" she asked.

It had been the question I'd been asking myself for a fortnight but I found I didn't want to discuss it with Karen, or with anyone, until I'd spoken to Chelsea about it. So I shrugged and said, "I don't know. I have some ideas but... We'll see."

She seemed to take that as a dismissal, which, in a way, I suppose it was. She stood up to go and I rose to shake her hand again.

"I am in your debt," I said, as earnestly as I could. "Don't hesitate for a moment to claim what I owe you."

I watched her walk away, unsure that she really understood how much I would do if called on. I had already spoken to Kazima about putting a hefty bonus in her next pay packet but that was nothing to what I owed her.

I sat down, smiling, remembering how I had paid off Dicko as soon as I was mobile. He'd been amazed at the little extra I'd added to his agreed rate and was falling over himself to let me know how eager he was to drive me around again if I needed it. Ronnie was absolutely scandalised. He couldn't believe how I'd been "throwing my money around like a drunken sailor," the minute he wasn't around to keep an eye on me. But I knew from the cops that Dicko had waited for me well past the agreed time and had then gone to the nearest police station to tell them I was probably in trouble. It would have been too late to help, as it turned out, but it was the thought that counted.

I walked over to stand by Chelsea's grave. I closed my eyes and pictured her in front of me.

"I suppose you know why I'm here," I said. "Since you're in my head, you know everything before I even say it." In my imagination, she smiled indulgently. "It's been really hard without you and I think it will just get harder." I hadn't meant to say that but picturing her so clearly hurt more than I expected. I hurried on, to get it out before I couldn't speak at all.

"I'm going to start a business. I'm going to get my private investigator license and run an agency. I've looked into it all. It's not that hard and I don't even need to make any money at it. Thanks to you, I'm set up for life – as long as your business keeps going. Even so, I've done a business plan and all that. Ronnie got a good laugh out of that. He thinks I'm a complete nerd. Mind you, you should have seen the look in his eye when I told him I'd need him to work as a paid consultant, you know, guide me, make sure I do things right. The chance to do more detective work – even after what happened – had him drooling like a dog watching me eat a chop. I'd ask him to be my partner only he says can't get his license back. He won't tell me why. He probably beat up a customer or something. You know what he's like.

"I know it sounds stupid – childish, even – but I really feel like I need to do something about all the bad things I've seen. You know what I mean?"

"You always wanted to be Batman," my image of her said and laughed. It sent another stab of pain through me to hear even the memory of her laughter.

"Is that what it is?" I asked, hoping it wasn't. "The thing is, although I stumbled around like a drunk, I still managed to find Anning and bring down Opperman and Debra. And what if I could do it again? Wouldn't that be something really cool and worthwhile to do with my life?" She raised an eyebrow. "Yes, I know I was scared all the time. Really, really scared. And I know I nearly got myself killed. And I know I had a lot of help. But I did it, hey? And maybe I could do it again. Even one more time would be worth it, don't you think?"

She smiled. She seemed proud of me. Or did she? I didn't know, to be honest. I had always thought she was proud of my achievements, that she admired me, but, lately, I hadn't been so sure. Maybe it was all just indulgence, like a mother telling her child how great its crappy drawing is. It was love, for sure, but maybe that's all it was.

As I struggled with my anxieties, her image faded and I couldn't get it back. I opened my eyes. The world around me seemed unusually solid, the light unusually harsh. "Goodbye, darling," I said to the ground with her dead body in it. I turned and walked away, disturbed and uncertain, to start building my new life.

Thank You

Thank you for reading *Bright City Deep Shadows,* the first of my Luke Kelly crime novels. I really hope you enjoyed it as much as I enjoyed writing it. If so, I'd be grateful if you'd leave a review on one of the book retail sites, your blog, or pasted to a wall on the nearest underpass. There will be more books about Luke's adventures. To stay informed of when new books of mine are about to appear, please visit my website and sign up for my newsletter.

About the Author

I am a writer living in Queensland, Australia. A former research scientist, IT consultant and award-winning software designer, I now live and write, mostly science fiction, in a quiet corner of the Australian bush with my wife, Christine, and a Tonkinese cat called Minsky.

Other Books By Graham Storrs

Crime Stories

Sisters: The Complete Short Story Collection

The Luke Kelly Crime Series:

Bright City Deep Shadows
Bright City Lost Souls
Bright City Dark Love
Bright City Old Wounds

Science Fiction

Cargo Cult
Heaven is a Place on Earth
Mindrider
Time and Tyde

The Timesplash Series:

Timesplash
True Path
Foresight

Novels in the Placid Point Universe

The Rik Sylver Trilogy:

The Credulity Nexus
The Sentience Machine
The Dissonance Factor

The Canta Libre Trilogy:

Emissaries
Supplicants
Warriors

The Deep Fracture Trilogy:

Loner's Deep
Omega Point
Nadezhda

Acknowledgements

As usual, I would like to thank my wife for her support and encouragement.

While there is typically only one author, it always takes a whole group of people, working behind the scenes, to get a book into production – beta readers, editors, artists, designers, layout specialists, and so on. It may be invidious, but I'm going to single out just one of these, my friend and fellow writer, Chris Giacca, for his help and guidance on local Australian idiomatic speech. Chris is an amazingly careful reader and the text is definitely better – and more authentic – for his input.

Also, as usual, despite the legion of people who have helped, any problems that remain with this novel are all my own doing.

Contact the Author

I am always happy to hear from readers, so don't be shy. And if you enjoyed this book, don't forget to post your review.

Follow me on Twitter: @graywave

or on Facebook:
facebook.com/GrahamStorrsAuthor

For details of all my novels and short stories, visit
grahamstorrs.com

www.ingramcontent.com/pod-product-compliance
Lightning Source LLC
Chambersburg PA
CBHW061326170626
46817CB00001B/342